Pinch Me

I must be dreaming

Pinch Me

I must be dreaming

||| GLENDON SWARTHOUT |||

St. Martin's Press
New York

LIBRARY OF CONGRESS CATALOGING-IN-PUBLICATION DATA

Swarthout, Glendon Fred.
        Pinch me, I must be dreaming / Glendon Swarthout.
            p.   cm.
        "A Thomas Dunne book."
        ISBN 0-312-11383-8 : $20.95
        1. Man-woman relationships—Fiction.   2. Middle
aged persons—
    PS3537.W3743P56   1994
    813'.52—dc20   94-12909
                                             CIP

First edition: September 1994

10 9 8 7 6 5 4 3 2 1

for
Owen Laster

A lively understandable spirit
once entertained you.
It will come again.
Be still.
Wait.

Theodore Roethke

To ask her to marry him, and to be sure she said yes, Don Chambers took Jenny Staley for a ride in a hot-air balloon.

Both of them were divorced, Don for five years, Jenny for twelve.

Both sold real estate.

Once she said that when she was a little girl what she wanted most was a star to put under her pillow. Now what she wanted most was to go up in a balloon. So soon after that, the sooner the better his desire advised, Don contracted with a balloon company and popped for $250 for an hour's ride and set the date and picked Jenny up that afternoon at five and drove her to a dusty lot on the outskirts of north Phoenix, Arizona. Parking in front of the acreage's only tenant, a one-room, concrete-block shack painted hot pink, he led her around back past the building's rooftop sign—

BALLOON FLIGHTS
"Champagne Wishes and Caviar Dreams"
Dawn Ascensions & Late Afternoons
DAILY—INQUIRE WITHIN

And there was her surprise—a yellow, white, and purple bag fifty-five feet in circumference inflated with 56,000 cubic feet of hot air and hanging seven stories high and underneath, a wicker basket waiting. "Oh, Don!" she cried, and clapped her hands. "It's what I've dreamed of ever since I was a little girl."

He grinned and caught a tear in her eye and disbelieved she could be so beautiful unless she loved him. "Then today's your lucky day, let's go!"

The balloon tugged at the ropes, which were held by a man and woman who were members of the crew and would follow to landing in the "chase vehicle," a pickup truck. From the basket, a bearded young man beckoned. Like children, Don and Jenny went hand in hand to the basket and clambered aboard. The beard said his name was Max and that he'd be their pilot. Were they ready? But before they could respond, the ropes were suddenly let go and swoosh! Up, up, straight and silently up! The basket swayed and they swallowed their hearts and grabbed for each other and also the grab bar around the top of the basket.

It was as though the great hand of God reached down to earth and snatched Don Chambers, age forty-two, and Jenny Staley, age thirty-eight, suddenly up, up, straight and divinely up into a new life.

Deus ex $250.

"Wow!" admired Jenny.

"You like?" asked Max.

"Sensational. What a view!" agreed Don.

One, Max, talked all the time. Two, the basket was small, only three by four feet, and crammed with propane gas tanks and instruments and Max. Three, when he pulled a handle overhead and ignited the dual burners in the throat of the bag, they couldn't hear themselves think, much less converse. They sailed along the south slope of Camelback Mountain at five hundred feet, and the sight of the big smoggy city and its suburbs supine under a big blue sky was sensational. Max talked about piloting. You steered with the wind, which varied in velocity and direction according to altitude. You ascended by "burning," by cutting in the burners, which put out 12 million Btus between them, and descended by pulling the deflation line, which released air out a vent near the top of the bag. It was April, the citrus trees were in bloom, and they wafted along on the fragrance of orange blossoms. Max asked if they'd like to play Peeping Tom, and when they asked what that meant, he said he'd show 'em. He pulled a line and the balloon descended slowly till they drifted sixty to seventy feet above the ground, almost at treetop level. From this height they could spy into houses through windows and arcadia doors. This was an affluent section of Phoenix, most of the plush homes had walled patios with swimming pools, and as they lurked above one patio, a fat lady, in the nude and wearing hair curlers, sunbathing on a plastic raft in her pool, looked up and let out a shriek and tipped over the raft. On another patio, on a lounge, a bare-assed guy was banging a bare-assed girl until three Peeping Toms looking down deflated his frogal. Outraged, the guy jumped off the girl and hurled a full can of beer up at the basket.

"Get outta here, you bastards!" he roared.

Max burned gas and took them up to five hundred feet again. Don was embarrassed and frustrated. Watching patio pornography and listening to Max and his big mouth was not the romantic moment he had blown a bundle for, and not only that, the ride was running down by now. He had to get things organized. Since he was damned if he'd put the question in front of a stranger, he decided to use the burner sound as cover.

Max talked about his instruments and burned. Don put his arm around Jenny's waist and spoke into her ear. "Jenny, I love you."

She shook her head.

He raised his voice. "I love you."

She couldn't hear.

"I love you!"

She heard that.

Max stopped burning and said he had two important instruments. One showed him the rate of climb. He burned. Don shouted.

"I've only been out with you eight times, but I knew the second time you were the one!"

The other, Max said, was a pyrometer, a gauge that showed the temperature in the bag so that the pilot could control it. He burned.

Jenny cried in Don's ear. "You haven't even kissed me!"

"I know! On purpose! So you'd know how special I think you are! How serious I am!"

Max stopped burning too soon, and Don could have killed the gassy sonofabitch. Max said the only real danger with a balloon was power lines—you put power lines and propane gas together and you have a problem.

"Why're we going down?" Don demanded.

"Not too long till landing. I'll rip the top in about ten minutes."

"Well, I'm not ready!" Don couldn't stop shouting. "Take us up again, goddammit!"

Max pulled the handle and his beard.

"Anyway, I love you and I think—I hope—you love me!" Don shouted in Jenny's ear. "And what I got us up here for was to ask you to marry me! Jenny, will you please marry me?"

She turned his head in order to cry in his ear. He waited.

"No!"

"Why not?"

"Windy."

"Windy?"

"My grandmother."

"What about her?"

These were their first words since the landing. Don Chambers was mad and miserable. Jenny Staley was desolate. They had ordered double marts in the Beef & Bung, a California chain restaurant. This one, a carbon copy of countless others, featured an Africa of greenery, things like brass elephant heads on the walls, things like "Mud Pie" for dessert, and a menu etched into the blade of a massive meat cleaver sharp enough if you were sauced enough to slice off a finger. The doubles came, and Don slugged his down to the olives.

"What about Windy?" he repeated.

"She lives with Sue and me."

"I know. And I've never been introduced. I've never even been inside your door."

"On purpose—like your not kissing me. But I decided long ago not to involve any man with my family unless I was serious about him."

"Thanks."

"I'm serious now."

"Thanks."

"Don, I'm so sorry."

"Back to Windy."

"She's ninety-one."

"Amazing."

"Not today it isn't."

"Is that her real name?"

"No. Mate. Mate Coon. When she was a young ranch wife she was very quiet, so of course the cowboys called her 'Windy.' Now it fits. Anyway, I owe her everything. She's been mother and father to me twice."

Don flagged a waiter and ordered a mart, another double, for himself. He knew what she was talking about because she'd talked about it before, on their dates. Looked at one way, he supposed, the story of grandmother and granddaughter was tear-jerker tragic. Looked at on the tube, "Windy and Jenny" was pure soap opera—another title might have been "Sisters in Sorrow." The first segment was set in 1911. A girl of eight, Mate, later Windy, was mule-teamed west to Arizona from Garden of Eden, Kansas, in a wagon—not a covered, just a wagon. At nineteen she was wed to a rancher named Wade Will Coon. In time, Wade Will and Windy had a still-born son and Jenny's mother, Frances, and a Model T Ford they called their "liver-shaker" and a spread out of Holbrook on which they ran a thousand head. Then they had three years of drought and went broke and Wade Will stuck a Colt .45 in his mouth and pulled the trigger. Tune in to 1934. Windy the widow moved herself and baby to Phoenix, bought a house with her mite, took in boarders and roomers, and made a laborious living out of hash and clean sheets. Her daughter, Frances, grew up pretty as a picture and married Fred Turner and had her own daughter, Jenny. Now it is 1972. Fred and Frances Turner are killed in an auto accident on the Apache Trail, and Jenny, sixteen and orphaned, is taken in by her grandmother, who is sixty-nine.

We flash ahead to 1976. Jenny Turner, only a year from graduation at the University of Arizona in Tucson, marries Bucky Staley. She is twenty and two months along. She bears a daughter, Sue. She bears Bucky for six years. He has dancing eyes and waving lashes and sparkling teeth and rippling muscles and beans for brains. He lacks a center of gravity. He zigs and zags, from job to job and apartment to apartment, chasing opportunity and bouncing checks, and finally, after waiting six years for him to become a big boy, to accept fatherhood and make the payments on matrimony, Jenny takes Sue and leaves and divorces him.

Cut to 1982. Dark of night. A knock at the door of Windy Coon's humble abode. It is Jenny, homeless and helpless again, holding little Sue by the hand. To the old woman, seventy-nine now, it is a reincarnation. There she herself stands, nearly forty years before, with the baby Frances in her arms. Slow dissolve, with music, to the next twelve years. Grandmother and granddaughter live together like infantry under fire. If they are lonely at times, and weary, and embattled, they have each other and Sue, and they have survived the worst that mere men and dirty death can do to them. They are heroines. "Windy and Jenny" will run, it seems, forever, and rank high in the ratings. But wait—tune in tomorrow—when a tall, dark stranger takes Jenny up in a balloon and asks her to marry him.

The waiter brought Don's double and a meat cleaver and they pretended interest in the blade.

"You can't leave her," Don said.

"Ever."

"Uh, what about a nursing home?"

"Never. Besides, she wouldn't."

"Who looks after her when you're out?"

"Sue."

"But she goes to school." Sue, he also knew, was in her second year at Phoenix College and hoped to go, eventually, to Arizona State and major in computer programming. "What then?"

"She worked her schedule so that she has classes just three mornings a week. Windy does fine alone—well, she has left the stove on high once or twice and burned the kettle to a blob."

Don was careful. "How is she mentally?"

"She's not senile, if that's what you mean. She's—well, in and out, you might say. It's funny. She'll be talking in the present when suddenly—blip—out comes something from years and years ago, like a Polaroid picture, clear and in color. But she's fine for her age. She watches TV all day. When Sue's gone, she remembers to take her pills because we put them in little paper cups in a row with the times on them."

"Pills," Don said. "What shape is she in?"

Jenny was careful. "Not bad, for ninety-one. Oh, she's lost a lot, of course. She wears cataract lenses, so her peripheral vision's not good. She's apt to bump into things."

"Bump into things."

"That's partly because she has limited mobility. Osteoarthritis in her hips and shoulders. She gets around with a cane."

"A cane."

"She's on Indocin and Ascriptin for that. And on Persantine for poor circulation."

"Poor circulation?"

"Then there's the Parkinson's."

"Parkinson's?"

"Tremors of the head and hands. Symmetrel helps. As for the diabetes—"

"Diabetes!"

"What's called the 'adult-onset' kind, fortunately, not the insulin-dependent kind. We can control it with diet. We have to hide sweets from her, though, which makes her angry, which is bad for her high blood pressure."

"High blood pressure!"

"Yes. She's on Lasix—that's a diuretic—and Aldoril. That dilates the blood vessels and relieves pressure. Then she has . . ."

"No more, no more!" Don groaned.

"What's wrong?"

"I'm not feeling well. Where am I—Pill City? How do you know all this stuff?"

"I talk to her doctor."

"She can't be long for this world."

"Who knows? According to the doctor, if you live to eighty-five today, you have a very good chance of making it to a hundred."

"No thanks. I want to tick off in my sleep the day I hit sixty."

"You say that now. Just wait."

"Wait." Don glowered into his glass, next fired down the dregs of the double, then glowered at Jenny. "Let me get this straight." He removed the olives from his ice and inspected them. They were small and ignoble. He buried them under the ice. "As I understand it, even if you love me—which you haven't said—and even if I asked you to marry me—which I did—you won't because you have to wait till your grandmother's gone, which might be nine more years, and so do I." The maxi-marts were getting to him. "Have to wait, I mean."

Jenny was silent.

"In which case," Don continued, drying his fingers on the front of his Christian Dior shirt. "I wish she'd shuffle off t'night."

"You don't mean that."

"The hell I don't."

"You can't."

"Well, maybe I don', maybe it's the booze, I don' know, but I love you an' this is awful. We're s'pose' to be talkin' moonlight an' roses an' all I hear's high blood pressure an' poor circulation."

"Don, give me your hands."

He gave, and they held hands across the table.

"Now look at me."

He looked, and caught another tear in her eye.

"Don, dear, thank you."

"For what?"

"The lovely balloon ride."

"Oh."

"I love you."

"You do?"

"Madly. I knew on our third date you were going to be the one."

"Knew on the second."

"And I will marry you."

"Really?"

"As soon as I can."

Just then Don had the flash.

"But Don, we must wait. I can't desert Windy. Sue mustn't have the responsibility, she's too young. And a nursing home is out."

"Jenny, how many bedrooms in your condo?"

"One. We're crowded, but a one-bedroom was what I could afford."

"How d'you sleep?"

"Windy and I share the bedroom. Sue has the davenport— that's temporary, till she goes away to school."

"Les' go."

"Where?"

"Show you. Got an idea." Don crashed up, dropped some bills

on the table, and took Jenny's arm. "An' if I don' do it now, on four marts on a full heart an' an empty gut, I may never."

*

His vodka valor evaporated on the way out to Scottsdale, but not his resolve. He had too much time, money, and emotion invested in Jenny Staley to let her off the hook now. He loved her. She loved him. He was ripe for remarriage. So was she. They were made for each other. So his job, as he saw it, was a sales job, and selling was Donald William Chambers's middle name. He could sell a polygraph test to a politician. He could sell herpes II to a saint. What he must do in the next hour was talk three women into buying an idea, and moving an idea, and it seemed to him it should be no more tricky than moving a high-priced house. The secret? The higher the price, the softer the sell.

Within a month after he had shipped himself to Arizona five years ago, Don had taken a three-week cram course, passed the exam, and joined the staff of Rancho Grande Realty. Everyone was getting in on the real estate act—gas pumpers who scarcely knew escrow from escargot, retired ladies and gents who wanted extra bucks for bingo, and housewives who had never sold anything to anybody except a roll in the hay to their husbands. And the reason they were all running around with "Open House" signs was that the Phoenix area was breaking out in one of its periodic growth rashes. Housing was a better gamble than gold. Commissions grew on trees like citrus. It couldn't last, it never had; bust must follow boom, everyone admitted; but while the crap table was hot, why not have a piece of the action?

Within a year Don had become, in the lingo, a "high roller." He had clawed himself up the realty ladder from hustling four-to-the-acre tract houses going for fifty thou to the quarter-million and higher market, and on this luxury level you operated very differently. First you got your listing, your property, an exclusive listing hopefully, new or resale, and set your price, say, at half a mil.

Then you got your clients. Either they flew in first-class from the East and you met them at Sky Harbor, or they were already here, toughing it out at the Biltmore or Camelback Inn while house hunting. One look and you knew they were loaded, which was why you dressed as though you were. Away you chauffeured them in your Sedan de Ville, the kind of wheels they were accustomed to. You showed the house, probably in Paradise Valley, where poodles ate off sterling silver and even the burglars had brokers. You kept your mouth shut, opening it only to mention amenities such as the spaciousness of the servants' quarters and the remarkable microcircuitry of the alarm system. After the walk-through, you took them to lunch at your country or tennis club—Don's was the Squaw Peak Racquet Club. You ordered drinks, excused yourself to make a phone call so that husband and wife could confer, and when you returned you closed the deal, often for cash. Oh, to show his sharps, the husband might knock you down ten thou, and the wife might want her Roman bathtub retiled, but in general the whole thing was a classy piece of cake. Right house, right people, soft sell. Now tonight, he had the right idea and his sell would be as soft as a baby's behind after oiling. The only problem was the people. Windy Coon and Sue Staley were unknowns, and he'd better peg them properly before he began his pitch. This was a deal Don had to close. This was a commission he had to have. Jenny—and living with her happily ever after.

"Where are we going?" Jenny asked as he ran a yellow light and swung the Sedan de Ville left onto Scottsdale Road heading north.

"We can have dinner later."

"Tell me."

"Next episode: 'Windy and Sue Meet a Tall, Dark Stranger.' "

She lived in Oasis North. He lived in Oasis South, just two blocks from her. Both developments had been slapped up by the same builder, and done by the architect who apparently mass-designed most of the condominium set-ups in Scottsdale—thirty-two units, mortarwash over frame painted Navajo white, red-tile roofs, covered parking, pool, sauna, Jacuzzi, many palm trees and much landscaping tended by undocumented workers, one bedroom sixty-nine thou, two bedrooms–two baths eighty-nine thou, fifty a month maintenance. Don had bought his new, twenty percent down and thirty years, while Jenny's had been a resale, cash to mortgage.

He pulled into a parking slot at Oasis North and she led the way to her door, then paused.

"Don, are you sure?"

"Death, taxes, and dishes."

But the second he stepped through the door, he wasn't. In the living room sat a very old lady with a cane across the arms of her chair. The cane was wood, and heavy, and the handle was carved into the head of a rattlesnake reared to strike, jaws wide, fangs sharp. The old lady sat four feet or so from a TV set. The set was tuned to a rerun of "Mr. Ed" on an independent channel that ran them all day between commercials for used car lots and hair transplant clinics. The old lady, her cataract lenses glued to the tube, did not acknowledge the intruders. The audio, including a mechanical laugh track, was bomb loud.

"Hi, Gram!" cried Jenny. "I'd like you to meet a friend of mine—Don Chambers!"

"Glad to meet you, ma'am!" Don shouted.

Nothing.

"I'll get Sue!" cried Jenny. "She must be in the bedroom studying!"

"Didn't hear you!" Don shouted.

"Sue!"

"Oh!"

She left the room and Don sat down on the davenport and waited for conversation. What he got was the sitcom.

"Well, Ed, what'dya think about that?" inquired the fabulous talking horse's owner.

"Whhhoooaaaa, Wiilllbuuur," neighed Mr. Ed.

"I'm more than a friend!" Don shouted.

The only response was the damned laugh track. This was as bad as Max the Beard and his damned dual burners. Don looked his client over. She was big, but the flesh had fallen with time from her bones the way it does from a rickety horse or cow. Her face was stark, like that of an ancient Sioux chief in a tintype—fierce nose and chin, high cheekbones, bulging brow, and her straight iron hair was pulled into a tomahawk bun. A skull with hair and skin on it. Whether or not Windy Coon was an authentic Arizona pioneer, she dressed the part. She was costumed in faded Lee Rider jeans, a tunic of crinkle gauze, an ornate squash-blossom necklace of turquoise and silver, and beaded squaw boots.

Jenny brought Sue. "Don Chambers, a friend of mine! Don, my daughter!"

Don rose and shook hands. "More than a friend!"

Sue shook her head. "Can't hear you!"

At eighteen, Sue had her growth, and a lot of it, and a lot of Bucky Staley—dancing eyes and sparkling teeth and rippling muscles. And though her mother was honey blond, Sue's hair was black and short and shining. She was too good-looking to be a computer programmer.

"He took me for a balloon ride!" Jenny cried.

"I love her!" Don shouted.

"He what?" Sue cried.

"Just a minute!" Jenny went to her grandmother's ear. "Gram, can we please have the TV off a minute?"

The old lady lifted her cane, extended it to the set, and with the point punched the on-off button. "Talking horses, what foofaraw."

In the silence, everyone seemed to sag.

She looked at Don. "Chambers, huh? What d'you do?"

"Real estate."

"Hmpf."

Whatever that meant. Don took it to mean, when applied to a male, contempt for any profession less masculine than chasing and castrating cattle.

"You a divorced man?"

"Uh, yes."

"How many times?"

"Just once."

"Any kids?"

"I have a son. He's in college now, in California."

"Why're you here?"

By now Don was beginning to do a slow burn. He certainly wasn't here to be third-degreed. Soft sell, hell—this was one he'd have to bulldoze.

"Windy," he said, "that's what I want to tell you. I hope I can call you Windy." He crossed the room and bent over the TV set, facing her. "I love Jenny. She loves me. I just asked her to marry me."

"Oh, Mom!" cried Sue, and embraced her mother.

"Don, maybe this isn't the right . . .," Jenny began.

"But she said no," Don interrupted.

"Oh, Mom, why?" cried Sue.

"She claims she can't leave you and Sue," Don said to Windy. "Then I got a great idea—she doesn't have to!" He tried to fix the old lady's eyes with his, but behind the thick cataract lenses hers seemed to swim. "I know how we can do it. I live just down the street, in Oasis South, in a two-bedroom condo. Well, you can all move in with me! Jenny and I'll have my bedroom, and you and Sue can share the other. You'll even have two TV sets: mine in the living room—it has remote control—and this one right in your bedroom! Won't that be great? I know we'll all be happy—and Jenny and I really will." Don straightened and smiled his sunniest, close-the-deal smile. "So how about it, Windy? Will you say yes and come live with us so we can get married?"

There was a long wait. Don broke out in a sweat. Windy Coon's eyes swam from Don to Jenny to Sue and back to Don.

"I have trouble with my bowels," she said.

Jenny and Sue sat down suddenly.

"Get bound up all the time," she said.

Don backed to the davenport, sat down by Jenny, put elbows on knees, chin in hands, and contemplated the carpet.

Windy pulled a Kleenex from her tunic, pushed up her glasses, and dabbed at tears. "Her folks was killed in a car crash," she explained to no one in particular. "Such a dear little thing, sweet sixteen. I took 'er in an' raised 'er like my own. Then a hull lot later, she got loose of that no-good Staley, an' there she was on my doorstep again, her an' little Sue, an' I took 'em in again. She's all I got, her an' Sue. I have t'sleep in the room with Jenny. Have t'get up in the night sometimes."

Jenny and Sue looked at each other.

"I've lived too long," Windy snuffled. "Up on the ranch, when we had a critter sick or hurt or too old, we took pity on 'er an' shot 'er. Too damn bad you can't do that with folks."

Jenny got up, came to Windy, and sat down on the floor between her and the TV. "No, you haven't, Gram. Lived too long. You'll make a hundred, I'm sure of it, and the newspapers will want to know how you did it, and we'll all be so proud of you." Jenny spoke softly, but the others could hear. "It must be very hard for you, dear. Even to think about moving to a new place. But I want you to know you don't have to. If you want to stay right here, where you're used to everything, why do. Your happiness comes first. Don and I'll be glad to wait. Do you understand me? We'll do whatever you want."

Windy Coon stared at her granddaughter, trying to comprehend. And then she must have, for one tremulous hand was raised and came to tender rest on Jenny's head. It caressed her. The caress was at once a hail and a farewell, a blessing and a reminder of lives shared—of joy and dust, loss and hash, rage and laundry, of struggle and memory and fear and dreams seen through the unwashed windows of the years. And watching that hand on the head of his beloved, Don was moved. Now he understood Jenny's no. If love could lift you like a bag of gas, love could also be a good strong rope.

"D'you love this dude?" Windy asked.

"Yes," Jenny said.

"D'you want t'marry 'im?"

"Yes, Gram, I do."

Windy Coon removed her hand and sat back nodding. "Sue," she said, "fetch me my gun."

The girl gaped. "Your gun?"

"Step lively, missy."

After his sweat, Don was shaken by a chill. Sue returned with a huge, relic Colt revolver and gave it to her great-grandmother, who examined it.

"Wade Will's," she said. "Only thing of his I got left. Shot himself with this gun, out of pride. If a man don't have pride, he's no man."

Suddenly she hoisted herself, upped the weapon, and pointed it directly at Don. A bolt of fright sheared through him. For all he knew, the old lady was either wrecked on a dozen different drugs or, after nine decades of sanity, had finally snapped her cap. Reflexively he leaped to his feet and stood as though presenting his breast to a firing squad.

"Gram!" cried Jenny.

"Windy!" cried Sue.

"Hush," Windy chided. The barrel of the Colt waggled as she tried to focus on her target. "Now listen, Chambers, an' listen hard. You be good t'my girl."

"I will!" shouted Don.

"You be damn good t'her," Windy warned, "or I'll blow a hole in you big enough t'throw a bucket of shit through."

She lowered the gun, and while Don collapsed in a chair, took up her rattlesnake cane, extended it to the TV set, and with the point punched the on-off button to a roar of canned laughter.

*

"To us," Don said.

"To us," Jenny agreed.

They touched glasses. To celebrate, they were having champagne at Madame de Farge's. There was a French restaurant on every corner in Scottsdale, which called itself "The West's Most Western Town."

"Don't you want to order?" Don asked.

"I'm still not hungry—too excited. Too much has happened too fast—a balloon ride, a marriage proposal, Windy willing to move—in one evening! I don't believe it!" Jenny shook her head and smiled. "Don, darling, I do love you—and I'm so happy!"

"I haven't been so happy since Carol said yes. To a divorce."

She sobered. "But do you really realize what you're taking on? Three of us barging in on you—a girl of eighteen, an old woman who needs constant care, and I have to be gone a lot, sitting on houses. Can you take it?"

"The more the merrier."

"You say that now. Just wait."

Don hauled the bottle from the bucket and poured. "Wait. Let's never use that word again. Listen, luv, I love you. I've rattled around alone too long. I'll bunk with the Argentine Army if I can live with you."

She looked at him. "That does it."

"What?"

"Will you please come 'round the table to me?"

Don rose and came around the table and Jenny stood to meet him and put her arms around him and he put his around her and they kissed. No one would have guessed it was their first. So ardent and extended and French was it that they got a béarnaise of applause from the other diners.

"That does it," said Don, shaken, when they were reseated. "Set the date."

"The date?"

"The wedding, what else? How about tomorrow?"

"Tomorrow!" Jenny swallowed champagne the wrong way. "Tomorrow! Oh my dear, think of what I have to do! There's my furniture. And putting the house on the market."

"Give me an exclusive?"

"And you must have things to do."

"Move my toothbrush."

She laughed. When she laughed, Jenny had an endearing habit of tilting her head back and letting go. Then she slipped and thought. "I could manage it in two weeks, I suppose."

"Two weeks." Don considered. "It's a deal. Where? County building? Vegas? A church?"

"We'll have to talk about that. Don, people are staring at us."

"I know. Rating us X."

"Let's duck out."

"L'Orange?"

"Let's go have a cheeseburger."

"And fries."

Don left enough long green on the linen to appease the waiter and they made a quick exit. Not quick enough, however, to avoid the fishy eye of Madame de Farge, who sat in the foyer knitting.

*

They passed into the restaurant patio. It was night now, there was a moon, and the shiver of palm trees, and a fountain played. To his surprise, Jenny stopped and grabbed Don like a grab bar and held him tight and whispered. She was sorry, but she had to use that word again. She couldn't wait. Two weeks to make love. Her whisper and the scent of orange blossoms in the air and her felinity against him were too good to be true, so to prolong the pleasure, he squeezed her and teased her. But he thought, he murmured, that what she hungered for was a cheeseburger. At this she kissed him and gave his lower lip a cat nip. He couldn't wait either, he confessed, and why should they? If kids today could swan-dive into the sack scarcely knowing each other's names, why should mature, consenting adults in love and about to wed wait till they were practically mental cases? He was right, she whispered, teasing back, why should they—or was fast food more important to him than sex? At this he stuck the tip of his tongue in her ear and made her melt. Where, he groaned, her place or his? This made her laugh, and they headed for his car without breaking embrace, lurching with lust like sailors on liberty. Don had an erection. Jenny's nipples were hard as rocks.

*

But first she had to have a walk-through of his condo in Oasis South, which would be her new home. Except for the extra bedroom and bath, it was a clone of hers in Oasis North, featuring the same "Southwestern Look"—beamed ceilings, white walls and tile floors on which you could easily go flying, a minus of bookcases, a plus of (too much of in fact) Mexican decorative tilework in the kitchen and two johns, and everywhere leaded-glass light fixtures fresh off a truck from across the border.

They entered a bedroom with a nude poster of Ginger Lynn, the Hollywood porno princess on one wall and one of the Lone Ranger on another and a Claremont McKenna College pennant over a Carta Blanca beer sign on a third. "My son's room," Don explained. "Ron."

"What will he do when he comes home and finds Windy and Sue in here?"

"He won't. Oh, two weeks at Christmas and one at spring break. Summers he counsels at a boy's camp in Colorado. So it's no strain—he can bunk in a sleeping bag anywhere."

They reached the end of the line, Don's bedroom. He stepped in for a moment, then invited her. "I was just checking."

"For what?"

"Babes under the bed."

It had the look of a motel room a criminal couple had stripped and skipped. They had stolen the prints from the walls, the rugs from the floor, the TV from its stand, the blankets from the king-sized bed, and the Bible from the dresser, leaving only the phone, rumpled sheets, and two crumpled Coors cans in a corner.

"Raunch City," Don said.

"Disgusting," Jenny said. She sat down on the side of the bed. He took a rusting, collapsible beach chair.

"Well," Don said.

"Well indeed," Jenny said.

Now, unexpectedly, they were shy with each other. On their dates they had talked a streak about Jenny's girlhood and Bucky Staley and her rough row since the divorce. "I couldn't see the point in finishing college with a degree in Fine Arts. I sold tickets for TWA, I made appointments and sent out bills for a gynecologist, I clerked at Goldwater's Department Store, and so on. I did everything but collect aluminum cans." About Don's boyhood in Michigan and his divorce from Carol. "She was something else. Carol was the kind of girl who had to name her kid Ronald because his father's name was Donald. Even worse, she liked living in Detroit." About baseball and Sue and money-market funds and Ron and splitting commissions and inflation and movies and men and women and how they made idiots of themselves. Now it was time *not* to talk.

"Jenny, listen," Don said. "There's something I'd better unload. The last five years, since I came out here, I've done the whole bachelor bit—the singles scene. I wore shirts open down to my navel. And chains. I cruised. I bedded."

She nodded. "All right, thank you. I should tell you, too. I had a serious affair a few years ago. With the gynecologist. I lived with him, sort of on the side. I loved him, I really did, and he loved me and hated his wife—you know. But in the end he didn't love me enough or hate her enough and finally I bailed out. Damaged. Since repaired."

Don nodded. "Fair enough. But listen, I'm a changed man. About six months ago I got sick of spending so much time in the sack with so many women, so I tried this new thing. Abstinence."

"Abstinence?"

"Total. It's the latest. You just don't. And I haven't, for six months."

"What are you saying?"

"I'm apt to be an animal."

She tilted her head and laughed. "So am I!"

They grinned at each other.

"Well," said Jenny.

"Well *indeed,*" said Don.

"Do you mind if I take a shower first? I feel the need."

"Sure, oh sure." Don jumped up and bowed. *"Mi casa es su casa.* Here, use my john. Should be towels and all."

"Gracias."

She closed the door, and as soon as he heard the glass shower doors close and the water start, Don blew the bugle and charged. Swiftly he swept the pretzels and potato chips out of the bed with his hands and smoothed the sheets. Rapidly he tore off his shoes, sox, slacks, and shirt, thought about taking a shower himself, and decided no. She'd be through first and have to wait. Hastily he surveyed himself in a full-length mirror the way Jenny would see him in a minute, and was shocked. He was wearing a bikini brief, little more than a string and a ball bag, which was the sexy way to go these days. His was bright red, a chic creation by Pierre Cardin, but now it looked silly as hell and sure as hell would to Jenny. She might laugh. He whipped it off, then thought he'd better not confront her naked because she might be wearing his robe when she emerged, so he put the bikini back on, then sat down on the bed again and waited. The shower stopped. He waited, chewing on a fingernail. And waited. What in hell was she doing? Then he got up, carried the beer cans into the kitchen, returned, took off his red bikini again before the ball bag ruptured, then faced the john door.

"Jenny, what are you doing?!" he shouted.

"Using the squeegee."

"Using the squeegee! What in hell for?"

"You're supposed to squeegee the doors after you shower or you'll have terrible water spots on the glass. I know because my shower's the same at home. Sue and I always squeegee."

"But why now? There's a right time and a wrong time to . . ."

"Because I'm your guest, Don. I won't be responsible for water spots on . . ."

"I never squeegee!"

"It shows. Your doors are . . ."

"Goddamn my doors!"

"I'll be through in . . ."

"Goddamn my squeegee!"

Don ripped open the door, plunged into the john, slammed open a shower door, stepped into the stall, and lunged for Jenny and the squeegee. Laughing at the sight of him, teasing, she held it behind her so that Don, who began to laugh with her at himself, had to put an arm around her to reach it, and together they slipped and slid into a sensual, ceramic waltz. "I'll squee your gee!" he threatened. "Careful!" she cautioned. "We could break something important!" Slyly she got the squeegee into her other hand and behind his back, and laughing, a little demented, Don skidded her against a tile wall, at which Jenny lifted a shapely leg and slithered it around his hip. Then they stopped laughing and started kissing. The squeegee fell to the floor. But just as he was about to enter her, and coitus was about to be accomplished, it was interrupted by a ring of the phone in the bedroom.

"Oh, no," he groaned.

"Don't answer it, darling," she moaned.

"I've got to . . . clients flying in from Connecticut tomorrow . . . want something around half a mill . . . maybe it's them . . . Jenny, I've got to . . . I'm sorry."

"You're sorry?"

Like a blind man examining an elephant, Don felt along the walls and out of the shower and the john. The phone, on a stand by the bed, was still ringing. With wet hand he put it to wet ear.

"Hello?"

"Donald?"

Long-distance.

"Who is this?"

"This is your father."

"Dad! How come you're calling? What time is it? Must be midnight back there!"

"Donald, I am lying on my living room floor."

*

Don's damp posterior descended to the bed. A curious Jenny stuck her head through the john door. "It's my father, in Michigan," Don told her. "He's lying on his living room floor."

"Donald, who are you talking to?"

"A friend, Dad. More than a friend. Dad, why are you lying on your living room floor?"

"I was walking around in the dark."

"In the dark? Why?"

"Oh, I do sometimes, when I can't sleep. And I tripped on something and fell. At first I couldn't move, then I crawled to the phone. I am in great pain."

"He fell," Don told Jenny.

"Probably broke a hip," said Jenny. "They do that—Windy did. It's their favorite bone."

"But Dad, why didn't you call the hospital?" Don demanded. "Have them send an ambulance?"

"I will, soon as I hang up. But I wanted to hear your voice again before they take me away. Son, I think this may be the end."

"Oh, Pop, no!"

"I fear so. And I want to see you again before I go. Can you come home, right away?"

"Oh, Pop, sure I can! He thinks it's the end," Don anguished, but Jenny was back in the john. "I'll get the first plane out of Phoenix—I'll be there tomorrow!"

"Bless you, Son. I'll hang up now and call the hospital. It'll be good to see you again."

"Yes, call 'em right away. Dad, I'm so terribly sorry about this."

"I'm in great pain."

"See you tomorrow, Pop!"

"Tomorrow."

"Take care!" Don grimaced. "That's a dumb thing to say. I mean—see they take care of you!"

"I will."

"Good night, Dad."

"Good night, Donald."

*

Don dropped the receiver and flipped through the phone book and called airlines. Jenny came out and sat down beside him just as he finished phoning.

"American," he said. "They've got a redeye out at one-ten, gets into Chicago at six-ten. Then I lay over till seven-thirty and catch United to Lansing, then rent a car. I'll be in Owosso before noon."

Only then did Don notice he was naked and she was fully dressed. "Oh my God," he groaned. "Us."

She kissed him on the cheek. "Never mind about us—this is an emergency."

"But what about the wedding? I don't know how long he might linger—I'll call you every night. God, I'm glad you were here. Jenny, what if this is the end? My God, my father."

"We can wait, dear. If it's just a hip, he'll be all right. Though it might be a stroke. But I don't think it's a stroke or how, if he's paralyzed, could he get to the phone? Don, you've never told me much about your father."

"He calls me Donald."

"Your mother's dead?"

"Twenty years ago."

"What's his name?"

"A stroke?"

"What's his name?"

"Harry. Harold Chambers."

"I thought Chambers."

"I have to pack!"

"How old is he?"

"Eighty-three."

"What about your clients?"

"What clients?"

"The Connecticut couple."

"Oh my God, yes. Jenny, will you please call my office in the morning and tell 'em what's happened and have 'em put somebody else on the Connecticuts? They're due in at ten-ten, TWA."

"I will."

"I've gotta be on that bird in two hours! You realize how much loot I'll lose on a half-mil sale?"

"Maybe you won't."

"Oh yes I will! I've gotta pack! What if he dies? I won't have anyone!"

"You'll have me."

"And my son."

"And Sue."

"Windy?"

"All of us."

"Listen, Jenny, this won't make any difference. In two weeks we marry, no matter what. So you go right ahead with the arrangements—okay? My father!"

She took him in her arms like a child. "Don't worry, dear, he'll be fine. You won't believe what recovery powers they have. I'll help you pack now."

"On the living room floor."

"I love you, Donald."

"Oh my God."

As soon as the DC-10 was airborne out of Phoenix, a beat realtor clicked off the overhead light, reclined the seat, closed his eyes, and was crashing asleep when an elderly woman beside him asked if he were going back east on business. To be polite, and elicit sympathy, he replied no, he'd just had a call from his father in Michigan who had fallen and been ambulanced to the hospital more dead than alive and said he wanted to see his son one last time.

"Lucky you."

"Lucky?"

It would have been unfair to say of Harold Chambers that he was a failed father because he had never aspired to success. He liked to say of himself that he "hoed a straight row." Born on a farm, he had eventually gone to work in the accounting department in Owosso, and there he had hoed his row for fifty years. He retired at age seventy-five because his eyes were going, his books were so fouled up they had to bring in a CPA, and because the company gave him a pension and some furniture and told him kindly to get lost.

"I'm seventy-one," said Don's seatmate, "and I'm going to Elkart, Indiana, for my mother's birthday, believe it or not." Her glasses, in the shape of butterfly wings, had rhinestone rims. "She's one hundred years old tomorrow, believe it or not."

"A hundred? Really."

"A hundred is right. She's killing my husband and me. We'll be in the ground before she is."

Harry Chambers was consistent. He belonged to two organizations, Rotary and the Masons. He had two hobbies, trout fishing and raising raspberries, and was skilled at both. He wore white shirts and two suits, a blue worsted and a black worsted, and white socks. He had seen only two states in the Union, Michigan and Arizona, because he did not give a tinker's damn for the rest. He had missed service in two World Wars, being too young for the first, too old for the second. He had never voted for a Democrat. The penultimate tragedy of his life was Thomas E. Dewey's loss to Truman in 1948 because Dewey had been born and raised in Owosso.

"Oh, come now," Don said. "Surely at a hundred she can't be too long for . . ."

"Eats like a horse, sleeps like a baby!" snapped the butterfly lady. "She's in a nursing home in Elkhart—costs us a fortune and we're retired ourselves. Oh, she gets a little from the government, but not half enough. And she's on the long-distance phone every other day, collect, daytime rate, begging us to come back and see her. We make three or four trips a year as it is, and it's eating us up."

In his eighty-three years on this earth, Harry Chambers had done only one thing out of character. At thirty-nine he proposed to Lila Reed, who was twenty-eight. She accepted him. The town was dumbfounded. The single woman staffer on the *Owosso Daily News,* she was a looker, vivacious, and far too sharp for the local swains, none of whom had had the nerve to put in a bid. The concensus of opinion, finally, was that she was Harry's last chance and he was hers. Reflecting on the match when he had grown up, Don could understand her acceptance. She was a mover and shaker. She believed she could change the bookkeeper, could uproot his raspberries and turn him into a fly fisherman, could remake him into the equal she needed and deserved, and for a while she did her damnedest. She had Don. She stayed home with him until he started school. She worked like hell on Harry. But while she might shake her husband up now and then, she could not move him. In despair, she crossed him off as a liability, returned to the newspaper, and redirected her dreams to the asset of her son. He disappointed her, too. An ordinary child, a middle-level adolescent, Don went in due course to the University at Ann Arbor, then dropped out after two years of engineering to take a job in Detroit. It was the penultimate tragedy of her life. She died at fifty-two, two months after her grandson, Ronald, was born to Don and Carol—not of cardiac arrest, Don was certain now, but of a heart she broke herself. She had lost twice, and Lila Reed Chambers—her byline in the paper—could not, would not, cope with defeat. She had married a stick-in-the-mud and was stuck with him. She had brought into the world a son who would little alter that world. Her son did not resent the judgment. Don loved his father, but loved his mother more. He respected her. She was creative. If she had failed, twice, it was not her fault. Had her origins been big-city, she might have had a champagne-and-caviar career. Owosso gave her only cold cereal.

"Well, listen," Don suggested. "Why don't you move her out to Phoenix and put her in a nursing home? That would save . . ."

"She wouldn't move if the damned home burned down. Dear Lord, don't think we haven't tried! She says all her friends are there in Elkhart, and they are—six feet under, pushing up daisies. But when we tell her that, she starts to cry." The woman pushed up her rhinestone rims and with a hanky wiped away a tear. "She cries buckets—long distance, collect, daytime rate—she just wears us out!"

After his wife's passing, Harry Chambers continued to till the limited acreage of his life as though nothing had happened. He lived in the same house and went to the same work. He had more money now—his own savings plus what Lila had put away, and her salary was higher than his—but did not spend it. Don flew him out to Arizona for two weeks in the spring, all expenses paid, and took him to watch the Oakland A's exhibition games in Phoenix. Last year two bouts of flu had prevented his coming, so father and son had not seen each other for two years. They alternated weekly phone calls, however, which seemed to suffice.

Don thought that maybe if he got a pillow the woman would take the hint and let him sleep. He popped his call button, asked the stewardess for a pillow, got one, and settled into it.

But she was nonstop. "May the good Lord strike me down, I can't help it," she continued. "But I wish my poor mother'd gone to the great nursing home in the sky twenty years ago." She put away her hanky. "A hundred years old. I'm seventy-one. If this goes on much longer it'll kill both of us, my husband and me both—he's got emphysema bad, and his arteries are hardening up like cement."

Not that the bonds between Don and Harry Chambers were buddy-buddy. Harry disapproved of much of what his son was and did, and Don knew it. His optimism rubbed Harry the wrong way because it was such an obvious legacy from Lila. Divorce, particularly Don's from Carol, was an abomination. And Harry undoubtedly cursed the day his son pulled up stakes and moved from Michigan to Arizona. That was desertion, plain and simple, and deliberate. And if divorce and desertion were not reprehensible enough, Don had committed the cardinal sin of quitting a perfectly good job in industrial Michigan to gamble on finding another out in the land of lizards and cactus. That was really dumb. Rolling stones gathered no moss. And when Don found a job, and was a success at selling real estate, and when the moss of commissions began to roll in, Harry could take no pleasure in it, for himself or for his only child. He merely let Don pick up the tab every time, from dining out to peanuts at the ballpark. He sent his son a card for his birthday and an Owosso necktie for Christmas.

"You'll see, young man," said Don's next-seat neighbor. "Your father lives another ten years and you'll wish him gone, too."

Don was shocked. "I will not!"

"Oh, yes, you will. And when he goes, you'll dance a jig on his grave."

He was also bitter and weary and bored. Pushing up out of the pillow, he gave her a red and angry eye. "I will not! That's cruel and inhuman. I love my father and I hope he lives to be a hundred and ten!"

"Ha. You do now."

"Ma'am, you should be ashamed of yourself! Think of what your mother's done for you—you should hope she lives forever!"

"She just might!"

"Well, you think about it and shut up and let me sleep!"

Don retired into the pillow and slammed his eyes shut. But Mrs. Elkhart was insulted, and stabbed him through the eyelids with such baleful glares while flying over New Mexico and Oklahoma and Kansas that he couldn't catch a wink all the way to O'Hare.

*

Harry Chambers was out of surgery and asleep when Don entered the room at Owosso General and stood reverently at the foot of the bed trying to get a fix on the father he'd come so far to bid farewell. His first sensation was that he was in the wrong room. Two years ago, the last time Harry had vacationed in Arizona, he had been short, perhaps five-seven, but gross in girth, blown up to forty-four inches around the middle by the ice cream and pastry he couldn't resist. He still had ample hair, a blend of wan brown and gray, but kept it trimmed so short that he looked like a hired hand after a washbasin and sheep shears. The man in this bed was incredibly diminished, incredibly changed. His skin was ashen. The brow was strong but the chin was weak, so that the face was muzzy. The hair was stubble. The hands, clasped over the chest in funeral repose, were cross-hatched with blue veins and speckled with liver spots. There was a resemblance, though. Had this man been attired in shirt and tie and a worsted suit he'd have been a dead ringer for the late Harry Chambers laid out in a casket. Don's eyes filled. It was quite possible he was too late. He knelt at the side of the bed and took icy hands in his.

"Dad? Dad, it's Don," he choked.

The eyes opened. They swam around the room and floated in on Don.

"Son? Is that you?"

"I'm here, Dad.

"Give me my glasses."

Don found the cataracts on the stand by the bed among the water bottle and plastic glass and Phisoderm and thermometer and other trinkets provided patients at high prices and helped him put them on.

"Are you all right, Dad? What happened?"

"Now get me my teeth."

Don searched and located upper and lower plates in the bathroom, in a glass of water, and brought them to his father, who opened his mouth and fitted them with trembling fingers.

"What happened, Dad? Did you break something?"

Harry clacked his plates, reared up, and seized Don's hands in a desperate grip. "Do something for me, Donald, please!"

"Anything, Dad!" He tensed, waiting for what might be his father's last words. "Anything!"

"I have to know! Go to the office—come right back and tell me. Am I—is all this—covered by Medicare?"

*

"Hip. At his age the hip's about as brittle as a prick in a plaster cast. But we bang a Jewett's Nail in there and they're ready to go. Usually."

This was Dr. Arnie Skinner, Harry's physician, whom Don had tracked down in the hospital. Harry's doc, who had treated him for thirty years, had recently been treated to eternal rest. Skinner looked to be fresh out of residency and pulled on a long, thin cigar in a holder.

"What happens now?" Don inquired.

Skinner said they got hip fractures ambulatory again as soon as possible after surgery—three or four days. Then three or four months on a walker should do it. Hopefully.

"How is my dad? General health, I mean."

"For his age, terrific. He won't make the Olympic team, but he's good for a long haul."

"How long?"

"I'm a medico, not a mystic."

"He's eighty-three."

"Let's put it this way. I wouldn't borrow on the estate if I were you."

"What about mentally?"

"You mean, is he senile? Is he walking around a few short of a full string of fish? He is not. Anyway, senile's a cheap-shot word."

"Do you see him often?"

"Sure, he drops in all the time—some business, some social. We talk. People tell docs things they won't tell their own kids."

"Like what?"

They sat over coffee in the hospital cafeteria. Skinner blew some professional smoke. "Well, your old man's an unhappy old man. Lonely. All his friends have checked out by now. He sits and watches TV. I'd be depressed myself if I lived alone in that mausoleum of a house waiting to die or the sun to shine or who wins what on a game show. He's prone to respiratory problems, too—bitching Michigan climate. I know a hell of a lot better climate for him. Guess where?"

Don stared at young Skinner.

"You're right," said the doc.

"Oh my God," Don said. "I can't."

"Your father, your conscience."

"I can't."

"Why not?"

"It would destroy my life."

"I know. Decisions, decisions." Arnie Skinner grinned. "Hear the one about the very old couple goes into their lawyer's office one day and says they want a divorce?"

"I've heard it."

" 'How old are you?' the attorney asks. 'Ninety-two,' says the old gent. 'Ninety-one,' says his wife. 'How long have you been married?' 'Sixty-four years,' says the wife.

"I've heard it," Don protested.

" 'My God!' says the attorney. 'Why have you waited so long to seek a divorce?' 'I'll tell you,' says the old gent."

"I don't want to hear it," Don protested.

" 'We decided to wait till the children were dead.' "

*

Don visited Harry again that evening, then slept the night in his father's bed in his father's house. He was a stranger in the house now. The toys of the boy who had grown up in it were packed in a box, probably, in the basement, as were the books of the college sophomore come home for Christmas. Where was the boy now? Where the sophomore? Where the stripling husband and father who had sped up from Detroit on a day in Indian summer twenty years ago only to arrive late for his mother's dying?

He slept late in the morning because he was whipped, then made coffee and roamed the downstairs. It really was an old mausoleum of a house. In the living room a TV set and an armchair faced each other. The fabric on the arms of the chair was frayed. He looked out the kitchen window, and in the backyard, by the detached garage, the raspberry bushes were broken down and weedy. Dirty dishes were stacked in the sink. He washed and dried them. Then he thought of calling his office in Phoenix, but when he picked up the phone, the holes in the receiver were clogged with earwax. He cleaned out the holes with the point of a fingernail file and sponged off the phone. On another thought he went into his father's bedroom downstairs, stripped the bed, stuffed the sheets into a hamper already stuffed, and remade the bed with clean sheets. He wondered who did Harry's laundry. On the dresser was a photo of Lila taken when she was a bride. He went into the living room again, on the worn carpeting of which his father had fallen, and looked out a window. Around the house was a perimeter of huge oak trees and telephone poles, and along the power lines between the poles, he remembered, daredevil squirrels used to walk tightrope. He used to watch them, waiting for them to explode in smoke from high voltage. Where were the squirrels now?

He found an album on the sideboard in the dining room. It contained snapshots of his parents, which, he remembered, were once kept in a drawer table, loose. He wondered how many hours Harry had whiled away pasting them in the album on the assumption Don would cherish it someday. And when Don realized he wouldn't, that instead he'd probably pitch it, he got teary, hurried to the bathroom, shaved, then dressed hurriedly. He had to get out of that haunted house. Otherwise he'd start thinking about what Doc Skinner had suggested. The hell he would think about it. It was impossible. Jenny and he were marrying in two weeks. Windy and Sue were moving in with them. There was simply no room at the inn for Harry. That was the way it was, so why should he glum around the world carrying a load of guilt?

He breakfasted at a McDonald's, then drove the rental car north out of Owosso. The day was cloudy. He missed the southwestern sunshine. Everything was green, green in Michigan. In Arizona, in the desert, everything was brown and gray and sand. And in Michigan your sight was limited, trees bounded you, while in Arizona you had space and majesty and the eye could laser as far as the mountains would let it.

Eight miles north of Owosso he bridged Honey Brook. Don did a doubletake, stopped, backed, cut the motor, left the car, climbed a fence, and moseyed along the little stream. Honey Brook was haunted, too. It was here, when he was twelve years old, that his father had taught him how to brush-fish for trout.

Don Chambers dropped out of the U. of Michigan after two years to take a job in Detroit as a manufacturer's rep selling a line of small machine tools for the car industry. He aced the draft by being married in 1963 and siring a son in 1964. He married Carol Styles, a year his senior and an assistant buyer at Himmelhoch's, a ladies-wear retailer on Woodward Avenue. They were content. Fourteen years later he was still peddling tools to the tune of $21,000 a year and she was lingerie manager at $12,000. They had it made. They had a house, two cars, money in the bank, life insurance, and a kid. Then they flew to Phoenix in the winter for a combo machine-tool convention and vacation and Don went ape over Arizona. Carol did not.

Brush-fishing for trout meant that you worked a very small stream tough to reach. You used a telescopic rod, a stout line, and nightcrawlers. You had to sneak up on a hole soundlessly through the brush, often on hands and knees, or you'd spook the wary trout. Once you got within rod's length of a hole, which might be a passage through banks of watercress no more than a foot wide, you extended the rod and let the bait down into the water a few feet above the hole so that the crawler would sink and ride naturally with the current into the hole and the trout would think it a gift of God or something. It took Harry several holes and spooked fish before Don, age twelve, got the hang of it. Then they came to Harry's glory hole.

Don pressured Carol into a second winter vacation in Arizona, however, and when they returned to Detroit in March, and there was still snow on the ground, he asked her to shoot the moon. He asked her to join him in an adventure—to move West—to start life over. She refused. She loved Detroit. She'd been born there, her family was there, his father close by in Owosso, they had good jobs and friends, and he must be stark raving even to consider throwing all that away. Throwing *what* away? Couldn't she look down the road? Couldn't she see what they'd be ten years from now, twenty years? Zilches! No, she was sorry, she couldn't look down the road because she wasn't college-educated—Carol was forever zapping him about his two years at Ann Arbor. Well, he could, he asserted, and the rut they were in might be good enough for her but it wasn't for him and, besides, who in hell wanted to live in a rut? The breach widened. He began to call her "Harry" because she had more Harry in her than he did. She began to call him "Lila" because, like his mother, he was never satisfied. They began to have knock-down, drag-out fights over Arizona.

Musing along the stream, Don approached a real jungle of brush and bushes and remembered—inside it had been Harry's glory hole. He wondered if it was still there, thirty years later, and made up his mind to find out. He thrashed through the brush, got down on his hands and knees, and crawled toward the hole.

Don Chambers had his midlife crisis early, on the Edsel Ford Expressway. It was February, he was driving in a blizzard, and he had a flat tire. He pulled off and tried to change the tire in blinding snow and below zero and cut his hand on the jack and jumped up and down bleeding and waving his arms and howling like a madman and left the goddamn car and hitched a ride and paid the guy twenty bucks to take him home. That night he laid it on the line with Carol: move to Arizona with him or give him a divorce. She took the divorce—and Don to the cleaners. She got custody of Ron, the house, Don's life insurance, five hundred a month alimony plus two hundred child support. Don got to keep Ron summers, his two-year-old car, his credit cards, a rusty telescopic fishing rod, and the court graciously allowed him a grubstake of five thou from the joint account. He took off for Arizona in 1979 and a cloud of dust. He was thirty-seven and free.

But now, crawling along in his Yves St. Laurent slacks, he was not free. "Your father, your conscience," Skinner had said. In Don's opinion, he shouldn't have to face a decision like this. In his opinion he was a nice guy, no world-beater, but basically a nice guy. A solid citizen. He voted regularly and didn't cheat on his taxes—oh, maybe writing off 80 percent of his Sedan de Ville and 50 percent of his tennis club was a tad high, but he'd never been audited. And now, to have this monkey on his back just when the bluebird of happiness was singing his song—it was bad timing, and either way, whatever he decided, he had to lose.

After thirty years, Harry's glory hole was unchanged. Don sat looking at it. The sun burst out between clouds and the water was suddenly the color of honey. The hole, perhaps four feet deep and carved under the bank by current, was the result of a small water-fall over a semisubmerged log crosswise of the brook, and if there was any hole in Honey Brook in which a lunker lurked, this was it. Sitting there, Don remembered more. On the day when he was pupil and Harry teacher, Harry had crawled with him to the hole then stopped, thinking, trying to decide. He thought for a minute, then whispered, "That's my hole. You take it. Crawl up to rod's length, lay your crawler in the water upstream of the log, let the current take it over the log. Wait. There's a big one in there—I've missed him twice because I was in a hurry. He doesn't strike and run. He'll come out from the dark and take the bait and start back under the bank slow. So wait and watch your line move. Wait till it's almost to the bank, then let him have the hook hard." Father patted son on the shoulder. "Good luck."

The boy behaved as told. His crawler roiled over the log into the hole. The line stopped, then tautened and moved toward the bank. He waited, heart stopped and every sense on fire, then set the hook hard. Hollering to high heaven, out of Honey Brook he hauled a sixteen-inch trout. His father had given him his glory hole. Father had made son a gift of his life's fish.

Remembering the day, Don Chambers, forty-two and in love, who lived in a condo and sold real estate and voted regularly and interrupted coitus to fly across the U.S. to bid farewell to that fa-ther, began to cry like a child.

When he was cried out, he beat back through the brush and jogged along Honey Brook to the rental car and jumped in and spit gravel and hung a U and floorboarded it for Owosso General.

He swept a chair to bedside, sat down, and bent to be close to his father. Propped up by pillows, glasses on and choppers in and a day's convalescence under his belt, Harry looked much better.

"Dad," said an emotional Don, "I've got a proposition for you. Don't say yes or no till you think it over—but I hope you like it. We'll see."

Harry folded hands and twiddled thumbs.

"I don't think this is much of a life for you here, Dad," Don continued. "All your friends are gone, the winters are hell, and the house must cost you an arm and a leg to heat. Well, I was thinking. You seemed to like Arizona when you came out on vacations—how'd you like to come out permanently? I mean, sell the house and get on a bird and live with me? Sunshine the year round! There'd be just the two of us in my place—plenty of room. How does that appeal to you? Give it a thought. I know it'd be a wrench, leaving Owosso, but I'd love to have you, Pop. Take your time deciding. Take a couple weeks if you want, and if you say no, I'll . . ."

"I accept," said Harry.

*

He could have phoned Jenny that night, but he was overwhelmed by what he had done. He could have given her a buzz from Lansing the next day, where he turned in the rental car and a lousy Chicago connection gave him an hour to kill. At O'Hare, his westbound flight was delayed two hours, but he did not go to a phone. Instead, he had drinks and called himself a coward.

By the time Don got to Phoenix in late evening he had worked out his tactics. No flying in on Jenny and dropping the bomb—that was unfair and he was mentally incapable—not tonight. Instead, he'd play it cool and macho. Having left his Caddy at Oasis

South since he hadn't known how long he'd be in Michigan, he'd cab straight home, call her casually, make a date for tomorrow night, then by candlelight and wine lay the bad news on her calmly and regretfully, seasoning it with pride and manliness and self-sacrifice. But by the time he got to Scottsdale he had the shakes again at the enormity of what he'd done, and told the driver to make it Oasis North instead of Oasis South, overtipped him when they arrived, rushed the front door, rang the bell, and when Sue Staley answered, pushed past her into the living room and stood with suitcase in hand opening and closing his mouth like some kind of nut who didn't know who he was or what in hell he was doing there. Sue stared at him. Jenny Staley came in from the kitchen to stare at him. Windy Coon punched off the TV with her rattlesnake cane. She had a better show right in front of her.

"I don't believe it!" Don blurted.

They stared at him.

"I don't even believe what I've done!"

They stared at him.

"I've asked my father to come out here and live with me and he's coming!"

It took a moment for the cognitive dust to settle.

"Good," said Windy Coon. "Good." If there had been a place to spit her satisfaction, she would have. "I wasn't much of a mind t'move nohow."

"Well, I think that's just the pits," said Sue, curling a lip at Don.

He blinked at her. "The pits?"

"Where does that leave Mom?"

"Out on the end of a limb, that's where," Don declared. "And I've just axed it off. Sue was right. Windy should've slapped leather and shot me."

Jenny was sympathetic. "Dear, why don't you begin at the beginning?"

He did. Bits and pieces poured out of his bay like passenger luggage down a conveyor belt. Harry's hip. Doc Skinner's bright idea. That mausoleum of a house. The photo album. Harry's lonely life. Honey Brook. The glory hole and the sixteen-inch trout when he was twelve. "I sat there by that stream and just fell apart. Jenny, I cried. He's not an easy man to love, but he is my father, and I realized I hadn't loved him enough or done enough for him and this was my last chance. So I tore back to the hospital and asked him. I wanted him to say yes, I honestly did, but I guess I thought he wouldn't—he's never really been out of Owosso in his life—but my God he did, he said right away, 'I accept,' and only later did it hit me—what I'd done to us."

She had ferried him the two blocks to Oasis South in her car, and they were parked in the dark with the windows down. They were somewhat out of synch, for they had been separated and the first hot breath of summer was on their faces.

"He hates hot weather," Don recalled. "Well, here comes summer and here comes Harry."

"It's role-reversal," Jenny explained. "The parent cares for the child. Then, when the parent grows old, the child becomes the parent."

"Wait a minute," Don said. "What if we marry anyway and pool our funds? What if we buy a big house and move everydamnbody in with us?"

"Now you understand how I feel about Windy," Jenny said. "She's difficult at times, and needs an awful lot of care, but it's something *I* have to do. So do you."

Cramped from the flight, he put a knee on the dashboard. "What happened to the Connecticuts? You know, the couple?"

"Rose Bullock made the sale."

"Damn."

"She'll have to split the commission. You had the listing and the clients."

"I sure did."

"Speaking of that—I hate to tell you—but while you were gone, business slacked off. The people in my shop say we might be on the downside of the cycle. They say it happens every five years or so, and we're overdue."

"Oh, no. Just what I need. I know, Jen—let's get married anyway. After my old man comes we'll just sleep around in motels."

He couldn't see her smile, but he knew she did. Then they were silent.

"Well, it's over," he said.

"What?"

"The balloon ride."

"Down to earth, dear."

"Yup."

" 'Life is unfair.' "

"Who said that?"

"JFK."

"Oh."

"You must be exhausted."

"Dead." He dropped the knee. "Speaking of that, how's Windy's health these days?"

"Shame on you."

"I already am ashamed. I ask you to marry me, you say yes, then I say sorry, kid, I can't, I've invited my father to move in with me. I apologize."

"Don't say it."

"I have to. If there was dirt outside this car instead of blacktop, I'd get out and grovel."

Jenny thought about that, then maneuvered herself over the console of her Cutlass and wound her arms about his neck and turned his face to hers. The smell of her, of Patou or Binaca, revived him. "Now you listen, Donald Chambers," she said softly. "You are a lovely man and I love you with all my heart. If you hadn't asked your father, you wouldn't be the lovely man I love. Don, dear, we're not alone. Many people have problems like ours today, and solve them eventually. Or time does. So let's keep the faith. Let's be patient. We're young yet. We can wait."

Harry Chambers couldn't. Inside of two weeks he phoned to say he was home and getting around fairly well with a four-point walker and had put his house on the market—asking price sixty-two five.

"I think that's low," said Don.

"Charley Chase doesn't—the agent. Not for Owosso. Do you know how much your mother and I paid for this house in 1941?"

"How much?"

"Eleven five. And something else. You know what Skinner says? He says moving to Arizona out of the cold and damp's just the ticket for me. Says it might add ten years to my life."

"He does?"

*

Harry again, a week later. "Sold the house today."

"Hey, great, Pop!"

The line hummed. Don knew Harry was waiting for him to ask how much and was damned if he would. In the first place, it was none of his business. But in the second, Harry was dying to be asked, and not to would be inhumane.

"How much, Pop?"

"Fifty-six four."

"Less commission. I think that's way too low."

"Do you know how much your mother and I paid for this house in 1941?"

"I know, but it's still too low. You didn't take the first offer that came along, did you?"

"Yes, I did. Sold it on a land contract."

"A land contract? What in hell is that?"

Harry said they were common in Michigan. You got a substantial down payment, in his case twenty thousand. Then there were payments of so much a month for ten years, like rent, after which the buyer went to mortgage and the seller got the balance of the principal in cash. But in the meantime, until the mortgage, seller kept title to the property.

Don tried to think that one through. "Do you mean—are you saying—the deal takes ten years to complete?"

"That's about right."

"But, but—ten years to payoff? If you retain title, that means you're responsible for the next ten years to see the place is maintained and insured and taxes paid and so on. And you're paid on time every month. Dad, why didn't you consider me? How could I watchdog all that at this distance?"

"You won't. I will."

"But suppose you—you have to think—I mean, you might not be around ten years from now!"

"Don't be so sure, Donald. I told you what young Skinner said."

*

Ten days later Harry was on the horn again to announce he'd had a yard auction yesterday—hired an auctioneer, moved his worldly goods out of the house into the yard—every stick of furniture, every sheet and towel, every pot and pan—put 'em on the block and sold 'em to the highest bidder and cleared, after the auctioneer's ten percent, a grand total of $2813.14.

"Well, my gosh, Dad."

"My gosh what?"

"I dunno. I'm just surprised, is all. What about my toys? You know, the ones in a box in the basement."

"Sold 'em."

"What about the photo album with snaps of you and mom? On the sideboard in the dining room."

"Oh, that. Threw it in the trash."

Don was rendered speechless.

"Why I called, Son, I'm ready. My suitcase is packed. How long before you get back here?"

"Me? Why should I come back?"

"Why, to help me drive."

"Drive!"

"Of course. I can't drive all day long."

"But, but, I thought you'd sell your car and fly!"

"Sell it? How would I get around in Arizona?"

"How can you drive with your right hip broken?"

"Leave that to me."

"Are you licensed?"

"I am."

"They insure you? With your eyes?"

"They do. They know me here. Been driving for seventy years. Started out in my father's Pope-Tribune in 1912. Remind me to tell you about that sometime. When'll you be back?"

Don bit a fingernail. "Well, two or three days, I guess. I hate to leave right now—real estate is sort of on the skids out here. It's not very smart of me to be away."

"Donald, you know I can't drive clear across the country by myself."

Don sighed, deeply. "I guess not."

"We were going to Ovid to play baseball, a bunch of us boys. On a snake-track road through sand—not paved back then. Well, the accelerator stuck, and I didn't know enough to switch off the ignition and I couldn't run us up a bank or into some bushes because I couldn't get out of the snake tracks." Harry's plates clacked as he warmed to his tale. "Well sirree, away we went, faster and faster, that two-cylinder buggy just a-roaring and us boys holding on and yelling bloody murder—'Whoa! Whoa!' "

*

This trip Don flew by day. Charley Chase was driving Harry and his car down from Owosso to Lansing and returning by bus. Chambers senior and Chambers junior would meet in the Lansing air terminal.

Don deplaned in Lansing, got his bag, and at first sight disbelieved the sight. Could this plump little fellow, seated on a bench in a busy terminal wearing a porkpie hat and trying to see through cataract lenses and eating an ice cream cone be the man who, on a winter's night in Owosso long ago, joyed in the flesh efficiently enough to bring a son into being? Impossible. He looked like a child given a treat and abandoned by his family. A topcoat was over his arm, a four-point aluminum walker stood before him, and he wore a black worsted suit, brown shoes, a white shirt, and a purple tie with pink ducks. Don came up to him and Harry smiled and moved his cone and shook hands.

"Great to see you, Pop. Well, are you ready for the road?"

"Hold your horses. I'm not wasting this cone."

When he had finished, right down to the tip, they started for the parking lot. Harry's progress was painfully and maddeningly slow. He swung the walker out before him, planted the points, then lunged forward and let his weight into it and down, grunting now and then with the effort.

"Can I help you, Dad?"

"Nope."

"How long yet on the walker?"

"A month or two, Skinner says."

After forever they reached Harry's wheels, and Don was aghast. He had failed to check the garage behind the house in Owosso. What he was to drive across the continent was a big brown 1970 Buick Wildcat, a four-door sedan. It was a spectacle and a menace. All four fenders were mangled beyond recognition. One rear door was tied shut with rope. Cracks cobwebbed the rear window. The front bumper was battered into the grill.

Harry was proud of it. "You remember 'Aunt Min'—what I always called 'er. Near a hundred and ninety thousand miles and she runs like a top."

Don set his jaw. "Pop, why in hell haven't you bought yourself a new car?"

"Why should I? Cost a fortune these days! And they don't make 'em like Aunt Min anymore."

"I see you've had a few accidents."

"Well, a few," Harry admitted.

"You must have had a collision. Why didn't the insurance company repair it?"

"Would have if I'd told 'em. At my age, you put in a claim and they'll cancel you."

Don put a tentative toe to a bald tire. "When did you last change the oil?"

"Damned if I know."

"What about a tune-up?"

"You know, Donald, when Tom Dewey was campaigning he came back to Owosso. I shook hands with him! He remembered me!"

"Dad, this car's a disaster. Your rubber's shot, and probably your brakes, and—"

"Say," said Harry, miffed, "are we going to stand around all day jawing or are we going to Arizona?"

Don took the keys, stowed his one suitcase in the trunk with Harry's one suitcase, unlocked the rear door not tied shut, stowed the walker, unlocked the front doors, helped his father in, and slid behind the wheel. On the front seat was a cardboard shoebox. On the back seat under the walker were a small cardboard carton and a briefcase.

"Move 'em out!" said Don, starting the motor and forcing from Aunt Min's ancient guts through the exhaust a great fart of blue flame.

"What's that mean?" Harry asked.

"Oh, that's what they used to say when they started the wagon trains. Heading west." Don indicated the shoebox between them. "What's in that?"

"My pills."

Don nodded backward. "And the briefcase?"

"I cleaned out my safe-deposit box."

"The carton?"

"The urn."

"The urn?"

"Your mother's ashes."

*

By noon the next day it was apparent to Don that he would drive every mile of the two thousand and that they would make pee-poor time. Harry couldn't take his pills dry, which was all right because the Buick couldn't pass a gas station without stopping, which was all right because Harry needed incessantly to relieve himself. Don would get the walker out of the rear and while Harry was using the restroom and taking his pills Don would credit-card the quart of oil and the gallonage Aunt Min would guzzle between there and the next stop. Since it was also apparent that Don would pick up the tab for motels and meals, which he'd done last night because his father hadn't offered, it would have been cheaper for him, he figured, to sell the car for scrap and charter a Lear jet.

"We're not making very good time," Harry complained outside Springfield, Illinois.

"That's because we have to make so damned many stops," Don retorted. "Gas and pills, gas and pills. Why do you have a whole boxful of pills?"

"I stocked up," said Harry, taking the shoebox into his lap and starting to inventory. "There aren't so many. Let's see. I had a little heart attack a while back, and Skinner—"

"A heart attack!"

"Skinner's got me on three things. Coumadin—that's to prevent the blood clotting. Digitalis. Lasix—I don't know what that's for." Harry fondled the bottles like a miser his gold, reading the label on each. "Don't know what I'd do without these. Do you ever have acid stomach, Son?"

"No."

"I do. You can hear me belch a mile away. I like Di-Gel. My right shoulder gives me trouble, too—arthritis. I take Tylenol. What's this? Oh, yes. Persantine. Poor circulation."

This pharmacopoeia was beginning to sound familiar to Don.

"Then you've noticed I've got some Parkinson's. Symmetrel keeps that under control. And a slight touch of diabetes. Nothing I can do for that but stay away from sweets."

"Dad, I don't understand. Skinner told me your health is generally good."

"You asked him, eh? Well, it is. For my age. What's this? Aldoril? Aldoril? What's that for? Oh, yes. Blood pressure."

"Say, this is really lush farm country."

"Then I have prostate problems. If I had a dime for every time I have to go to the toilet, day and night, I'd be . . ."

"Just look at those cornfields."

"Skinner massages it. Which reminds me, I'll have to find a new doctor in Scottsdale."

"We're loaded with doctors. Overloaded."

"Well, that's the first thing I must do. I hear there's something new for arthritis—Tylenol isn't doing it. I think it's called Ascriptin—sort of a fancy aspirin. When I find a new . . ."

"Dad, I've got some news for you." As far as Don was concerned, it was either interrupt or head for the nearest hospital and get himself a complete physical. "Very good news."

"Oh?"

"I've fallen in love."

"Hmpf." Harry recovered the pillbox and set it aside. "Some little snippy?"

"No, a wonderful girl. Her name's Jenny Staley. Well, not a girl—she's thirty-eight."

"A divorced woman."

"Yes. Twelve years."

Harry sat on this information like a suppository. "Got a passel of kids, I expect. The woman."

"Just one, a girl, Sue. And Jenny lives with and supports her ninety-one-year-old grandmother."

"Ninety-one!"'

"A real Arizona pioneer."

"A real pistol, I'll bet."

"Anyway, aren't you happy for me, Pop?"

" 'Once bitten, twice shy.' " For ten miles a dour Harry twiddled his thumbs and his son's happiness. "Well," he said, finally, "I'd say you were better off with Carol. I'd say you've got yourself in a hell of a mess."

*

A pit stop beyond St. Louis to slake Aunt Min's insatiable thirst and reduce Harry's blood pressure, the latter brought his briefcase from the rear seat into the front, and when they were under way again, began to inventory the contents as he had his pillbox.

"Donald, I think you should know what I hold. I told you I cleaned out my safe-deposit box."

"You don't have to, Dad. It's really none of my business." On second thought, Don changed his mind. It *was* his business, or would be. "Unless of course you want to."

"Well, I should. It'll all be yours someday, and at my age, you never know. Say, that's another thing I'll have to do right away— find a good, sound bank."

"We're also overloaded with banks."

Harry took several thick packets of stock certificates and bonds in rubber bands and fingered through them, reading aloud the names of various equities. He had been a conservative investor, buying only blue chips—IBM, Morgan, Exxon, AT&T, General Electric, Union Pacific, etc.—plus some triple-A municipals and some U.S. Treasury bonds.

"About a hundred-forty thousand here, roughly," said Harry, evincing the same pride he had in his car. "Then there's the twenty in cash from the house, and I had a good bank account—I've got a

||| 50 |||

cashier's check for all that—you add it up and I'm worth in the neighborhood of two hundred thousand."

Don was sincerely surprised. "That's a nice neighborhood."

Harry was returning the packets to the briefcase. "And I shouldn't have to touch capital. I have a small pension from the store, and the income from these, and the house payments, and Social Security—government keeps raising that every year."

"Keeps raising my taxes, too. You senior citizens are breaking our backs."

Harry ignored that. "I take in well over fifteen hundred a month. I should be in fine shape for my old age. Oh, yes, here's my will, signed and witnessed. And I'll put the cash in time certificates." He snapped the briefcase shut. "Fine shape—unless I go dotty and have to go into a nursing home. I hope not—they'll go through two hundred thousand like termites." He looked meaningfully at his son. "Then I'd have to depend on you, Donald."

That ticked Don. He wanted to say—then? Depend on me *then*? What about *now*? Pop, if you're so affluent, why in hell don't you peel off a couple shares of IBM for fuel and lodging and food and maybe a mart for your dear, dutiful son who's carting your valuables and ass across the country in this heap at his own expense? He simmered for a mile or two, then decided to slip in his own stiletto.

"One thing, though, Dad, we have to remember. You've socked away a bundle, but Mom contributed. She worked a lot of years on the paper and saved a lot. Probably a hundred thou of that is hers."

Harry bristled. "Oh, no, it isn't."

"Sure it is. Be fair."

"No, it isn't. She didn't work that long."

"But she made more than you did."

Harry was now very hot under the collar. "She did not. And in case you're interested, I don't care to talk about it anymore. Or her."

*

Don, however, did. And after they bid bye-bye to Joplin, Mo., he asked the burning question.

"Dad, why do you have Mom's ashes? Why aren't they in the cemetery in Owosso?"

"Well," said Harry, shifting uneasily, "I'll tell you about that."

"I wish you would."

"Well, I bought a plot in 1943. For the two of us." Paid a hundred dollars for it, and perpetual care. It's in the most desirable part, trees and shade. Then after the war, space got short in the cemetery and the price kept going up. I was getting offers all the time. By the time she died, that plot was worth twelve hundred. So I had her cremated. Kept her ashes in the garage."

"Did she want to be cremated?"

"I don't know."

"What if she didn't?" Don demanded. "What if she wanted to be planted at home, in that beautiful place?"

Harry was on the hot seat now. "I don't know that she did. Anyway, what's the difference? She's gone."

"Swell. Oh, swell. And what'll you do with her ashes in Arizona?"

"I don't know." To conclude the conversation, Harry pulled down the brim of his porkpie and played drowsy. "And I don't care."

"You've got to do something!"

"I'll worry about that when the time comes."

Don was not through. "And what'll I do about you, when your time comes?"

Harry came to. "I don't give a damn. Well, yes I do. Don't cremate me."

*

And then, on the Will Rogers Highway, tooling for Tulsa, Harry wanted to drive.

"Oh my God, Dad."

"It's my car."

"But your hip! Have you driven since?"

"I have. Two or three times."

"You can't see to the side!"

"Who needs to?"

"How're your reflexes?"

"What're you talking about?"

Harry made a convincing case. Oklahoma was flat as a pancake, the highway was six lanes wide, each three separated by a wide, grassy, sunken median, and traffic was desultory. Besides, they had just lunched, Don was sleeply and could use a siesta.

So they pulled off, Don came around the Wildcat, got out the walker, followed Harry around, helped him behind the wheel, brought the walker back, stowed it in the rear, took the passenger seat, and a confident Harry, peering through cataract lenses, steered them onto and down the Will Rogers at the lawful 65 mph.

Don's eyelids drooped.

Harry's eyelids drooped.

Don dozed.

Harry dozed.

Don was bumped into panic.

Aunt Min was off the road altogether. She rattled and roared down the sunken median below highway level toward a concrete culvert at Indianapolis speed!

Harry snored.

Don yelled!

||| 3 |||

Don Chambers couldn't care less that he was dead because Heaven turned out to be an infinitely better deal than he had
ever dreamed.

He owned his own cloud, free and clear. On its fleecy upper
surface were a tennis court, a swimming pool, a well-stocked bar,
a closetful of designer men's wear in his sizes, a stereo set with
Klipschorn speakers, and a giant-screen TV. New Age music filled
the air. Jenny fluttered down on gossamer wings to greet him. Her
face and form were divine. She wore only high heels and a
teddy—Don had seen pictures of teddies on models in department-store brochures but never one in real life—of ivory satin lavished with lace and blue satin beading. She came toward him,
folding her wings, smiling. He opened wide his arms to take her
and the teddy in, to drape her on the bed of his undulant cloud
and diddle away an eternity of terrific sexual activity.

But just as he was about to embrace her, voices blared over the
music, mortal voices, and dragged him from the dream. He slit an
eye at the clock. It was five-ten in the morning. He had driven
twelve hours yesterday, almost five hundred miles, all the way to
Phoenix from Tucumcari, New Mexico, because his father was
tired of the road. Groaning, he hauled himself out of bed and into

the living room, and there was Harry, in BVDs, watching a Mexican movie on the tube.

"Dad, for God's sake!" he cried. "It's five o'clock in the morning!"

"I know that," said Harry mildly. He had not yet put his plates in for the day, and gummed his words. "I always get up at five. 'Early to bed, early . . .'"

"Does it have to be on so loud?"

"If it isn't, how can I hear?"

*

They found a safe place for Lila's ashes: on the floor of the closet in Harry's room. They found a bank. Harry opened a savings and a checking account and rented a safe-deposit box. Don's doctor was an internist who socked him a hundred bucks a throw. Harry wouldn't hear of that. They found him a G.P., who went for forty-five. They found some snappy sport shirts and slacks for him at Sears, where he insisted on shopping because he owned a hundred shares of the stock. They found a Buick dealer whose service manager offered to do a complete hysterectomy on Aunt Min, removing and replacing everything including the ovaries, for twenty big ones. Harry wouldn't hear of that. And Don found out more about his father, in the first two weeks they bachelored together, than he really wanted to know.

Harry was a vidiot. He loved the remote control, but seldom used it, preferring to pick one channel and let it roll. His tastes were eclectic. Game shows, soaps, old flicks, local news and national, sitcoms, wrestling, talk shows, documentaries, bike races, dramas—all were grist for his entertainment mill and he nodded through them all, from 5 A.M. to 10 P.M., with impartial pleasure. He liked a lot of volume, too. To make phone calls or do paperwork, Don had to shut himself in his room. Then, when Harry hit the sack at ten, and Don wanted to catch the news and maybe the "Tonight" show, Harry complained he couldn't rest for the racket.

Don was dubious. He took his father to a war movie one night and Harry slept through the rifle fire and artillery like a log.

Don would sometimes urge him to get outside, get some fresh air, go sit under a palm tree by the pool. It was June now, the temps in Scottsdale were hitting 110° daily, and Harry said it would be a cold day in hell before he went outdoors in such a "fiery furnace." He turned the air-conditioning in the condo down to 72°; Don usually kept it at 78°. Harry said he sweat like a hog at 78°. Don said he couldn't afford 72°. They compromised on 76°, but when Don would come home after a hard day's hustling, the AC was set at 72°.

Harry did go out now and then, though, to keep the Buick's battery charged, he said, and on such occasions, reflecting on the traffic, Don grew cold, despite the heat, with apprehension until his return. He remarked that, since Harry was now a resident of Arizona, he should buy Arizona plates and take the exam for an Arizona driver's license.

"Why?" inquired Harry.

"Well, if you have an accident, driving with Michigan plates and a Michigan license, the cops will come down on you hard."

"Then I won't have an accident," said Harry, and shifted to the attack. "Why're you gone so much? What're you up to?"

"Earning a living, Pop."

"Hmpf," said Harry. "I thought you were already rich."

That was another sore point with Don. His father was tighter than the paper on the wall. As he had contributed nothing on the road, he contributed nothing to the running expense of his new home. Don sent out their laundry and paid the bill. Don bought the groceries. When they went out to dinner, Harry did not even fumble for the check. And the reason they dined out often was that Harry couldn't abide Don's cooking. To watch his weight, he specialized in salads and small, rare steaks. Harry was a roast and potatoes and gravy man. He liked pie for breakfast. Don liked juice and coffee. But if there was a difference of opinion about diet, there was none about housework. Don did it all. Harry couldn't help with the dishes, couldn't make a quick pass at the place with a dustcloth, couldn't even make his own bed—his hip bothered him, he claimed, it wasn't coming around as it should. Consequently his son became his servant, toting cups of coffee to the TV, fetching glasses of water and pills from the pillbox, waiting on his sire hand and foot.

Even his feet posed a problem. Too wide at the waterline to reach them, Harry had been unable for a year to trim his toenails. They were bent up and bent down and ingrown and hard as horn. Don tried clippers and scissors and tin snips and profanity, to no avail, then took him to a podiatrist who did a neat job and charged him fifty dollars. Harry frothed at the mouth. *Fifty* dollars to trim toenails! He threatened the receptionist with his walker. He threatened the podiatrist with small-claims court and the Better Business Bureau. Don dropped a fifty on the counter and bustled his father out of there, but Harry didn't lose altitude for two days.

The payoff came one night at Harry's bedtime, after he had turned off the tube and clumped for his bedroom. The matter had been on Don's mind, and on his nose. "Dad," he said, "would you like me to draw a bath for you?"

"Why?"

"I thought you might enjoy one."

"Well, think again."

"How often do you take a bath, by the way?"

"When I need one." Harry glared. "And when I'm damned well ready."

*

Don shook his head. "Biggest mistake of my life. No, take that back—Carol was. But inviting him out here comes a close second."

Without Jenny's ear to bend, her shoulder to cry on, he didn't know what he'd do.

"I'm living with a stranger. This man and the father I remember from years back are two different people. What about Windy?"

"Oh, absolutely." Jenny was positive. "She used to be gentle and soft-spoken and sweet—the perfect granny. Now she can be a real trial sometimes. I guess they all change."

Don had just begun. "Pop was never perfect. But if he was never generous, at least he wasn't cheap. I paid for every meal, every motel, and every gallon of gas from Michigan to Arizona. Now he doesn't contribute a dime or lift a finger. If he wasn't outgoing, at least he wasn't a hermit. He won't even go sit by the pool and talk to people. He squats in front of that set all day and feels sorry for himself. Harry was never a backslapper, but he could at least smile once in a while. Now he's mean. I mean *mean*. And no sense of humor whatever. He might not have been placid either, but at least he wasn't pig-headed. Jenny, I'll say it—he's turned into an old bastard. He's unpleasant as hell to be around. I can't do anything right. Nothing suits him. He never says thank you. He won't read the paper. He never asks about me. He never asks about Ron, his own grandson. The whole world is bounded by his old hide. He bitches about everything—the cost of things, Washington, how hot it is, what I cook for us." Don threw up his hands. "I think about him and *think* about him—and I can't find one damn thing to love. Or even like."

She shook her head. "Poor darling."

"He's ripping me up. Grinding me down. Wearing me out."

"We have to empathize. It's very hard, but we have to put ourselves in their positions. He's used to living alone, isn't he?"

"Well, sure. Twenty years."

"That's one thing. Then there's this move—the first time ever, to a strange environment. Maybe he's a little frightened, insecure . . ."

"That'll be the day."

"I'm not taking sides, Don. I'm just . . ."

"Do you realize, Jenny Staley, if I hadn't asked him out here we'd be married now and happy as clams? My God, I'm getting old myself! I found a gray hair on my chest today!"

That made her tilt her head and laugh and look beautiful.

"Okay," he said, "laugh and be beautiful, but I need help. What'll I do?"

"Be patient."

"Patient!"

"Time squeegees all wounds."

He grinned and grabbed her hand and kissed it. "Let me ask you something, girlfriend. Where have all the twinkly, rosy-cheeked, wonderful old folks gone these days? The only place I see 'em is on television, being nice to their kids and grandchildren and pitching products. Where the hell have they gone?"

"Away, I guess." Jenny sighed. "Like Tin Lizzies. And melodeons. And Sadie Hawkins Day."

"The only ones I know are tough to take. And they shouldn't be. They should live so long—well, they are. And if they make it past seventy they ought to pinch themselves every morning and be damn glad they're alive and—what's this?" Don noticed a thread sticking out of a seam in his Jean Merde jeans. He tugged at it. "I'll tell Pop off tonight. He's lucky to be—wait a second." He forgot the thread. He looked at her. "Eureka! Another sensational idea from my fertile brain! We'll get 'em together!"

"Who?"

"Windy and Sue and my old man and us! You know, togetherness! Windy's friends are gone, you said. I can't move Harry off his butt to meet anybody. Don't you see? When you and I marry, we'll all be related, sort of, so let's get the family acquainted! Dinner tomorrow night!"

"Oh Lordy." Jenny frowned. "Are you sure?"

"Sure I'm sure!"

"Oh Lordy. Where?"

"Where else? Picacho Pass!"

They had drinks at Jenny's condo. Don bartended. Windy's order was predictable—shots of bourbon washed down with tap water. Harry never drank, but Don wanted to loosen him up a little so Mickey Finned him with a blend of whiskey and ginger ale, which he swigged as though it were straight soft drink, which he thought it was. He was thirsty and sweaty. Don had urged him to wear some of his snappy new sports attire from Sears, saying that Picacho Pass was nothing if not informal, but Harry opted for his usual shirt, tie, and black worsted. He requested a second ginger ale, and Don obliged. Despite the lubrication, however, the social machinery functioned only fitfully. There were too many monkey wrenches. Windy disliked Don because he had tried to talk her into moving and Harry because he was Don's father. Harry disliked Jenny because she was a divorced woman and his son would have been better off with his original wife and Windy because she was Jenny's grandmother and Sue because she had asked him, upon his entry, if he wouldn't like to take off his coat and tie. Sue still bore a grudge against Don for leaving her mother at the altar. Don and Jenny did their best with the weather and current events, but all were relieved when Don announced they must hit the trail if they were to make his reservation. Seating arrangements in his Sedan de Ville were as follows: Don and Jenny in front, Windy and her cane and Harry in back with Sue to separate them, and Harry's walker in the trunk.

Things went smoothly during the ten miles from Scottsdale. Everyone commented on the natural beauty of the desert as seen through a multiple-car smashup, with police cars and paramedics and local TV crews covering the multiple-car smashup.

Their table was ready. Picacho Pass was a long, low, barny tourist trap featuring country-and-western music that emanated from a guitar, a fiddle, and two sets of adenoids. The walls were covered with horse tack, a huge hooded grill blazed mesquite and fought the air-conditioning to a draw, and suspended from roughhewn beams above hung thousands of severed neckties snipped from dudes who should have worn, according to the management, western garb. Don's party was no sooner seated of course, and a waitress come to take drink and dinner orders, when, before Harry could stop her, she had deftly divided his tie with scissors, stepped up on a chair, and thumbtacked the pink ducks to a beam while the orchestra sang "Wear a tie to Picacho Pass, Lose a tie and kick yore ass!"

Harry took the joke and the general hilarity in good grace, although Don sensed he was seething inside, and ordered a sloe gin fizz. The last drink of hard liquor he'd had was in 1939, he said, and it was a sloe gin fizz, he recalled, and he enjoyed it. Don had misgivings about a sloe gin fizz on top of two whiskeys, and whether Windy could handle a double bourbon after inhaling at least three shots at the condo, but was not about to monitor his elders' drinking, so he ordered a mart for himself and attempted to get the conversational ball rolling at his end of the table. Sue was seated at his left, Jenny was at his right, and Harry next to Jenny across from Windy. Harry, meanwhile, attempted to break the ice with Windy.

"How did you lose your husband, Mrs. Coon?" he inquired.

"He shot himself," said Mrs. Coon.

Harry swallowed some sloe gin the wrong way and had a coughing fit. Jenny had to pound him on the back.

"Well, well, isn't it nice we can all be together," said Don warmly.

Harry tried again, this time with a concern he and his dinner partner might have in common.

"Are you constipated, Mrs. Coon?" he asked loudly, as though she were hard of hearing.

She stared at him like a TV screen. So did Sue and Jenny and Don and several other diners.

"I have a lot of trouble with my bowels," Harry continued.

"Tell me about computer programming," Don said quickly to Sue.

"Well," said she, "I'm really into it. I think the future's in software."

"I can tell you just the thing," Harry continued to Windy. "Dulcolax, D-u-l-c-o-l-a-x. They call 'em 'torpedoes.' You take one of those, Mrs. Coon, it'll blow you sky-high."

"Tell Sue about your son," said Jenny quickly to Don.

"Say, why don't we all go to the salad bar?" said Don quickly to the table, rising red-faced.

Don carrying his father's plate as well as his own, Jenny carrying her grandmother's, too, the five wended slowly down the line without mishap until the return to their table. Then, unfortunately, Harry's peripheral vision being limited and his system suffused with a variety of spirits, he somehow hooked one of the points of his walker behind the leg of a highchair at another table, and trying vigorously to extricate it, tipped the highchair and the baby in it over onto a table occupied by a beefy man dining with his family. The baby lay screaming face down in a puddle of A-1 Sauce while the father erupted from the table.

"Mommy, mommy, Joanie's drowning in the steak sauce!" yelled the family's six-year-old.

"My God, my baby!" panicked the wife, yanking her bawling babe out of the spicy puddle.

"Why, you old fart!"

Don jumped between his discombobulated Dad and the beefy man, now doubling his fists to flatten Harry.

"Sir, sir, please, he's eighty-three! He's got more chemicals in him than duPont makes, and he's been drinking tonight, too. His peripheral vision's not good, either, and his hip's out of whack . . ."

"What the hell do I care about that? He assaulted my baby!" huffed Jumbo.

"Sir, sir, I'll be glad to pay for your dinners, all of 'em. Please!" Don was bouncing back and forth in front of the angry man, keeping him away from Harry while balancing full plates in either hand.

"Okay, and this salad's on you, too!"

The beefy father reached underneath to tip both plates of salad onto Don's chest, the Roquefort and Italian dressings mixing nicely to run down the front of his sport shirt.

Dinner was served. The same meal was served all and sundry at Picacho Pass—a two-pound "cowboy steak," pinto beans, corn on the cob, and slabs of garlic bread. Halfway through the meal, Don realized to his dismay that his father's dentures—which fit him improperly because they had been slapped up for two hundred bucks at a while-U-wait dental clinic in downtown Detroit—would make it practically impossible for him to eat anything but the pinto beans and garlic bread. He looked down the table for corroboration. Yes, Harry's steak and corn were untouched, but his pinto beans were gone and he had preempted the whole basket of bread. The only consolation was that Windy, her appetite appeased, had decided to pay some attention to her partner, and was now preempting him.

"Harry, you wouldn't b'lieve the troubles we had with calvin' up on the Slash-Bar-C. Some of them young heifers like t'died givin' birth!"

"Oh, dear, she's had too much to drink," said a worried Jenny. "Don, please tell Sue about Ron."

"Okay, glad to," said their gracious host, still paper-toweling his shirt off. "Well, he's a winner, Sue—though I may be prejudiced. Twenty years old and six feet tall and lean and blue eyes like Paul Newman. Sophomore at Claremont McKenna College over in Cal—he'll be taking finals in two weeks. Majoring in business."

"He sounds yummy," said Sue. "So how's your relationship?"

"Sometimes them young heifers'll sluff a calf, we call it," Windy continued. "Sluff. Premature. All's you can do is wrap 'em in gunny sacks an' pour the warm milk down 'em. But you can't save 'em."

"No?" asked Harry, pretending interest.

"Great," said Don. "We're best friends. When he was eighteen he had the choice of living with his mother or me. He picked the West, thank God. We've driven all over it together, when he came out summers."

"Then sometimes, when it's the first calf, it'll damn near kill 'em," Windy continued down memory lane. "I recollect Little Nell. We had 'er in the corral b'cause she was due. Come out one mornin' an' there was the calf—half in, half out of 'er, already dead. Tried pullin' it out of 'er by hand an' couldn' budge it."

"Oh?" No longer hungry, Harry put down a slab of garlic bread.

"What's he like?" Sue asked. "I mean, you know, as a person?"

"Saddled up my horse an' tied a rope to the front feet stickin' out an' hauled away, but that didn't work neither."

"Well, Ron's very conservative."

"I like that," Sue approved.

"So what we did, we got us another rope aroun' Little Nell's chest an' tied it t'the corral fence. So's we could get some purchase. Then hooked up the first rope, aroun' the calf's feet, to our Model T Ford."

"He doesn't smoke, doesn't do drugs, won't live with a girl, drinks only beer. Takes the pure path. Oh yeah, sometimes he sucks oxygen."

"Sucks oxygen?"

"Well, we give that T the gas an' away she went an' out come the calf an' say, you could hear Nell yippee-i-ay a mile away!"

Harry had gone pale.

"Yes, he has his own tank. Pure oxygen."

"But why?"

"Say, Harry, how old are you?"

"I'm eighty-three."

||| 64 |||

"You on Social Security?"

"Yes, I am. Aren't you, Mrs. Coon?"

"Hell, no."

"Oh, Lordy," Jenny gasped. "Your poor father's in for it now!"

"Why?" Don asked.

"Why oxygen?" Sue repeated.

"I'm ninety-one an' I could get Old-Age Assistance, too, an' I don't an' won't," Windy declared. "Won't take a damn cent—I got too much pride, Harry! No damn welfare for me!"

"Because he has a theory," Don explained. "Oxygen purifies the blood, and the blood goes to the brain, so the brain is purified. Or the thought processes or something."

Harry bristled. "I am *not* on welfare. I paid into Social Security for years—now I'm just getting back what's rightfully mine."

"D'you need it?"

"No, I don't. But it's mine, and . . ."

"Horseshit!" Windy shoved her dishes aside with bourbon belligerence and gave the gas to her subject. "You've already got a helluva lot more'n you ever paid in, so now you're gettin' somethin' for nothin'—if that ain't welfare, what is it?"

"He sounds swell, your son," said Sue to Don. "But I want to know just one thing."

"Well?"

"Then what do *you* do—live off your granddaughter?" Harry demanded. "D'you call that pride?"

Sue looked Don in the eye. "How long are you gonna leave my mother on the hook?"

Windy blew sky-high. She pushed back her chair, drew the rattlesnake cane from her lap like a six-gun, and, extending it across the table as though reaching for an on-off button, punched Harry in the chest. "Don't talk t'me like that, you old turd!" she cried.

"At least I don't live off my son!" cried Harry.

Windy punched him again as Don, Jenny, and Sue sat paralyzed and looking horrified. "The more y'give old folks, the more they'll take!" cried the Arizona pioneer. "After a while, they claim it's their right!"

"Stop that!" cried Harry, trying to move his chair to escape the cane and toppling the walker with a crash. "Just stop that!"

Windy punched him again. "Greedy geezer! Goddamn government's made you into a beggar!"

"No wonder your husband shot himself!" cried Harry, face flushed, one hand fending the cane, the other clutching the stub of his necktie. "If I had to live with you, Madame, I'd take poison!"

"Why, you old bastard!" shrieked Windy, and then raised the cane to strike him over the head as Don, Jenny, and Sue shot to their feet in unison with numerous other patrons of Picacho Pass.

"You old bitch!" yelled Harry.

She raised the cane higher. Harry then did the only thing he could do in self-defense. Seizing the two-pound cowboy steak from his plate, he hurled it at her full force. The rare sirloin grazed the side of Windy's head, knocking off her gray wig, and there the old lady sat, bare as a Bermuda onion.

*

Later that night, on his way to his room to retire, Harry paused. "Son," he asked, "do you really intend to marry that woman?"

"Yes, Pop, I do."

"Well," said Harry, "you are marrying into the damnedest family I've ever met. And I don't care to meet them again. That old woman is crazy. The girl looks like a tart—painting her eyes, at her age. Your lady friend seems passable, but if she's anything like her grandmother, you're in for a peck of trouble." He belched— the pinto beans. "Take my advice, Son—get rid of the whole damn bunch. You have made a big enough mess of your life as it is."

Don gave him a level look. For a moment, for the first time in his manhood, he hated his father.

*

Three days later, Harry moved out.

Don came home from a long hot day showing high-priced houses to a woman from Pittsburgh, who, it turned out, had come to Phoenix with her husband for a convention, had done all the shopping she cared to, and now, to pass the time till the convention was over, wasted Don's time looking at expensive property. Harry sat in his TV chair, packed suitcase at his side, pillbox in his lap.

"Donald," he began, "I have something to say. It's been grand of you to take me in, and I'm grateful. But I'm not happy here. I'm used to living by myself. So the last couple days I've scouted around and found just what I need. What worries me is how you'll take this. The last thing in the world I want to do, Son, is hurt your feelings."

Don did not—repeat *not*—split his sides laughing. Don did not—repeat *not*—faint dead away with delight. Instead, he put on a sincere and solemn face. "Dad," he said, "my feelings don't count. If this is what you want, I want it for you. You have your own life to live, and a lot of it left, hopefully. Well, what've you found? Where?"

Harry upped himself into his walker. "Come on. Bring my bag and box and I'll show you."

Don in his car followed Harry in Aunt Min down Scottsdale Road to Camelback and over to 68th and south to McDowell—a thrill-filled trip during which his father ran a red light, made a left turn from a right-hand lane, and almost broadsided a cement mixer. What he had found was a one-bedroom apartment at the Eventide, one of many "retirement centers" in the Phoenix area designed to serve both the immigration of senior citizens from out of state and the profit motive. It boasted a swimming pool, covered parking, nurses on call 'round the clock, and a dining room in which nutritious, well-balanced meals were available at reasonable cost. Don had heard about the Eventide. Locals called it "Toothpick City." For around the corner, within easy walker and wheelchair distance, was a cafeteria, and every evening most of the residents said the hell with nutritious, well-balanced meals, took off for the cafeteria, gorged themselves on starches and carbohydrates, and returned to the Eventide removing the residues of the feast from their dentures with toothpicks. Harry's apartment was carpeted and draped and applianced and furnished in the latest Levitz luxury and set him back seven hundred dollars a month, including all utilities except the phone. He had, moreover, engaged the widow lady next door, a Mrs. Bustard, to come in for an hour each morning, do his laundry, wash up yesterday's dishes, make his bed, and generally slick up the place.

"I think this is swell, Pop," said Don after a survey. "I'm sorry to see you go, of course, but I have to admit, this is the ideal setup for you. Just one thing—are you sure you can make it on your own?"

"I am. I have for twenty years. Put my bag on the bed, will you?"

Don did. "Well, if you ever need me, night or day, I'm as near as your phone."

Harry was trying simultaneously to support himself on the walker and open his suitcase. His hip for some reason had stiffened up, and his mobility was still limited, but he would not go to his new doctor about it, not at forty-five dollars a crack. Don opened the bag for him. "How much are you paying the lady, by the way?"

"Mrs. Bustard? Well, we haven't talked that over yet. I thought I'd offer a dollar a day."

"A dollar a day!"

"She's only coming in for an hour. Besides, she's a widow—they'll work cheap to be around anything in pants." Harry winked. "Gets their hopes up."

Don watched him try to hang a shirt on a hanger with one hand. "What about dinner tonight? Would you like me to take you out?"

"Going to the cafeteria around the corner. I hear the food's mighty good."

"Okay." Don hung the shirt up for him. "Just watch the desserts."

"*You* watch out for that screwball family."

*

Don's instinct, once he had said good-bye and good luck, was to sprint for the nearest public phone and tell Jenny to gussy up, they were wining and dining, he had tidings of great joy. Instead, he sneaked next door to make Mrs. Bustard's acquaintance. She was a small, teachery woman in her seventies with bird eyes and a beak for a nose and a whistle in her breath that indicated pulmonary problems. Her look pecked. Her sleeves were rolled up. As soon as Don identified himself she invited him in, but he stayed at the door and thanked her for hiring out to his father. She said no thanks—she had the time and the health, and with the price of groceries these days, a penny earned was a penny saved to spend on Stouffer's.

"Speaking of that," Don said, "you're going over for an hour a day, he tells me, mornings. What's he paying you?"

"Darned if I know." She frowned. "Odd—now that I think of it, he never mentioned pay."

"Well, he's going to offer you a dollar a day."

"A dollar a day!" whistled Mrs. Bustard. She bit a lip and seemed prepared to bite both. "Why, the old skinflint! Begging your pardon."

Don nodded. "That's all right. That's why I'm here. When he offers, take it. But you should have six dollars an hour, and I'll make up the difference. It'll be our secret—I'll slip it to you once a week, when I'm over here. That way everybody's happy: you get what you should, I get help my father needs, and he thinks he's getting a bargain. Is that satisfactory?"

She was no hesitater. "Now you're up my alley. It's a deal."

Don smiled. "One other thing, Mrs. Bustard. My father's not young any more, and he—"

"How old is he?"

"Eighty-three."

"Social Security?"

"Yes."

"Pension?"

"A small one."

"Got a bit tucked away, too, has he?"

She fired these questions at her visitor as though he were in elementary school.

"Oh, well, Dad's comfortable—let's put it that way. But he's limited physically, as you saw. Also, he's setting up housekeeping in a big, strange city—trying to make a new life for himself. I work, I can't be over here every day, so will you look out for him?"

She wore pants and earth shoes and propped an earth shoe up on a pot of petunias. "Meaning what?"

"Meaning, if he doesn't look well, or doesn't act normal, or there's anything out of the ordinary—you know . . ." Don brush-fished for words. "What I'm trying to say is, I want my father to be happy here at the Eventide. I'm in the phone book—Donald Chambers—and you can reach me through Rancho Grande Realty. So will you please just sort of watch over him?"

Mrs. Bustard stuck out a hand. "Consider it done. I'll drop in on him now and then—unexpected."

Don shook her hand, and then, to his surprise, she winked one of her sparrow eyes. "He won't mind," she said. "Listen, I read men like books—I've had three husbands. Widowers like a woman around."

*

He sensed something was wrong the second he caught up with Jenny and she wouldn't say hi or stop running and the only way to tell her his tidings of great joy was to run with her.

"Dad's moved out! He's got his own one-bedroom at the Eventide—you know, Toothpick City—and the lady next door's going to do his housework. I can't believe it. As of today he's gone and I'm free and rattling around alone at my place. D'you see how this adds up?"

Jenny ran. A goddess in an aqua jog suit floating through mythology on blue-and-white Nikes. Don ran.

"Jenny, listen. We've got it made! I have room now—for you and Sue and Windy and Sue's computer and Windy's pistol! Say when!"

Jenny ran. Don ran. His Bally loafers hurt his feet. He considered himself in Olympic shape at forty-two—tennis and saunas and clean living—but he was beginning to puff.

"Jenny, goddammit! Will you please marry me right away?" he puffed.

"No," she said.

He had called her from the nearest public phone and got Sue, who said her mom was jogging along the bank of the Salt River Project irrigation canal. She usually ran her two miles in the morning, before work, but this morning Windy was unwell and Jenny had taken her to the doctor so she was running this evening. Sue told him where, and Don zoomed over and found her Cutlass parked and drove on two blocks and got out and intercepted her on the canal bank.

"No!" he yelped. "Not again! Why not?"

"Because it won't work," she said, maintaining her pace. "Sorry, Don. But it won't."

"Why in hell not?"

"Been thinking. Dinner the other night. Picacho Pass. A disaster." Jenny synchronized her speech with her respiration. "Our old people hate each other. Windy doesn't like you. You'll uproot her. Take me away from her. Sue doesn't trust you. Thinks you'll never marry me. Thinks we're sleeping together. Very conservative. Like your son. Put us all together under one roof—like a zoo! And unfair to you."

"Not true!" Don, running, had begun to whistle like Mrs. Bustard. Possible pulmonary problem? And his Gian Marco shirt was wet through. "Stop!" he whistled. "For God's sake! Talk to me!"

Jenny slowed, glanced at him with some apprehension, then walked to the off side of the canal bank, sat down by the trailing limb of a eucalyptus tree, and watched as he staggered after her and dropped and sat working his lungs like any weekend athlete. He dragged off his Ballys and massaged his feet. They sat in silence for some time. In the distance the McDowell Mountains turned a delicate lilac in the dusk. The movement of water in the canal was imperceptible. It was run-off water from winter rains in the north along the Mogollon Rim gathered in reservoirs and let down from dams to the deserts to grow cotton and melons and swimming pools. Behind them a big red ball of sun rolled off the world and bounced back the last light between earth and sky.

Jenny changed the subject. She asked Don how long since he'd sold a house, and he had to think back—it must have been two months ago, his longest dry spell. He'd been so hassled, flying back and forth to Michigan and resettling his father in Arizona, that he hadn't noticed. She said she had noticed—her last sale cleared escrow nine weeks ago. Everyone was facing it: the bottom had finally dropped out of real estate—residential at least. The pro salespeople were hanging on, they had to; but the fringers, the housewives and hobbyists and fast-buck artists, were falling like flies. "Didn't you see the multiple-listing book last week? Four thousand active listings in the Valley, and there were eighty-some sales. Two percent." Don had his wind again. He said he had noticed one thing: his last two floor times at the office came up zero. "Floor time" was the three or four hours each top salesperson in a realty firm got on a rotating basis each week to take all incoming calls to the firm from other brokers and, more important, potential clients, whether looking to buy in general or calling about a specific property where they'd seen the company sign.

"Likewise," Jenny said.

"I could make more sitting babies than houses," Don said.

"There you are," Jenny said. Don asked where the buyers were. Jenny replied no one knew, but they'd stopped coming in from out of state, just stopped, and for the natives money was tight and prices were as insane as ever. "Not only that, it's dirty tricks time," she said. "Last week I showed a house Rudy Petersdorf was sitting on—I had to introduce my couple to him, of course. And he got their name and somehow their address. Well, two days later Rudy grabbed them and sold them something else." Jenny picked up a handful of sand and threw it at the canal.

"I can top that," Don said. "I got a call from a guy in Illinois. He was flying out and wanted to buy, had cash. But I didn't get the call myself—John DeLillo got it and told the buyer I was out of town and he'd be glad to pinch-hit for me. I found out about this later. Anyway, DeLillo met the guy at the airport and sold him a five-bedroom with a tennis court. Cash."

Jenny threw another handful of sand at the canal.

"You're beautiful when you sweat," Don said. "You're a beautiful sweater."

She stood, as though she hadn't heard. "So that's another reason. It wouldn't work in the first place, and in the second neither of us can afford it."

"Two can live cheaper than one."

"How about four?"

"Listen, Jenny, suppose. Suppose things don't improve. How long can you hold out, money-wise? Now, be honest."

"Not long. I have car payments and condo payments and monthly maintenance. Sue's college costs. Windy's medical and drug bills you wouldn't believe."

"Doesn't she have anything?"

"She could get SSI (Supplemental Security Income) and Medicaid, but she won't. As you heard."

"Sue said something about Windy being unwell this morning. Anything serious?"

Jenny frowned at him. "Don't say it. Don't even think it." She changed the subject again. "What about you? Money-wise."

"Me? Well, outside of exhaustion and blisters and severe depression, I'm fine."

"Money-wise."

"Honestly?"

"Honestly."

"I'm not about to retire. The fact is, I'm living pretty close to the bone. When I was making it big, I was spending bigger. Oh, I have a little in a money-market fund. But I'm paying on my Caddie and the condo and the club membership, and Ron's private college is killing me, and I have to ship Carol five hundred a month—alimony." He stood and grinned, trying to soften her up. "At least my old man's well-fixed. If I had to support him—food stamps."

She didn't soften. "How long?"

"Depends."

"How long?"

"Couple of months."

"Months!"

"You said to be honest. Hey, I just thought of something—how much equity d'you have in your place?"

"Thirty-three thousand."

"Ah. I've got over forty in mine. Better use mine." He brightened. "I know how to get enough bucks to see us both through. Here's what we do. We tie the knot. Then I move in with you and Sue and Windy. Then . . ."

"And sleep where?"

"Well, lessee. Windy and Sue share the bedroom. You get the davenport and I'll take the floor. Then we put my place on the market and sell it."

"To whom?"

"To whom?"

"These days."

"Oh. Damn."

Jenny got up and walked along the canal bank in her original direction. He followed in his socks.

"I love you," he said.

"We have to be practical."

"Love *is* practical."

"Someday maybe. Not now."

"You know what I think?"

"What?"

"I think you're scared, Jenny Staley."

"No. Intelligent."

"I think you're scared to marry again. Afraid it'll be bad again. And you're using tough times and your grandmother and your daughter to hide behind. I could hide, too—I'm almost as broke and depressed as you are—but I won't. I love you enough to gamble. I love you enough to clean out my checking account tomorrow and rent a balloon and . . ."

Jenny started to run again, turning her head from him. "I love you too much to marry you now!" she cried over her shoulder, running faster.

"The hell you do!" he shouted, running after her until he hit some gravel and it hurt his feet and he had to hop and stop. He was sure she was crying. It was all over between them but the shouting. Their first fight was their last. He watched her diminish in the dark. "The hell you do!" he shouted, mad and miserable, then turned and started running back down the canal toward his car carrying his Ballys, running even though he didn't have to and his feet hurt as much as his heart.

*

The first crisis in Harry's new life Don mediated by phone. His father called the morning after he had moved into the Eventide to say he had just fired Mrs. Bustard. Don was appalled, and wanted to know why, and Harry was glad to tell him. The widow had come in that morning for her first hour as a domestic and proceeded to make herself a cup of tea and Harry a domestic proposition. She proposed to give up her apartment, move in with Harry, and split living expenses—the arrangement would be cheaper and more companionable for both of them. Harry was appalled. She argued that many elderly people shacked up together nowadays—that way no one suffered the loss of Social Security due to marriage. Harry heated up and declared it the most immoral thing he'd ever heard of. She said, nuts, this was a new era, and advised him to get with it. Harry ordered her to take her tea and get lost. Don listened patiently and said to stick around, that Harry had to have help, and he'd see what he could do. This was Don's floor time at the office and nothing was happening, so he tied up the phone for the next hour making a series of calls, first to Mrs. Bustard, then to Harry, then to Mrs. Bustard, then back to Harry, and, after much negotiation, effected a settlement satisfactory to both sides. Harry would forgive and forget and rehire Mrs. Bustard for a dollar a day. Mrs. Bustard would cease and desist any and all propositions to her employer.

"Besides," said father to son, "if I want a woman living with me, I'll get my own. I'll marry again."

"Marry again!" exclaimed Don, appalled.

"Yes, marry again," said the salty Harry. "Hadn't thought of that, had you?"

The next crisis in Harry's new life Harry refused to entrust to Mountain Bell. He called Don and told him to come right over to the Eventide, he was in terrible trouble. Don said he couldn't. Harry said he had to. Don was snappish. It was early afternoon, he was sitting on an $875,000 house in Finisterre, an opulent development in Paradise Valley, and though he hadn't any lookers, he wanted the afternoon free to brood about Jenny. He had neither seen nor called her, nor she him, since the breach by the SRP canal. He asked why the matter couldn't be discussed over the phone, at which Harry started to snuffle and said if Don had any regard for his father, he'd come over PDQ.

When he got there it was to learn that Harry's "terrible trouble" was financial. A man, it seemed, had phoned him the day after he moved into his apartment and made an appointment—he was evidently tipped off to all new arrivals at the Eventide—and two men showed up and offered him an opportunity to turn a 200 percent profit in two years by investing in unset diamonds. They were well-spoken, well-dressed men—a Mr. Murphy and a Mr. Korrick—and claimed to be fellow-Rotarians with offices in Scottsdale. They showed him the diamonds, several rave letters from successful investors in the past, and a statement from the American Gemological Institute in New York City that officially certified the cut and weight and present appraised value of the gems. Harry was sold. He was not one, as he phrased it, to "look a gift horse in the mouth," which in this case meant a 200-percent capital gain in two years. Therefore he went to his bank the next day, brought home a certified check to Mr. Murphy and Mr. Korrick, and exchanged the check for diamonds. The two well-dressed, well-spoken gents went on their way. This morning Harry tried to call them at the Scottsdale number on their letterhead. The phone had been disconnected. On reflection, Harry sniffed the faint scent of rat. He next applied to the phone company for the number of an American Gemological Institute. He next took Aunt Min and his investment to the nearest jeweler—who rocked him fifty dollars—for another appraisal. Shaking like a leaf, he returned to his apartment, where, in rage and agony, he called his son and heir.

"How much did you give them?"

"Ten thousand dollars."

Don made a face. "What did the jeweler say?"

Harry held up a small leather pouch. "Oh, they're real diamonds, all right."

"How much, Pop?"

"Three." Don nodded. "Then you are out seven thou."

"No, I'm not! I won't be!" Harry, standing, gripped his walker as though to twist it like a pretzel. "I want you to get my money back!"

Don looked at him, then looked in the phone book for the number of the Anti-Fraud Division of the office of Attorney General of the State of Arizona. He put in a call and eventually reached someone in authority and told his father's tale of woe and listened for a while and said thanks and hung up. Still standing, Harry waited.

"You've been had, Dad," said Don. "Those guys are long gone by now, out of the state and out of reach. It happens all the time in Arizona, old people being taken. Phoenix is Sucker City. If you'd only read the local papers, you'd . . ."

"Oh, no!" Harry let go of the walker and sank heavily into a chair as the fate of his seven thousand dollars sank into his comprehension. He seemed confused. He took out his upper plate, studied it, then replaced it. Then he whistled a little tune.

"Father," said Don. "Father, why in hell didn't you call me before you turned over that kind of money to strangers?"

Harry whistled. The tune, so far as Don could make it out, was "Pop Goes the Weasel."

"I could have checked on them for you."

Harry whistled. Behind cataract lenses, his eyes swam the room, avoiding Don's.

"I could have put on the brakes . . ."

Harry whistled.

"Well, it's water over the dam now," said Don. "What we have to do is see to it that something stupid like this doesn't happen again. One thing we could do—I admit it's drastic, but it works. We go to a lawyer and you give me power of attorney. I do all your banking and pay your bills and give you an allowance. Then nobody can sell you a gold mine or some prime acreage or a bridge over the Salt River or . . ."

"Pop Goes the Weasel" ended abruptly. "I'll be damned if I will!" cried Harry. "Not the way you spend money!"

Don, seated, sat up straight. "Are you insinuating that I'd use your money to . . ."

"This is all your fault anyway!"

"My fault!"

"Yes! For bringing me out to this damned shyster shithole in the first place!"

*

That evening Don brought in fast food because he was too low mentally to cook, and ate in his living room and drank beer and watched TV. That is, he sprawled before the set in swim trunks and let one channel run and trivialize its share of the viewing audience halfway to suicide and felt sorry for himself. Jenny was being unreasonable and unfair. Here were all these echoing rooms, just waiting for a family to fill them. And here he was, lonely as hell, a man needing a woman. Even his loins were lonely. And there she was, two blocks away, a woman needing a man, a lorn lady pining for the pillar of strength and perfect husband he could be. She was being unreasonable and as unfair as his old man. The nerve of Harry—blaming Don for his being sweet-talked out of seven thou, pointing the finger at his son instead of fingering his own greed and stupidity. Lord only knew what disaster the octogenarian would walker into next. In any event, both of them—his love and his father—were being unreasonable and unfair and ripping him off emotionally. How much was he supposed to take? He had half a mind to go out to the sauna and stay in it until he dehydrated himself to death. The doorbell chimed. He answered it.

"Hello, Don."

He nearly fell out of his trunks.

"May I come in?"

She drifted in and Don kicked beer cans into a corner and stuffed fast-food wrappers under a cushion and turned off the TV.

She wore a lipstick and a sort of see-through dress and high-heeled spectators, and no one would have bet she had ever done anything more laborious in her life than lift ladyfingers.

"You look, uh—splendid," he said.

"So do you," she said.

"I do? If I'd known you were coming over I'd have worn a tie."

Usually that would have made her laugh, but tonight she had something important to say. "I'm here to apologize, Don. I've been unreasonable and unfair. I wasn't running away from you the other evening—I was running away from responsibility. I've never done that before." She stepped behind a chair and held on to its top. She had obviously composed a speech. "I was also running away from myself. From the best in me. And I've been ashamed ever since. Well, I came tonight to say three things. One—Don, I love you. Two—I love you enough to marry you now no matter what. Three—"

"No matter what?" he interjected. "Our families, the hard times, the whole bit?"

"Yes."

"When?"

"Whenever you want."

"Tomorrow?"

"Yes. Well, I have floor time in the office tomorrow. But the day after—absolutely."

"Jenny, I can't tell you—"

"And three"—she hesitated—"I guess I'll say it right out. I want you. I want you physically so much I can't wait till tomorrow or the day after." She was almost blushing. "So, Don, if you'll forgive me, and if you want me . . ."

"*Want* you!"

"Just let me go in your bedroom for a minute, then I'll come out. I bought something—I hope you'll like it. Talk about extravagance, I . . ."

"*Like* it!" He moved toward her.

She moved away. "No, not yet darling. Just let me go in your room and . . ."

"Go!" he cried.

She smiled and he let her pass without touching, and so that he wouldn't get his glands in an uproar while waiting Don whirled around the living room, picked up the beer cans, retrieved the fast-food wrappers from under the chair cushion, and raced them to the kitchen and the garbage can.

"Don't take a shower!" he pleaded as he passed his bedroom door.

Now she did laugh. "I won't!"

By the time he returned to the living room, there she was. Jenny Staley wore the high-heeled spectators and a teddy—the pictures of teddies in department-store were the only ones familiar to Don—of ivory satin lavished with lace and blue satin beading. It was his dream all over again. She came toward him. He opened wide his arms to enfold her and the teddy, to lead her into his bedroom—he suddenly realized he hadn't made the bed—and lie with her and enter upon eight hours of terrific sexual activity. Just then the doorbell chimed.

"*Who* in hell?"

"Don't answer it," she begged.

The doorbell chimed again. Twice.

"I better. Solicitors aren't allowed in here, so it must be somebody I know. Whoever it is, they're out, gone, good-bye."

He went to the door and opened it.

"Hi, Dad."

It was Ron, a suitcase in each hand.

Covering for Jenny, Don barred his way. "What are you doing here?"

Ron tried to push past him. "Aren't you glad to see me?"

"Well, sure, of course, but—" Don had a quick look over his shoulder. She was gone. He let Ron in. "But you're supposed to be taking finals!"

"I'll explain about that." Ron put the suitcases down and started for the door. "Have to get the rest of my gear."

Don backed toward the hall as though to barricade his bedroom door. Ron returned with an oxygen tank and tubes and face mask.

"How'd you get here?" Don asked.

"Thumbed. A real nice guy picked me up in Blythe and brought me right to the door."

He went out again and came in carrying a cage and a kind of contraption. Jenny entered, fully dressed.

She stared at Ron and the cage. Ron stared at her.

"Ron," said Don, wishing he had a shirt on, "I've got a surprise for you. This is Jenny Staley, a friend of mine."

"Hello, Ron." Jenny smiled.

"Well, more than a friend," said Don. "The fact is, we're about to be married."

"Really?" Ron looked Jenny over and his bare father over and put one and one in bed together and was clearly concerned. "Gee, that's swell, congratulations," said he unenthusiastically. "I've got a surprise for you, too. This is Bobby."

He set the cage down. In it was a big brown buck rabbit with a bent ear.

"A rabbit?" asked Don.

Ron went to close the door.

"Why a rabbit?" Don asked.

"Well, he's a pet now. But I bought him for an experiment for a psych course." Ron stretched his six feet and big ears and blue Paul Newman eyes behind steel-rimmed glasses out on the davenport. He wore jeans and sandals and a grubby T-shirt on which was printed "In the Beginning, Everybody Was A Fetus." He rubbed his eyes. "Boy, I am really bushed. Say, Dad, what about Gramps? Is he asleep?"

"He's not here. He moved out last week. To the Eventide, a retirement center."

Ron was clearly concerned. "That's terrible! Why'd you let him do that?"

"He wanted to. I couldn't stop him. Anyway, he's doing fine—happy as a hog in deep mud. Don took a chair. Jenny took another.

"Ron, I want you to know you're welcome," said Don. "This is your home. But why are you here? You told me this was finals week."

"I'm not taking finals, Dad." Ron sat up, tense. "I hate to lay this on you all at once—but I've dropped out of Claremont McKenna. I wasn't exactly burning up the academic track, but that's not the real reason. I'm not basically a business major, I decided. I'm thinking of switching to English."

"English!" Don made a face. "What can you do with English?"

"I don't know—maybe write. Fiction, I don't know, or nonfiction. But I'm dropping out for a year and living at home. A lot of guys do it. That is, if it's okay with you."

Don opened his mouth, looked meaningfully at Jenny, then closed his mouth.

"I want work experience," Ron continued. "I need time to get my head on straight—about changing majors and what I want to do in life and all. You know—I'm sort of having a *pre*-midlife crisis."

Don nodded.

"So you're going to be living with your father for a year," said Jenny.

"And the rabbit's going to be living with your father for a year," said Don.

"Well, sure," said Ron. "I can't just dump him out in the desert." He got up and opened a door in the cage and lifted the animal out by the loose skin around its shoulders and held it with his other hand under its rump. "Listen, let me show you what Bobby can do. I want to prove to you I haven't exactly been wasting my time in school, Dad—*or* your money."

With a foot he pushed the contraption into the center of the room. It was a car, a kind of miniature go-cart. Its frame and chassis were made of plywood, its toy wheels were aluminum and rubber-tired, it had a seat with a hole in it and seat belts and a steering tiller and a foot pedal and was powered by a six-volt storage battery behind the seat.

"I built this car myself," said a proud Ron. "I call it the Rabbit Rabbit—what else? I told you, I was doing this paper for a psych course, but I never finished it because I couldn't train Bobby to steer. I've got him to respond to verbal commands, but—here, I'll show you." He let Bobby down to the floor and pushed the little car to the far side of the room. "Go, Bobby!" he commanded.

An obedient Bobby perked up his good ear and hopped across the room to the vehicle and hopped into the seat.

"See?" said a proud Ron. "Amazing, huh? Well, just wait." He lifted Bobby, adjusting him in the seat so that he sat almost upright, and began to belt him in. "You put his tail down through the hole—I even thought of that, for his comfort. Then you buckle the belts—can't expect him to do that—one just above his hindquarters and one over his belly; then put his right hind foot on the pedal—which activates the battery—and then one paw on the steering tiller." This done, Ron stepped back. "Now watch," he said to Don and Jenny. "Maybe this time he'll get smart and steer—you always hope. One of these days!"

Don and Jenny sat like statues.

Ron bent over for a Grand Prix start.

"Go, Bobby, go!" he commanded.

The well-trained Bobby depressed the pedal with his right hind foot. There was a hum. The Rabbit Rabbit moved forward, gaining momentum. Bobby removed his paw from the steering tiller. As his audience held its collective breath, the car hummed faster and faster across the tile floor in a straight line until it crashed head-on into the opposite wall with such impact that the unfortunate animal was thrown forward against the seat belts and one of its ears, the permanently bent one, whapped against the wall and the limp, belted Bobby hung over the steering tiller in a state of shock.

"Holy jumpin' Jesus," groaned Don.

||| 4 |||

Even with Harry momentarily out of his hair, it seemed to a harassed Don Chambers that his problems were multiplying like hares.

First and foremost was his drop-out, oxygen-sucking son, whom he loved more than anyone on earth after Jenny, and maybe as much, but differently. With that talent for bad timing particular to the young, Ronald Chambers had come home. To talk alternatively about getting a job or writing short stories or enlisting in the Marines. Or listen by the hour to the Eagles' classic "Desperado" or Samuel Barber's "Adagio for Strings" on the stereo. Or read *Crisis Investing* and take chromium pills. Or damage walls and woodwork trying to teach a poor dumb animal to drive a car. Don blamed most of this on California. Ron's conservatism, however, came from God knew where unless it was hereditary—a trickledown of Harry's bile and Carol's reactionary blood. The son disapproved of practically everything the father did. Two examples. Don and Jenny must eschew the sack and preacher their relationship pronto. And his grandfather should be brought back to Oasis South. Then they could all live together happily ever after, Ron and Don and Jenny and Sue and Windy and Harry—Windy and Harry especially. Ron believed in the old-fashioned extended family, of which the elders must be an integral part, whittling and shelling peas and cackling tales before the hearth. In short, in Don's opinion, after two years of higher education at a cost to him of twenty-five grand, his kid had become a nerd. Guess who had to borrow the Sedan de Ville to look for menial labor? And guess who had to pay for the pellets to fill the food dish for the bunny?

Bobby was the least of Don's problems. Given the run of the condo, he hopped up into a chair and slept off the trauma of the last head-on and recharged his battery until the next time Ron buckled him into the Rabbit Rabbit. He was clean, too, washing his face and ears regularly with his paws and dropping his droppings fastidiously out of sight, in closets and under beds. The only thing Don disliked was the rabbit's habit of hopping up on the bed during the night and snuggling flat out on Don's chest for security. It was not restful to wake up and feel Bobby's battered ear on your cheek, and lock gazes with Bobby's big brown victimized eye.

But what in hell to do about himself and Jenny was question *Numero Uno*. Had the real estate biz been rolling right along, had there been *mucho* money, the solution for them would have been simple: marry and pool funds and buy a big place and let whoever wanted to live in it live in it. But she still hadn't sold a property, neither had he, the wolf was at their doors, and there was no such thing as a drawing account in a realty firm. When you sold, you got your percentage, and not until. Jenny had just missed a car payment. Don had just drained his money-market fund of its last five thousand dollars and lent her enough to make the payment. He had to force the check on her, saying he would take his interest in sex. She had to have a car, he insisted. Without wheels, what would she do—backpack clients from house to house? Which would she rather do to keep the Cutlass—accept his loan or work the street outside Saks Fifth Avenue as a *haute couture* hooker?

Then one midmorning, while Ron was sleeping in, Don's horoscope in the newspaper riveted him to his chair. He was an Aries, and on this day he was advised to "Seize opportunity by the throat. Find a way out of your dilemma by overcoming opposition. Strike while the iron is hot." He hadn't had such a significant horoscope in weeks. He racked his brain. At length, when the meaning of the message hit him, he shaved, dressed, and hopped out to his car in nothing flat and drove to Oasis North. This was the moment, logic and astrology told him so. Jenny would be out. Sue would be at school. His opposition would be alone.

*

But with TV she was never alone. And she had the TV up to so many decibels that he had to walk in unannounced after the door chimed in vain. And then it wasn't iron which was hot, it was aluminum. As he passed the kitchen door, heat assailed him, and he found she had left a stove burner on high under her instant coffee water and boiled it away and melted the kettle down into a mass of metal which had glommed up the grid under it. It was a wonder she hadn't burned down the whole development. He turned off the stove and made a mental note to call Jenny to call an electrician and went on into the living room and leaned in front of Windy Coon and switched off "Let's Make A Deal," a new/old game show. She wasn't startled, she merely scowled at him. Not a good beginning, but Don didn't give a whoop. No soft sell this time. He wouldn't seize her by the throat, but he did intend to knock on her if he had to. She represented opportunity.

He said he was sorry to barge in like this, but there was something he had to discuss with her in private, something very important. "You know, Mrs. Coon, that Jenny and I want to be man and wife. I mean, wife and man. Remember the night I asked if you'd mind moving to my place with Sue so we could be, and you said yes, you would? And how happy we were, remember?"

"Howdy, Chambers," said she. "How's that old bastard father of yours?"

Don would not be detoured. "Well, that was two months ago," he continued, "and since then it's been one lousy thing after another. We couldn't all live in my condo because my father fell and broke his hip and came to Arizona to live with me. Then he moved out and Jenny and I thought everything was set and then my son Ron came home and now there isn't room there and not enough here because this is a one-bedroom. Unless I sleep on the floor. With the rabbit."

Don stopped. Thought about, none of it made sense. Said out loud, it made even less.

"What I'm trying to say, Windy, is times are hard and we can't afford to buy a bigger place, but Jenny and I still love each other very much and want to get married very much. Do you follow me?"

She didn't change expression. But she stood her cane upright before her and pointed the rattlesnake's fangs at him.

"There's only one way out, Windy," he said. He drew a deep breath. This was blastoff.

"Nursin' home," she said.

"Uh, uh, yes." She'd said it, not him. "That's right."

"Do me a favor, Chambers," she said. "In the kitchen. See if it's time I take a pill."

"Glad to." He went into the kitchen, noted that the molten aluminum on the burner was cooling, surveyed her pills in a row of paper cups on the counter, found an Indocin for arthritis and a Persantine for poor circulation in one marked "11 A.M.," drew a glass of water, and brought pills and glass to her. She polished off both pills in one gulp and gave him the glass.

"It's the only way, Windy," he repeated. "To make enough room here so I can move in with Jenny and Sue. A nursing home."

She clutched at the turquoise settings of her squash-blossom necklace. "Her folks was killed in a car crash," she said. "I took 'er in an' raised 'er like my own. Then later, there she was on my doorstep again, her an' little Sue, an' . . ."

Don interrupted. "Windy, I know all that—you told me before. Believe me, I hate to talk about this—I couldn't in front of Jenny—

but I don't see any other way. Windy, listen, Scottsdale's full of very nice nursing—"

"No," she said.

"Why not?"

As though on cue, a tear appeared below the rim of her right cataract lens and trickled downstage of her cheek. "When I was a young wife," she quavered, "up on the ol' Slash-Bar-C . . ."

"Why not?" Don demanded.

"Because I ain't goin' anywheres an' set an' wait t'die, that's why."

Don stood there, the glass still in his hand. He seemed unable to get rid of the thing. "But they have lots of activities and good nursing care and television and we'd come visit . . ."

"No." Now her left cataract produced a tear, which promenaded down that cheek. She set her jaw. "Nope, I won't go. An' you can't make me."

In the past a woman's one tear, whether his dear mother's or his ex-wife's, had always melted Don down. Two or more, with a soft sob lobbed in for a curtain line, had always cut him off at the balls. But this morning he was not undone. He had a funny feeling the old girl could turn them on at will. She'd been around a long time, she'd learned a lot of theater. She could believably point a pistol at a villain, she could keep her dignity when de-wigged. If she could show him guile, she could also show him grief. It was a great act, but he'd be damned if he'd buy a ticket.

"All right!" he said grimly, waving the water glass at her. "All right, you've been mother to Jenny, twice, but she's been like a daughter to you—a daughter you wouldn't let go! Has it ever occurred to you the last, best thing you can do for your kids is give 'em their freedom? Huh, has it? She's thirty-eight years old—isn't it time she had hers? Huh, isn't it?"

That reached her. She pulled a Kleenex from her tunic, pushed up her glasses, dabbed at her cheeks, then put on another face, a fierce one. "Don't you dare talk to an ol', helpless woman that way, you dirty damn dude!" she cried. "What're you tryin' t'do—gimme a heart attack?"

Don sat down on the davenport and moved the glass to his other hand. "Windy, I'm sorry, but I have to be frank," he said, trying another tack. "I don't want to hurt you, but I'm here for Jenny's sake. And mine, I admit. You forget, she's got her own life to live. She's had a lot of tough breaks—well, I'd like to give her a break. But how can I if she has to go on caring for you, worrying about you? It isn't fair, Windy. She wants to be married—she needs to be married—and so do I. How long do you want? How much more can you ask of her? You think about it. I'm sorry I have to say these things, but I love her, too, Windy. And I'm the guy in the middle. You think about it."

Don rose, deliberately did not look at her, and took the damned glass into the kitchen and stuck it in the dishwasher. He'd wait her out. He'd wait her out if she sat there till she fell apart. He looked through the kitchen window and walked into the living room past her and looked through a window at the Oasis North pool and watched for a time some "undocumented" tree-trimmers peeling palms.

"Chambers," she said.

He turned.

"Who'd pay my freight?"

He hadn't thought of that. How much did a nursing home set you back a month? A few hundred? Five?

"I would," he said.

"Then you win."

He moved toward her. "Are you sure?"

"Sure as shootin'."

He believed her, but it was still too good to be true. "Are you—are you doing this of your own free will?"

"Yup. With a boot in the ass from you."

"I didn't mean . . ."

"I needed it. I give it a think an' you're right. I'll go. It's time. If that dear, sweet girl wants you, she can have you—I won't be no burr under her saddle." Windy took up her cane preparatory to punching the TV. "But you hear me, Chambers. Like I told you b'fore, you be damn good to 'er."

"Oh, I will, I swear it!" Don pulled the handle of happiness and began to gain altitude. "Windy, I can't thank you enough! This makes everything possible! Oh, wow, will this send Jenny to the moon!" he babbled. "And we'll find you a terrific home and come see you every . . ."

The phone rang.

"You get it," Windy ordered.

He got it. "Hello?"

"Don? Don! Why are you there?"

"Jenny? Jenny! Jenny, I have the most wonderful news!"

"I've tried everywhere to reach you!"

"Windy's moving into a nursing home! We've just had a heart-to-heart talk, and she's . . ."

"The police called your home and office and your office told them to try me and I've called Ron and your tennis club. I thought the last place you'd be . . ."

"Jenny, darling, you're not listening to me! Windy's moving out! Of her own free will! That gives me the other bed in your bed-room—we're home free! So name the date, baby, because . . ."

"Don, your father's in a barbershop on Brown Avenue in his car!"

"So what? Everybody gets a haircut. Sue'll still have to sleep on the davenport, but . . ."

"Don, you're not listening to me! Don, your father is in a barber-shop on Brown Avenue in his car!"

"What are you talking about?"

"I'll say it for the third time. There's a barbershop on Brown Avenue and your father and his car are in it! In the barbershop! At the same time! Your father and his car! Both!"

"Father? Car?"

Father and car!"

*

The Scottsdale police had blockaded one lane of Brown Avenue with a patrol car and two others were parked with lights flashing and one officer was directing traffic and another was controlling the crowd on the sidewalk before the O.K. Tonsorial Corral. Don left his car in the street and shoved through the crowd and identified himself to an officer. It was easy to see what had happened. For some reason Harry, who had evidently been angle-parked in front, had guided his Buick like a missile up over the curb, across the sidewalk, and directly into the interior of the barbershop. There was no door now, so Don stepped into the O.K. Tonsorial Corral through the gaping orifice that had once been a wide plate-glass window.

Inside, it was a demolition derby. Harry had really pulverized the place. There were wrecked chairs and manly magazines and shards of window glass and pieces of porcelain washbowls and tangles of electric cord and a smatter of smashed blow-dryers and other equipment. The room reeked of shampoos and rinses and conditioners and carbon monoxide. There had been two barber chairs. Aunt Min had taken out the first with General Motors ease and proceeded to slam the second into the rear wall of the shop. The trouble was, it was occupied—by an elderly old sport who was pinned in the chair between the wall and the Wildcat's grill. He was red-faced and waving his fists and bleating about calling Senator Goldwater, and it appeared he could not be extricated from the chair until the ancient sedan was extricated from the shop. A number of people welcomed Don. Some were swinger patrons and some were mere gapers and craners. Two men seemed to be the barber-proprietors. They were rigged out in Nino Cerruti jeans, mustaches, snap-button Western shirts of bright salmon, bolo ties, and red cowboy boots. One was burly and swearing a blue streak. The other looked fairly fey and was weeping. Then there were two stalwarts in the natty tan uniform of the Scottsdale force.

Don had other, more immediate concerns. Aunt Min's motor was still running, her tailpipe burping black puffs of apology. On her roof rested a barber pole. Her windows were rolled up, her doors locked, and inside her, beside his walker, face beaded with sweat, squinting ahead as though he were trying to read eternity or the fine print in an insurance policy, sat the Owosso Kid. Something about the big brown sedan and the little old gent behind the wheel with his porkpie hat tipped forward reminded Don of the Rabbit Rabbit and Bobby up against the wall again.

"You Donald Chambers?" This from one of the Scottsdale uniforms, young and gung ho.

"Yes."

"Is that your father in there?"

"Yes."

"I'm Officer Diaz. Sir, he won't come out of there. He won't say anything to anybody. We could break a window and haul him out or tow the car away with him in it, but at his age and all, he could go into cardiac arrest or something. Can we maybe talk him out?"

"I'll try," said Don.

He tapped on the driver's window. His father recognized him. Don pointed, then pushed his way around the car to the rear door and his father reached back and unlocked the door and Don got into the rear seat and closed the door.

"Hello, Dad," he said.

"Donald," said Harry. "Oh, Donald, I'm so glad you're here."

"Are you all right?"

"I'm fine, just fine."

"Good. Why don't you turn off the motor?"

"Okay." Harry turned the key.

Don was determined to keep his cool even though it was hotter than the hinges of hell inside the sedan. "Tell me what happened, Pop."

Harry twisted around. "Donald, do you know what they tried to soak me for a haircut? Twenty dollars!"

"Tell me what happened."

"Well, I came in here to get a haircut. After I got it I asked how much and that big sonofabitch there said twenty dollars. Well, I saw red. I told him haircuts in Owosso are ten dollars and that's what I'd pay. I put a ten-dollar bill on the chair and walked out. Do you blame me?"

"Father, listen. They don't have barbershops in Scottsdale. They have hair-styling salons. You got a styling."

"I didn't want a *styling*—I wanted a *hair*cut!"

"And the going rate for a styling is twenty dollars. Plus tip. What happened then?"

"Well, I tried to put my walker in the rear door, you know, this one, tied with a rope, but I couldn't untie the rope so I threw it— the walker—in the front seat and got in and started it and I was so damned mad and the barber, that big sonofabitch there, stood in the doorway swearing at me and, and—I guess I got confused. I must've put it in drive, not reverse, and gave it the gun. I just wanted to get away from here. Or maybe it was my hip. Anyway, I yelled 'Whoa! Whoa!' but I couldn't stop, and this is how I ended up."

"I see," said Don.

So did everyone in the O.K. Tonsorial Corral. Every window in the car including the windshield and except for the rear window cobwebbed with cracks was full of faces peering.

"Donald, tell me," said Harry. "How much damage d'you think I've done?"

"I don't know. Off the top of my head, I'd say ten, fifteen thousand should satisfy the shop."

"Oh, my goodness. I think I'd better put in a claim this time."

"I think I would."

"They'll cancel me."

"Probably. But your fine shouldn't be more than a hundred or so."

"Fine?"

"The police take a dim view of people driving their cars into places of business. 'Operating a motor vehicle in a reckless manner'—I think that's how the law reads."

"Oh, my goodness. I'll lose my license."

"Probably."

Officer Diaz and the other uniform were looking into the Buick goldfish bowl and waiting, as were about ten other curious citizens. The burly stylist was still swearing and his partner still weeping. Beyond the hood, trapped in the barber chair between Aunt Min's grill and the rear wall of the shop, the elderly old sport was close to myocardial infarction.

Harry belched. "My stomach's upset."

"So's mine."

"Well, well." Harry sighed. "I'm afraid I've complicated your life lately, Son."

"A little, Pop."

"That's all right," said his father. "You'll be well paid for it one of these days."

*

Ron found a job installing underground sprinkler systems. It paid eight dollars an hour and he could ride to and from work with one of his crew. Toiling outdoors in one-hundred-plus heat took its toll by the time he came home in the evening. "Welcome," Don would say. "Welcome?" "To the wonderful world of work," Don would say. Ron would shower and crash. Or Don would ask, "Which is it today?" "Which what?" "Fiction or nonfiction?" Ron would shower and play Samuel Barber. Or Don would inquire,

"Aren't you even going to ask how's Bobby?" Ron would shower and get out the tank and tube and suck oxygen. He was too shot down by manual labor or dismayed by capitalism to help his father cook or do dishes. Don had to do both, and the housework as well, since he'd let his cleaning woman go to save bucks. In the process of getting his head on straight, Ron seemed to have lost all interest in teaching bunnies how to steer vehicles, so Bobby got a break.

*

Harry didn't. Society threw the book at Harry Chambers. His caper cost his insurance company fourteen thou, and Harry his coverage. Traffic court laid a fine of ninety dollars on him for operating a motor vehicle in a reckless manner and another fifty for driving with a Michigan license—which had expired—when he had become a legal resident of Arizona. The party was over. Fate and the high price of a haircut had grounded the old Pope-Tribune pilot at last. It was time to part with Aunt Min. Harry said he was too sentimental to do the deed himself, so signed the title and handed Don her keys and sent him out into the automotive world to get full value. After a day of beating the used-car bushes, Don came back in a taxi and handed his father three one-hundred-dollar bills. Harry looked at them and roared up over the curb again. That car was worth a thousand dollars if it was worth a cent! Those damned dealers must have seen Don coming!

"Did the best I could, Pop," said Don.

"Just goes to show you! Send a boy to do a man's job!"

Don changed the subject. "What'll you do now, to get around? Taxis?"

"Taxis? I've heard about taxis—they'll jigger the meter and rob you blind. I expect you to take me when I need to go."

"I can't always," Don demurred. "I have to work for a living."

"Selling real estate? That's work?"

"There's Dial-a-Ride. You just call the Senior Citizens' Center in

Scottsdale and they'll pick you up right at your door and bring you home."

"For how much?"

"For free. I think you tip the driver."

"How much?"

"How do I know? A dollar?"

"Hmpf." His motor of ire still running, Harry folded the memory of Aunt Min away in his wallet. "I'm not tipping anybody, not at my age, and not for a service they should provide for old people. The government should take care of our transportation."

Don couldn't resist. "That means I'd pay, Pop. I'm the government."

"Hmpf. If you are, no wonder the country's going to hell in a handbasket."

*

Don, Jenny, Ron, and Sue took Windy Coon to the nursing home that Saturday. Jenny said she couldn't do it alone, she might disintegrate, and besides, it was time Ron and Sue met since they would soon be semi-related, and besides that, this was something an entire family should do together. And besides that, Don added, in case Windy balked at the last minute and started shooting, there was safety in numbers. Jenny wasn't amused. It had required several days for her to be convinced and to convince herself that this was the right move at the right time, that Don hadn't applied undue pressure on her grandmother, and that Windy was making the move of her own free will and generosity. And when she learned that Don on impulse had offered to pay the shot—which she certainly couldn't—she was even more apprehensive. She asked if he had any idea what it cost to put someone up in a nursing home. He said no, but it couldn't run more than four or five hundred a month—how big could the bite be for a bed and three meals and a piano for group singing? Jenny looked at him and shook her head.

All of Windy's worldly goods were contained in one suitcase, a set of old saddlebags, and a faded flour sack. Don stowed them in his trunk and the funereal five set off in the Sedan de Ville. Don had to carry the conversation, and did his best to keep it light and polite. He asked if July was hot enough for everybody. It was. He asked Jenny if she could see any vital signs in the house-and-hustle business these days. She could not. He asked Sue how was summer school at Phoenix College. She asked in response how anyone could possibly comment on summer school anywhere. He asked Ron how he liked installing underground sprinkler systems. Ron tried, replying he was really into it. For the first time he was beginning to appreciate the work ethic, the nobility of labor, etc., all of which went over like a lead balloon and after which Ron clammed up. Don didn't know what in hell to ask Windy. Everyone was overconscious of her of course, wondering if she knew where she was going and what was going on. She sat stiff and upright, cane before her, in the back seat with Ron and Sue, ticking away like a terrorist device. It was a lousy ride. It was like accompanying a casket on a first-class flight with only a piece of paper to attest that what was in the casket was dead. You wondered. What if the paper was fake, what if you suddenly heard bumping around in the cargo bay? Windy spoke, suddenly.

"I want some ice cream."

"You shall have it!" said Jenny.

"Right away!" said Don.

"All you want!" said Sue.

"Any flavor!" said Ron.

"In a cup," said Windy.

The detour to a Baskin-Robbins prolonged the agony fifteen minutes, and they fell over each other procuring and paying for a cup of Pomegranate Rapture. Then they sat like lumps and watched her relish it with trembling hand and plastic spoon the way witnesses watch the condemned eat a hearty meal on execution eve. She paused halfway.

"Y'know," she said. "Y'know." They hung on her words. It was as though she were addressing the ages. "Y'know, the night Wade Will pulled that trigger, I heard it the hull way t'the house. Up there on the ol' Slash-Bar-C you could hear a critter bawl a mile away nights. Dry air. Well, I was in bed an' heard it, down by the corral, an' I knew what it was. It was like that lead had went clean through my head, too." She nodded, and had another spoonful of Pomegranate Rapture, and licked her lips. "I was alone. That was a Saturday, too, an' all the hands was gone t'town t'get drunk. Well, I dressed an' went down t'the corral an' there he was. My darlin', my husband. I'd lost my baby, too. An' we'd lost the ranch. But he had pride, that man." A thoughtful Windy finished the ice cream. "I was twenty-two years old," she concluded. "I never been the same since."

Jenny closed her eyes.

Sue closed her eyes.

Ron cleared his throat.

Don cleared *his* throat. "Ahem. Well, shall we hit the trail?"

"Move 'em out," said Windy.

Eventually they reached the home. Don pulled up in front to unload. It was a comparatively new home, called "Happy Hours," and it was lavishly landscaped, Don noted, with year-around lawns and mature olive trees. "Well, Windy, we're home. 'Happy Hours.' " Don smiled. "Sounds pretty good to me." He toted her one suitcase, his son her set of saddlebags and additional belongings in the flour sack. The ladies helped the old gal on her cane slowly up the lighted front walkway. "Wow, this *is* spiffy," nodded Don. "Better landscaped than the Hilton."

"Sue and I thought it was lovely when we picked it," agreed Jenny.

They were about to enter Happy Hours when the old pioneer stopped and put her arms about Jenny's waist and Sue's.

"Now listen, everybody," she said. "Let's not have no long faces. You come see me when you can, I'll be here. Chambers, you marry my girl right soon. Jen, you sweet thing, you be happy—that's all I want for you. Sue, you go on an' graduate, an' you, boy, you do likewise. As for me, I got my pride, too. I'm doin' what's right. I give it a good think an' figured it out. The last, best thing you can do for your kids is let 'em go." She removed her arms, drew herself up, and punched the sidewalk with the point of her cane. "So let's by God go."

They were met by the supervisor, who could have passed for Betty Crocker in her younger days. "And you must be Mrs. Coon. Welcome to Happy Hours. May I call you Windy?"

"Surefire," said the scowling old pioneer.

"Fine, I'm Mrs. Schultz. And your family's here with you, how nice. Let's all follow me to your room, Windy, and help you get comfy in your new home." Don fobbed her suitcase off on his son and while the others went with Windy to see her new digs, Don lingered in the reception area before going to the business office to complete arrangements. He'd never been inside a nursing home before, and found himself twitchy. A look down the road? There were a lot of old ladies and a few old gents sitting and staring or swinging walkers or gliding around in wheelchairs—the place was Prune City, no doubt of that—but he'd misimagined Happy Hours. He had expected linoleum, flaked ceilings, stacked bed-pans, morticians making pitches, the aroma of antiseptic, and last year's Christmas tree. To his surprise, what he was getting for his money was space and carpeting and drapes and decor on an almost executive-class hotel level. He headed for the business office gratified he could provide Jenny's grandmother with a luxury she had never known.

When he emerged from the business office ten minutes later, he appeared altered. He was pale. His step was unsteady.

A nurse, passing, asked if he needed help.

An old gent came up and offered him the loan of his walker to the front door.

*

"Darling, what's wrong?" Jenny was already outside. "Don, what's wrong with you?"

"Twenty-two," he said sepulchrally, not to her but to the world.

"Twenty-two?"

"Twenty-two hundred a month. Doesn't include nursing."

"No! Oh, Don, I didn't know! Sue and I looked at six different homes, and Happy Hours was the one—I thought *you* thought seven or eight hundred a month. Oh, Don, what have you done?"

"*Me*? What have *I* done?"

"First you talked her into coming here, and then me into letting her, and now . . ."

But they reached the Caddie and Don went at once to the driver's door and lunged in and started the motor and turned on the AC. Jenny slid in beside him, her face also pale. Ron and Sue sat together in the rear seat, faces red. The hot air and hostility in the car could have been cut with a knife.

"Well, Mom, I hope you're satisfied," said Sue.

Jenny flinched as though she'd been struck, and took a moment to recover. She turned to her daughter. "I am satisfied. It's a beautiful place. She'll be happy here."

"How do you know?"

"Try to understand," Jenny said. "It was the only way. Don and I want to marry."

"She wanted to die at home."

"And there wasn't room to . . ."

"So you made room. Now *he* can have her bed."

Another low blow, and Jenny shook her head. "Dear, someday, when you're older, you'll see that . . ."

"What if I do this to you someday, Mom, when *you're* old and gray?"

Jenny turned away.

"Warehoused," said Ron.

It was Don's turn in the ring. *"Warehoused?* At twenty-two hundred a month?"

"It isn't the money."

"You mean, it isn't *your* money."

"It's what it symbolizes," Ron said. "When they're old enough, they're disposable. Toss 'em out. Warehouse 'em someplace. It's how we show our gratitude."

"Now you listen," Don began, white-knuckling the steering wheel. "You don't have the faintest . . ."

"You gonna do this to Gramps, Dad?"

Don had no answer. He threw in the towel.

"Anyway, Ron and I just wanted you guys to know how we feel," said Sue.

Don was out cold, but Ron got in one last sucker punch. "The two of you are on our all-time shit list."

*

"I could've killed 'em both," said Don. "With my bare hands."

"I just know she'll be happy there," Jenny said. "You didn't see her room—it's lovely. She even has her own TV, with remote control."

"She *should* have. At twenty-two big bills a month, she should have her own satellite dish."

"Oh, Don—that's my fault. I never asked how much. I didn't dream . . ."

"Let's not lacerate ourselves."

"Yes, let's not."

"Change the subject."

"Right. How's your father?"

"Crackerjack. Zings me all the time. I can't do anything right."

"I can't either. Sue says so."

"Kill 'em. With my bare hands."

"It's the generation crunch," Jenny said. "People our age. We're in the middle, and they crunch us from both sides, the young and the old."

"Which is why we get old ourselves," Don added. "Fast."

Jenny was finally having her cheeseburger. Don's was plain, but a double of everything. He'd commented, when they came in, that this was how far they'd fallen in three months: from steak Diane at Madame de Farge's to mystery meat at Whataburger. They were dining inside, and just then a scuzzy young couple in cutoffs and tank tops and thongs and dirty feet entered with a baby. They parked the baby in a highchair directly behind Don and went to the counter to order.

Jenny crunched into her entree. "Are Ron and his grandfather close?"

"Best buddies. Ron's over at the Eventide oftener than I am. I suppose they sit around and cut me up—what a schmuck I am."

"They couldn't possibly. Donald Chambers, you are the most generous man I've ever known."

"That's me. Mr. Nice Guy." He salted his fries and mustarded his double burger generously. The baby behind him in the highchair began to scream at the top of its lungs. "My God," he said. "Just what we need." He picked up a French fry, turned, and stuck it in the baby's mouth. The kid stopped screaming at once and began to gum the spud.

"But Don," Jenny said, "how can you afford . . ."

"Not to worry. I wrote them the first check—it won't bounce. Windy's paid up for a month. You're the one, babe—you're in worse shape than I am. What can you do?"

"D'you want my pickle?"

"Yes."

"Well, I talked to some people in our office," Jenny said. "They've already second-mortgaged their townhouses. That may be the way I have to go."

"Don't unless you have to. Interest on two mortgages eats you alive." Jenny had stopped eating. "Hon, what's wrong?"

"I just realized." She blinked her eyes to keep back tears. "I'll be sleeping in my room tonight—if I can—and Windy won't be there! After all these years! She'll be alone in a strange room! Oh, Don, what if she wakes up and needs me?"

The baby had dropped its fry and started to scream again. Its parents, the dirty feet, were still at the counter, putting in a special order for Chateaubriand or something. Without even looking, Don extended his arm behind him and plugged the kid's mouth with another fry. Then he took Jenny's hand in his tender, mustard fingers. "Jen, please. Don't lacerate yourself. Listen, I'm getting a message. This is our chance. Now. I've checked into it, and all you need is a few bucks for the license and that's it. Okay, this is Saturday night. Monday morning we drive into Phoenix to the County Clerk and get the license, no waiting. We walk across the street. Any one of a bunch of Justices of the Peace will splice us, no waiting. So by Monday noon we've done it. The last time I proposed, we were up in a balloon. Well, glamorous this ain't, but it's the best I can do. The important thing is, let's do it now. While we can. Before some other goddamn thing happens. I ask you, ma'am, in this Whataburger—what about it?"

The baby gummed its fry. Jenny considered. "Then what would we do?" she asked.

"Why, we'd go home. To your place. We'd kick Sue's crabby ass out of there and screw the day away. And the night. Between repeated, heart-pounding, bone-bending acts of love I'd take you out to a wedding dinner. Taco Bell, maybe."

It was not another proposal of marriage but his attempt at humor which cracked her. She jumped up from the table and rushed outside into the night, Don after her. He caught her at the rear of the Whataburger, before she reached the car, and grabbed her and swung her desperately into his arms and though she struggled, would not let her go, and there among the big plastic garbage cans Jenny Staley had the breakdown she'd been building to. She cried up a storm. "I love you," he murmured, holding her hysterics close. But how could he love her when it was she, her family, who'd manipulated him into this whole horrible human mess? "I love you," he murmured. The day had been more than she could bear. Packing for Windy and carting her away and watching her spoon Pomegranate Rapture and saying good-bye to her and then the abuse by her bitchy daughter and his insensitive son. "I love you," he murmured, and sat down on a garbage can in his Givenchy slacks and gathered her into his lap like a little sister. Every time he murmured "I love you" she cried all the harder. But how could he love her when he had to pay for her car and her nursing home and her cheeseburgers? "I hate you," he murmured, at which she wailed and laundered well the shoulder of his Oscar de la Renta shirt. He caressed her shining hair. He made of her a grandmotherless child. "Dearly girl," he murmured, "forgive me for trying to be funny. I'm about as funny as a crutch. Or a walker. But I'm trying to save our sanity. We've got cannon to the right of us and cannon to the left of us these days, you and I. But as long as we can laugh and love each other, we'll survive." He kissed away her tears with his relish lips. "Will you marry me Monday morning?" he whispered.

"Yes," she whispered. Then she had a horrid thought. "But I am a hooker after all!" she sobbed. "I've just sold my bed to a man for a lousy twenty-two hundred dollars a month!" And she began to cry all over again.

"There, there," he soothed. "We must *all* fight inflation." That made her laugh and cry at the same time. "Now listen," he said, "if you'll be a good girl and get off my lap and let me get off this goddamned garbage can and come with me to the car, I'll tell you a secret. Will you?"

For a secret she would. He helped her blow her nose and they got into the Cadillac. He turned on the dome light so she could repair her makeup, then turned it off and teased her by sitting there whistling "Pop Goes the Weasel!" through his teeth.

"Don, the secret!"

"Oh, yes," he said. "Well, you ain't going to have to second-mortgage and neither am I. I know how to turn everything around for us."

"You don't."

"Yes, I do. It's been going on and off in my mind like a lightbulb ever since I left that business office. I'll take you home now. You've got much to do before Monday morning—decide what to wear at your wedding, how many bridesmaids, et cetera. Then I'm gonna go see a man and borrow enough money to take us on a real honeymoon and carry us till we start selling again."

She was doubtful. "What man?"

"Okay, we've been helping the hell out of our old folks—now it's their turn. Jen, on the way out here from Michigan my father told me how much he's worth. I was amazed. He's loaded. He and my mother together stashed away about two hundred thousand."

"No."

"It's a fact. I'm an only child, and someday I'll inherit—may he live forever. But not only that, he takes in over a thou a month, more than he needs to live on. Interest, dividends, house payments, Social Security, pension. So. So, I'm going over to his place—right now, tonight, after I drop you off—and hit him for a loan. A large loan. And he'll do it. I'll call you in an hour with the good news."

"Oh," she said.

They sat in the dark car thinking. The scuzzy young couple came out of the Whataburger with Cokes and their sound-asleep baby and made off in a pickup like bandits.

"Are you sure he will?" asked Jenny.

"Sure? Jen, he's my father!"

*

He chimed the chimes.

He chimed them again.

The living room was lit. Harry would be in bed or the kitchen.

He waited and chimed again.

He tried the front door. Locked.

He stepped to the window and stooped and looked in under the shade.

His father lay on the living room floor.

Don panicked. He ran next door to Mrs. Bustard's and hammered on her door until she appeared. "It's me, Mrs. Bustard, Don Chambers! It's Dad—he's lying on the floor and the door's locked!"

"On the floor? What's he doing?"

"He's unconscious!"

"He was all right after supper."

"Call an ambulance! Tell 'em emergency! I'll try to get in to him!"

She clucked. "He just wouldn't listen to me about that cafeteria."

"Cafeteria?"

"Those damned desserts. They'll kill half the people over here."

She headed for the phone. Don lifted the big pot by her door which held the petunias, ran back breaking his back with it to his father's apartment, and with superhuman strength raised it and heaved it through the living room window.

Kicking glass away, he rammed into the room like a Buick Wildcat and fought past the shade and dived for his father, who lay on his back with his walker on top of him. His eyes were closed. Don pitched the walker away and bent to his chest and listened for a heartbeat and heard one. With a groan of relief he sat back on his haunches and studied through teary eyes his poor, insensate father's face. His specs were askew. Carefully Don took them off. In one corner of Harry's mouth was a toothpick.

*

He called Jenny around eleven o'clock.

"Jen, I'm calling from Scottsdale Memorial, not from home. Dad's in here."

"No!"

"When I got to his place he was lying on the living room floor."

"Again?"

"Again. No broken bones this time. I got him to Emergency here by ambulance. He's probably had a stroke—not a massive one, they don't think. In the morning they'll run tests and see if he's paralyzed or his speech is affected or what."

"Oh, Don, dearest."

"I know."

"Will you stay there?"

"I guess so. Till they find out in the morning."

"Do you want me to come over?"

"No. You need your beauty sleep. God, I'm sorry. I guess Monday's off."

"I know."

They were silent.

"What a shame," she said.

"Whataburger."

"Don't make me cry again," Jenny said. "Let's just pray. That he's okay."

"Yes."

They were silent.

"I love you, Jen."

"I love you."

"Goddammit."

"We can. . ."

"Don't say it."

*

Well, he was only a name and number. Unwell, Harry was popular as hell. It occurred to Don that a new hospital patient with

III 108 III

Medicare and a supplementary policy and some money of his own was like a classic story that had just passed into the public domain. They were fair game for everybody. By the next morning his father's arrival at Scottsdale Memorial had attracted a whole platoon of ologists: a cardi, an ur, a radi, a path, a proct, a neur, and a wallet. Later, when these found out about his unhappy hip, they brought in an orthopedist and a therapist. The new patient was sedated, scoured, sensitized, sodomized by instrument, and scanned. He was pricked, probed, poked, prodded, and palpated. His essential juices were drawn and bottled and shipped to a dozen different destinations. There were conferences, and after two days, a consensus: basically, the plagues of age aside, Harry Chambers was okay. He had suffered a transitory ischemic attack, a minor stroke. But there was no permanent impairment of speech or hearing or motor ability beyond his hip, which was already dysfunctional, and he could safely be released tomorrow.

"Speaking of the hip," said Doc Bud Biller, "some therapy might help. Bring him in as an outpatient a couple times a week and let's have somebody wrestle him around a bit."

Laid back so far he was out of sight, Biller of Scottsdale Memorial was as young as Archie Skinner of Owosso General and Officer Diaz in the O.K. Tonsorial Corral.

"What about when he gets home?" Don asked.

"I'll have some pills for him to pop."

"I mean, he lives alone."

"Nobody near?"

"A nurse on call. The Eventide. And the old lady next door."

"Ah. Have her look in on him now and then."

Don stood with the doctor at the nurse's station. Biller pulled an Arizona lottery ticket from a pocket and started to scratch off the latex layer over the numbers with the end of his stethoscope.

"Another thing," he said, scratching. "He should have somebody with him nights for a week or so. An LPN—licensed practical nurse. On your way out, stop downstairs at the desk and ask for a list. Names and phones." He grinned suddenly, ear to ear, and waved the lottery ticket. "Bingo, I've won two bucks! How 'bout that? First winner I've had!"

*

Once, while Harry was living with him at Oasis South, Don had confided to Jenny that he was living with a stranger. That this man and the father he remembered from years back were two different people. That he couldn't find in this man, he was sad to say, one damn thing to love, or even to like. Now, on Harry Chambers's release from Scottsdale Memorial, Don Chambers was about to meet yet another stranger. He was about to be blessed, or cursed, with a third father. Don didn't and couldn't know this. Driving him home to Toothpick City he noted no difference. Don observed him closely, trying to scratch away the layer of reticence that covered his cerebral trauma, but as far as the son could tell, his sire was still his second father—the dear, liberal, selfless, lovable old bastard he had become in later life.

For example. On learning the price of a nurse was thirty dollars an hour, and that neither Medicare nor his supplementary policy would cover it, Harry decided a practical nurse would be impractical.

"But Pop, the doc says you have to have somebody with you nights."

"I've got somebody. You."

"I'm not a nurse."

"You're my son."

Don made a face. "All right, I volunteer. Biller says you'll be fine days. You can always call the nurse here, you know."

"Or the old bag next door. Bustard. If she isn't over here, she's spying on me."

For example. Harry was determined to continue going to the corner cafeteria for his dinner, and he could hash up his own lunch, but he no longer cared to make breakfast. He liked a hot country breakfast, pie, eggs and potatoes, the works.

"What about this Meals-on-Wheels business?" he asked Don.

"They'll bring a hot lunch right here. I don't know who pays for it—the taxpayers, I suppose. And they don't call it 'paying,' they call it 'funding.' "

"It's free to me?"

"No such thing as a free lunch, Pop."

"But I don't want *lunch,* I want breakfast."

"Sorry, no breakfast."

"Damn their socks."

And when, his first night as a practical nurse, Don showed up for his shift at 10 P.M., Harry informed him he'd prefer someone at eight.

"I just can't, Dad. I have to cook dinner and wash dishes and things."

"If you set out to do something, do it right. Send Ron over early. You come along when you can."

"Ron who? I never see him. Gone all day and after dinner he's out the door. Till all hours."

"Hmpf."

It was in the middle of that first night on staff duty, however, that Don woke up to the fact that he had still another stranger on his hands. That he now had to cope with an entirely different father. Don Chambers, meet Harry Chambers III. Because an event in his second father's brain, minor though it might have been medically, had transformed him into a third. Dead to the world in the twin bed beside him, Don was rocketed out of sleep and right out of the bed by a horrible halloo.

"There's a bear in the woods!"

Don reeled around the room in his skivs and tried to perceive what in God's name was going on.

"There's a bear in the woods!" Harry bellowed, and began to get out of bed himself. "I'll get 'im! I'll shoot the sonofabitch!"

Don sprang to this father and grappled him down on the bed and wrapped arms around him like a straitjacket. "Dad, Dad, this is Don! It's all right—there's no bear in here! You had a bad dream!"

"Oh? Oh," said his father, and went limp. "I did, did I?"

Upon which he lay back and snored away as though nothing had happened. But Don was so shaken by the experience that he could not have slept under sodium pentathol. He paced the apartment for a time, jumpy as a cat, then took up his post again beside his father and lay rigid, waiting.

It was well he did. At three in the morning, and again at four-thirty, Harry hunted bears in the woods, and had to be restrained and reassured and tucked in. By dawn's early light his son's eyes were bagged and his hands trembled as though he had picked up his own case of Parkinson's.

He phoned young Biller as soon as he fled home after making a hot country breakfast for Harry, who seemed none the worse for his ursine night.

"A bear in the woods?"

"That's what he saw, Doctor. Three times. I'm a wreck."

"A bear in the woods. Very interesting. I had one woman get up in the night and go outdoors and dance with Fred Astaire. Bare-assed. Well, your dad's hallucinating of course. It happens sometimes, after a stroke. He'll come out of it. I hope."

"What's wrong with him?"

"Who knows?"

"Could it be all the damned drugs he's on? Could he be OD'd?"

"The medication? Don't think so. Let's have a look at his file. Let's see, here we are. When he came to me he was on Coumadin, Digitalis, Lasix."

"He takes a lot of Tylenol."

"Bully for him. Let's see, and Persantine and Symmetrel and Aldoril. Wow. Now I've also got him on Darvocet and a potassium supplement."

"My God, Doctor—he's got more chemicals in him than duPont makes!"

"They love 'em. You don't pour the pills to the old folks, they'll go down the street to some quack. By the way, Chambers, why're you staying with him anyway?"

"He won't hire a nurse."

"You hire one."

"I can't afford it."

"Buy a lottery ticket. Get lucky."

The next night's duty was equally nightmarish.

"Look out for that devil!"

Don was out of bed like a bouncer out of a bar. It was past two in the morning.

"That man in the straw hat!" Harry howled, and pointed an arm at a dark corner of the room. "See that devil in the straw hat?" He began to climb out of bed. "I'll get 'im! I'll shoot the sonofabitch!"

Don grappled with his father and went through the reassurance routine and Harry snored away, only to repeat the performance sometime after three and again at five. There were no bears this night. This was devils night. Don bleared away much of it drinking black coffee in the kitchen. Why were old people so violent? Why were they always going for their guns?

*

"A devil in a straw hat? I'll be damned," was Bud Biller's reaction in the morning.

"Doctor, I'm dying. I haven't really slept for two nights."

"Devil in a straw hat, huh? Well, listen, Chambers, tell you what let's try. I'll call in a prescription of Dalmane. Give him one tonight at bedtime and see if that doesn't shut down his show."

"More chemicals? My God."

"Whatta you want? Herbs?"

Modern medicine offered barbiturates, Jenny sympathy. "Oh, you poor darling."

Don yawned into the phone. "I sat on a house this afternoon and passed out cold on the floor. Four hours. If somebody'd wanted to buy, I couldn't have sold. I'm losing all contact with the outside world. What's new? How's Sue?"

"I wouldn't know. School all day and out half the night. How's Ron?"

"Never see him."

"And Bobby?"

"He's the only sane one around. What about Windy?"

"That's the good news. I've seen her every day, and this should console you. Dear, my grandmother is happy at Happy Hours."

"How would she like a roommate?"

"Your father?"

"Me."

*

Dalmane did it. That night the father slept the sleep of science, his son that of the righteous. But on the way to the hospital that afternoon for hip therapy, Harry asked Don where they were going and why. And on the way home, Harry launched a long soliloquy about Laura and Joe and Heather and Alex and Tiffany and Spencer. It took Don to the front door to ascertain that these were some of the principals in "Ward One," a TV hospital soap on which Harry had become hooked while in Scottsdale Memorial. It also seemed, according to Harry, that their principal activity on the tube was playing musical beds. Harry slumbered soundly again that night, as did Don, and as did Harry the following night, without benefit of Dalmane. Don believed the worst was over. It was not. Harry caught him at the office later in the morning and issued a summons. Don arrived at the Eventide to find his father slumped at the small desk in the living room. Before him cancelled checks were scattered, and uncashed checks as well, and there was a bank statement. Harry was in tears.

"Dad, what's the matter?"

"I can't balance my checkbook!"

"No problem. I'll help."

"It's just not that!" Harry blubbered. "I can't add or subtract! I've kept books all my life, and I can't add two and two! My mind doesn't work right! How'll I ever do my banking?"

Don sat down. "Look, let me balance it this time and deposit those checks. All you have to do is endorse them."

"That's another thing—I can't seem to write my own name, not so's anybody could read it! Harry bawled. "What's the matter with me?"

Don listened to the whir of the air conditioning. "I don't know, Dad," he said presently. "And I don't see how you can do your banking unless you let me help."

"No!"

Don studied the Hopi overlay ring on his finger, wondering what he could get for it. "We talked about power of attorney before. If you'd give me one, just temporarily, I could . . ."

"Hell, no!"

That settled to his satisfaction, Harry subsided. He blew his nose with a handkerchief, then used the handkerchief to clean his specs. "They've got a lady therapist at the hospital," he said. "She knows her stuff, I'll tell you. My hip feels better already. And say, Medicare covers therapy, too."

Don knew there would never be a right time, but since the old man was on the upbeat, this might be as propitious as any. "While we're on the subject of money, Dad, I need to talk to you. I've got a problem myself."

"Oh?"

"Dad, I'm a little short. The truth is, I can make it to the end of the month and that's about it. It's very painful for me to have to tell you. You know how tough times have been in real estate—three months ago my income just stopped. You can't give housing away right now, much less sell it. Well, if I don't come up with some money soon, enough to tide me over till this thing turns around, I'll lose my condo. And my car. I've had a lot of extra expense, too."

Harry smiled. "Those darned kids."

"Kids?"

"On the TV show. In and out of bed together every day—you never saw such carrying on."

"Dad, listen to me."

"I'm listening."

"I have to ask you for a loan."

"How much?"

"Well, ten thousand would . . ."

"Ten thousand! I wouldn't lend ten . . ."

"You gave away ten thousand to those diamond guys. Strangers."

His father scowled. "Never do business with friends or relatives. That's sound practice."

Don stood. "I'll pay you interest—whatever's the going rate."

"Yes, I guess not."

"Pop, I need it! And you can spare it!"

Harry threw him a curve. "What extra expense?"

Don swung and missed. "Well, I had to make a car payment for Jenny."

"That was damnfool."

"You know we want to marry."

"Marry? On what?"

"So, in order to make room for me at her place, we put her grandmother in a nursing home."

That pleased Harry. "Ron told me. Good."

"Jenny couldn't afford it. So I offered to pay the bill for a while."

"You? How much?"

Don was getting in deeper and deeper. "Well, quite a lot."

"How much?"

"Is that all you can say? 'How much? How much?' All right—twenty-two hundred a month."

Harry's jaw dropped so far his lower choppers almost dropped out. "You mean, you're paying twenty-two hundred a month to put that old battle-ax away? What've you got her in—the Ritz? Harry shook his head. "I don't believe it. How anybody could be such an idiot. And you'd like me to lend you the money so you . . ."

"Goddammit, Dad, I'm in love!"

"Love shit."

Don stared at him as though trying to decide which father this was, the second or the third. He couldn't recall the first, the original. He began to feel an adolescent embarrassment, like that of a boy caught stealing. "I don't believe this either," he said thickly. "That you're making me beg. Your own son. I think I've been pretty nice to you lately."

"You should be. I expect it. Someday you'll get every red cent I have."

"I need some now! Why won't you help me?"

"Because the best way I can help you is turn you down. Flat." Harry hitched himself around in the chair at the desk, took hold of his walker, and hoisted himself to his feet. "Donald, I'm saying no for your own good. Apparently you've squandered your money—well, you're not squandering mine. I warned you about marrying into that family—they'll bleed you to death. Not only that, I question your judgment. You had a steady job in Detroit—you never should have left it. And you had a fine wife—you never should have divorced her. Well, you've made your own bed, I must say—now lie in it. This may teach you a lesson, my boy. You're not too old to learn."

They faced each other. Don began to feel physically ill. It was he who turned away, sickened. "Father, I am really hurt. You have really hurt me." He moved toward the door.

"You're going?" Harry asked.

Don could scarcely speak. "I don't like it here."

"You be back tonight. I'm not staying alone. And you be here at eight o'clock."

"I might not be."

"You'd damned well better."

Don stopped at the door. "You mean you really don't care if I lose everything. My own father. My house, my car, *every*thing."

His father clumped after him. "Just a minute." He reached Don and put a hand on his shoulder and smiled at him. "Son, I want you to do something for me. You scout around town—go to every supermarket in Phoenix if you have to. I want you to find me some raspberries. My mouth just waters for red raspberries."

*

"Nuttier than a fruitcake?"

"No. I'm not saying senile. But he'll be lucid for a while, then bring up something from the old days that has no connection. Is it the stroke? I mean, has he gone over the edge?"

"Maybe, maybe not," said Bud Biller.

"Will he pull out of it?"

"He might, he might not."

"Come on, Doctor."

"If I had a crystal ball, I'd be rich. Give me something else."

"Well, he can't do simple arithmetic. He can't sign his name legibly. He can't do his banking."

"Ah."

"And he won't give me power of attorney."

"I see."

Don could hear him tapping something on his desk, probably a pencil, thinking.

"Conservatorship," said Bud Biller.

"What's that?"

"You petition a court to be named his conservator. In some states it's guardian, in Arizona it's conservator. When petition's granted, you take charge of his affairs and him. Banking, everything. It's like being guardian of a minor—which many of them are, mentally."

"That's pretty strong."

"I know. But I have to suggest it to a lot of people with aged parents."

"He's only eighty-three."

"Some old dear souls need it at seventy."

"Oh." Don reached for a pencil and began to tap on his desk, thinking. "How would I go about it?"

"See an attorney. I understand you can also do-it-yourself, but I wouldn't want to."

"What would he do?"

"Advise you, I suppose."

"What might he say in this case?"

"Chambers, how do I know? I'm just an old-time country doc, buggying through the snow, selling castor oil and beating newborn babies' asses. I'm not an attorney. If I were, I'd be rich."

*

Don did not go to the Eventide that night. His phone rang off the hook after eight o'clock, but he hardened his heart. Let the old bastard hunt bears by himself. Ron was out as usual. Don and Bobby sprawled around on the bed and ate Milk Duds and ransacked every edition of last week's *Arizona Republic* until Don found the ad he'd recently spotted on a sports page. "Jeremy Snapkin," it read in small, dignified type. "Attorney-at-Law. Wills, Divorces, Bankruptcy, Drunken Driving, Tax, Immigration, Estates, Trusts, Palimony, Lost Luggage, Contracts, Reasonable Fees, Centrally Located in Scottsdale, First 15-Minute Consultation Free of

Fee." The guy was certainly versatile. And he certainly couldn't pass up a free fifteen minutes.

He consulted with Jeremy Snapkin the next morning. On the attorney's desk were two digital clocks, the face of one visible to the attorney, that of the other visible to his client. Every time a minute elapsed, and the digits flipped, the clocks ticked.

They shook hands and sat down and both checked the clocks and Don told his sad, filial story.

"So that's the situation, Mr. Snapkin. I'm thinking about a conservatorship."

"Call me Jerry. Hang on, I'll read you the law." He jumped, jerked a big book from a shelf, and found a page. " 'Arizona Revised Statute 14-5401, Article 4, Section 2, Sub-Section (a). Appointment of a conservator may be made in relation to the estate and affairs of a person if the court determines that: the person is unable to manage his property and affairs effectively for reasons such as mental illness, mental deficiency, mental disorder, physical illness or disability, advanced age, chronic use of drugs, chronic intoxication, confinement, detention by a foreign power, or disappearance.' " Snapkin shut the book and returned it to the shelf and himself to the swivel. "What are our grounds, Mr. Chambers?"

"Mental deficiency."

"Such as?"

"Well, he can't add two and two or sign his name. So he can't do his banking. And a few weeks ago he was aced out of seven thousand dollars in a diamond scam."

"Uhn-*huh*. Open-and-shut case, I'd say. He won't fight it, will he?"

"How can he? He's never been in a court before—neither have I. Besides, these days, he's a few sandwiches short of a picnic."

Snapkin looked at his clock.

Don looked at *his* clock.

He'd have bet the ink was still wet on Jerry Snapkin's bar exam.

He was as young as Dr. Archie Skinner and Dr. Bud Biller and Officer Diaz and all three of them were younger than Don, which didn't seem possible because *he* was young.

"Okay, I'll tell you what happens," the attorney said. "You're known as the 'Petitioner' and your father as the 'Protected Person.' I'll petition the court tomorrow on your behalf. Filing fee is sixty dollars—your cost. The court appoints a 'guardian *ad litem*' for your father—an attorney, but he's a formality and the county pays for him. Who's your father's physician?"

"Doctor Robert Biller."

Snapkin made a note. "The court will appoint him, too, and want his written report. That'll be fifty dollars—your cost."

The clocks clicked. Snapkin checked his. Don checked his. He was down to four free minutes.

"Then comes a hearing, a week, ten days from now. It's a hearing, not a trial. You'll testify, then your father if he's able. Then the judge rules, grants your petition, you sign papers and take over. We should be out of there in half an hour. They run conservatorships through there like cars through a wash."

"If you don't mind my asking, Mr. Snapkin, what'll you cost me?"

"Call me Jerry. How is your father fixed financially, Mr. Chambers? If you don't mind my asking."

"Oh, well, he's comfortable."

"Let's talk numbers."

"Well, a couple hundred thousand."

"Lovely. You the sole heir?"

"That's right."

"Six hundred. Unless he fights."

"He won't."

The clocks clicked. Snapkin checked his. Don checked his. He still had a free minute. The clocks and the young attorney made him nervous. Jerry Snapkin was small and robotic. His eyes and hands were jerky.

"How long've you practiced law, Mr. Snapkin?"

"Six months. Call me Jerry. But I've been through the conservator mill, believe me."

Don rose. "Really?"

"With my dear old widow mother, back in New Jersey. I've had her up before a judge three times. She's always booking cruises and buying her tickets—Caribbean, the Med, round the world—then she forgets to get aboard the goddamn ships and forfeits all money. Lost a fortune. She should be in a rubber room. I talk to her about a nursing home and she says 'A nursing home? But how would I travel?' "

Don edged to the door. "Really?"

Snapkin jerked out of his chair and around the desk and put an armlock on his client. "So I petition the court and go to the hearing and she takes the stand and suddenly she's not nuts, she's clear as a bell, talking about how she cruises the seven seas, and guess what?"

Don got a hand on the knob and tugged at the door. "What?"

"Petition denied! She wins!"

*

Don believed a dry martini on the rocks should be built, not made. To build the perfect martini you chilled two glasses in the fridge. You took them out, positioned two ice cubes side by side on the bottom, a third atop these, set a Spanish olive with a fourth cube. The olive was crucial. It must be extra-large, firm, well-shaped, and the pimento must not protrude. Such noble olives were not obtainable in a supermarket. Whenever Don went to Las Vegas, the home of the noblest olives in the world, he bought a gallon jar from a bartender buddy at the Desert Inn and carried it back to Phoenix under his arm. After this foundation had been laid—four cubes and the noble olive—you poured over it two ounces of a first-class vodka—this evening he used Stolichnaya one-hundred-proof because he needed a quick buzz—it was his last jug of Stolichnaya, incidentally, and the olive jar was almost empty—and let fall on the ice from an eyedropper one drop of Noilly Prat vermouth. You then waited a suspenseful minute. What you hoped to achieve was a just and lasting peace between Russian fatalism, Spanish passion, French arrogance, and American get-up-and-go. You waited a minute, then raised a tentative glass to your lips. You sipped. You smiled. You had built, not made, the perfect dry martini.

Don carried them into his living room and presented one to Jenny. They had met at his place because each had something important to tell the other, too important for the telephone.

"Tears," he said.

"Tears," she said.

They touched glasses.

"I second-mortgaged today," she said.

"You didn't."

"Dear, I had to. You're not making another payment on my car and you're not subsidizing my grandmother another month at Happy Hours."

"I couldn't," he admitted. "I'm down to the dregs myself. Well, where and how much?"

"Friendly Finance. Six thousand."

"At?"

"Ten percent."

"My God. And a pint of blood."

"Don, I had no choice. My bank said no and so did my S & L. Six thousand will see me through three months, if I'm careful." She sipped. "This is a splendid mart. All right, give me your good news."

"Don stirred the ice cubes with his finger and fired down half an ounce. "You asked for it. I asked my old man for a loan of ten thou. I told you he'd say yes. He said no."

"He didn't!"

"He really hurt me, Jen."

"Don, I'm so sorry."

"He's not responsible. Mentally he's a damaged man. This is about the third father I don't know. He can't do arithmetic, can't sign his name, can't do his banking. So I talked it over with Bud Biller, his doctor, and he had an idea." Don looked at Jenny.

"Well?"

"Well, I went to an attorney, and he's petitioned the court for a conservatorship. Making me my father's legal guardian under Arizona law. Taking charge of his affairs. They tell me it happens all the time."

"Lordy," she whispered.

"I know. But I had no choice, just like you."

"Does he know yet?"

"He has to. He had to be informed, the doc and somebody from the court have to write reports on his condition. The hearing's next Monday morning. My legal eagle says there'll be no problem—a simple case over and done with in half an hour."

"Have you heard from your father?"

"No."

"Why not, do you think."

"He's probably eating the carpet—or he doesn't know what it means. He's in and out now, like Windy. I haven't called him or seen him because what do I say? One minute I'm burned as hell at him and the next I'm sorry for him."

They sipped their perfect marts. Don thought about Jenny's second mortgage. Jenny thought about Don going to court. Sprawled flat in an easy chair opposite them, Bobby thought about rabbits.

The front door opened and who should walk in but Ron and Sue. Bobby took one terrified look at Ron and bounded out of the chair and out of the room, heading for a closet or under a bed.

"Hi," said the kids, sitting down.

"Hi," said their respective parents.

Sue wore an actual dress. Ron wore jeans and T-shirt on which was printed "Patience My Ass!"

"We've got something to tell you," said Sue.

She reached for Ron's hand. Ron reached for hers. They held hands. Don and Jenny waited.

"We're in love," said Ron.

"We're getting married. Right away," said Sue.

"Oh, no, you're not," said Jenny.

"Oh, no, you're not," said Don.

"Oh, yes, we are," said Sue.

"Oh, yes, we are," said Ron.

"Oh, no, you're not," said Jenny.

"I need a drink," said Don, steering for the kitchen with his glass and Jenny's. "Don't anybody say a damn word till I get back." He pitched in more cubes and sloshed vodka and vermouth out of the bottles and returned on the double, handing Jenny hers and tipping his high. "Oh, no, you're not," he said.

"Oh, yes, we are," said Sue.

"In the first place," said Jenny, "it's too soon. You scarcely know each other."

"Not true, Mrs. Staley," countered Ron. "We've seen a lot of each other since you cold-storaged Windy. Every night."

"All night," added Don.

"Mom, how can you say too soon?" asked Sue. "You told me you'd only dated Don eight times before he proposed."

"But I said no," argued her mother. "And besides, that's different. We're older, more mature."

"And divorced," reminded Ron. "You've both been around the track before."

"I resent that," snapped Don. "Besides, you're too poor. You don't have a pot or a window."

"And *you're* loaded?" queried his son. "At least I'm bringing home a paycheck."

"At least we don't have a second mortgage," added Sue.

"Is this how you get your head on straight?" Don demanded of his son.

"And what happens to computer programming?" Jenny demanded of her daughter.

"Well, we thought we'd both go to Arizona State this fall," said Ron. "Or maybe this winter."

"Arizona State!" cried Don. "When you could finish at Claremont McKenna, a good private college?"

"Don't knock Arizona State," warned Sue. "They have super athletic teams."

"You don't even have a car!" cried Jenny somewhat irrelevantly.

"You're forgetting!" cried Ron. "We love each other!"

"No, you're forgetting, goddammit!" cried Don. "So do we!"

"We thought you'd be happy!" cried Sue. "Windy's gone and I'd be gone and you'd have Mom's place all to yourselves!"

"Or this one!" cried Ron. "Gramps is gone and I'd be gone!"

"Wait a minute!" cried Don. "You can't marry! When Jen and I marry that makes you related—you're brother and sister or something! It's against the law! Your kids would have two heads!"

"Bullshit," said Sue.

"Sue!" cried Jenny.

"We'd only be related to each other by marriage," said Sue. "Nothing wrong with that."

"There's got to be!" cried Don. "It's unnatural! It's shirttail incest!"

Jenny picked the noble olive from her martini, stared at it, and began to cry. "You're too young! And this is too much for me right now! Why should you get married when we can't?"

Her tears and his Stolichnaya brought Don to a flash point. He swayed up from his chair and took a stalwart stance. "Now, you two listen to me! You can't, you won't, you shall *not* marry before Jen and I do! We're not going to be grandparents before we're even married! We've been trying for four goddamn months and it's been one goddamned thing after another and you are not dating three short weeks and waltzing down the aisle! It isn't fair! D'you read me? You'll have to wait—you'll have to suffer—we've had to!

Age before dumb! You'll have to wait—then if you still want to, the very day Jen and I make it with a minister, okay, it's your turn! As soon as we say 'I do!' we'll buy the rice and say 'Go, Ron! Go, Sue!' "

Bobby raced back into the living room and hopped into the Rabbit Rabbit and waited to be buckled.

*

Jerry Snapkin phoned. "He's fighting it. Your father."

"No."

"Yes. He wouldn't have the guardian *ad litem,* the court-appointed counsel. He's hired his own."

"Who?"

"A guy named Gus Goldberg."

"Oh, no!"

"I hear Goldberg's a shark."

"Oh my God."

"You told me he wouldn't fight, Chambers. He wouldn't even know what was going on."

"I didn't think he would."

"You must not know your father."

"How well d'you know your mother?"

Jerry Snapkin sighed over the wires. "Okay. Remember, I said it'll cost you more if he fights. Okay, see you Monday morning."

Don sighed. "Well, hell, it won't make any difference. When he gets on the stand he'll talk about Thomas E. Dewey."

"Thomas E. Dewey?"

*

Division 8 of the Maricopa County Superior Court was on the sixth floor of the county building in downtown Phoenix. Don reached it at ten of ten on Monday morning to meet Jerry Snapkin. He had never before seen the inside of a courtroom. This one was so well appointed, its paneled walls and deep carpets and indirect lighting and jury box and judge's bench and clerk's cubicle and attorneys' tables and sound system and spectator seating so deluxe, that it must have put the taxpayers in bondage right up to their balls. Snapkin was seated at a table before the bench emptying a briefcase jammed with enough papers to document a United States Supreme Court antitrust case. At the bottom of the case was his lunch, a sandwich wrapped in waxed paper, which he hastily stuffed back into the case as Don joined him.

"I don't have good vibes," he muttered to his client.

"Don't say that," muttered Don. "Why not?"

Jerry indicated a distinguished-looking gent with a mane of white hair seated at the opposition table. "Goldberg. I hear he's a shark."

"Don't say that, I'm shaky enough. You're supposed to pep-talk me."

"Twelve hundred."

"Twelve hundred what?"

"Dollars. Remember, I said it'll cost more if he fights. Double."

"Don't talk about that either, dammit. Not now. How come there's no audience?"

"People go to the sensational stuff, the trials—rape, homicide, so on."

"How come my old man isn't here?"

"I don't know. How come you dressed up so much?"

Don wore his classiest suit, a Christian Dior. "I thought I should. I've never been in court before. Why?"

"You look L.A., not Phoenix. Might make a very bad impression."

"Why didn't you tell me? Should I go home and change?"

"Too late now." Snapkin sighed.

Enter the Bailiff and the Clerk of the Court, taking places at a desk to the right of and below the bench and standing. The Bailiff banged a gavel twice. "All rise!" he proclaimed. "This Maricopa

County Superior Court is now in session, the Honorable Judge Hannah Lawhon presiding!"

Enter the judge. She wore black robes, gray bobbed hair, granny glasses, a severe expression, as though she had trouble in her bowels, and she was seventy years old if she was a day. She seated herself. All seated themselves.

"Why did we have to have her?" Don whispered.

"Luck of the draw. She's a tough old broad—that's why she keeps getting elected. She's on civil this term, but when she's on criminal cases they call her 'Hangin' Hannah.' "

Judge Lawhon adjusted her microphone. "Are you ready, Mr. Snapkin?"

"We are, Your Honor."

"Mr. Goldberg, I don't see your client."

"Your Honor, Mr. Chambers has limited mobility, and may be delayed. If it please the Court—ah, I believe he's here now."

There were loud noises at the rear of the courtroom. Enter Harry Chambers, who had undoubtedly been waiting in the wings for this moment, using his walker on the doors like a battering ram. Goldberg swept to meet him, to take his arm, to assist his client down the aisle to be seated with many a huff and puff at Goldberg's table. He removed his porkpie hat. Don hadn't seen his father for ten days. Harry wore his shiny black worsted suit. He was tieless, and the collar and cuffs of his white shirt were laundry-frayed. His appearance was calculated to be that of an aged, handicapped indigent alone in the world, bereft of family and friends, with one foot in the grave and the other in intensive care. Don was ashamed of him. And ashamed of himself. He wished to God neither of them were here. His father, worth two hundred thousand dollars, costumed to look like a charity case. Himself, on the brink of bankruptcy, swanked up in a French suit. Father did not look at son.

"What an entrance," muttered Jerry Snapkin. "I'm learning a lot. Goldberg should be on stage."

"We're ready now, Your Honor," Goldberg announced.

"Very well." Judge Lawhon surveyed her courtroom as though it were jammed with humanity. "Chambers versus Chambers. Since petition's being contested, this will be an adversary proceeding— examination and cross-examination as counsel deem necessary." She nodded at the Clerk of the Court. "Clerk will record that the report by Gerald Small, appointed Visitor, and the report by—let me see—Dr. Robert Biller—have been received and read by the Court." She addressed the attorneys. "Identify yourselves, gentlemen, and your clients."

"I am Jeremy Snapkin, Your Honor, and this is the Petitioner for Conservatorship, Mr. Donald Chambers."

"I am Gustave Goldberg, Your Honor, and this is the Protected Person, Mr. Harold Chambers."

Her Honor sat back. "Call your witness, Mr. Snapkin."

Don took the stand, was sworn in by the Clerk, and was led through name, residence, and relationship by his attorney. "Now, Mr. Chambers, will you tell the Court why you have petitioned?"

"Well," Don began. It came out a squeak. His throat was constricted. Every eye in the room was on him, including his father's now. He felt like a squirrel, crawling along a power line between telephone poles, walking tightrope, and expected any instant to explode in smoke and high voltage. "Ahem." He cleared his throat, and the sound system boomed. "Well, my father's been having problems lately. He fell and broke his hip. He did some damage to a barbershop with his car in Scottsdale and lost his driver's license. He was conned out of seven thousand dollars by some crooked diamond salesmen. Then, about ten days ago, he had a stroke. Since then he hasn't been himself. His doctor—Dr. Biller—tells me this sometimes happens after a stroke. He can't do arithmetic or sign his name. He can't do his banking. So I thought it might be a good idea to look after his affairs for a while, till he recovers. To protect him. I want to see him keep what's his and what was my mother's, who died many years ago. He's not getting any younger, and someday he might have to go into a nursing home. Which is very expensive. Anyway, that's why I petitioned to be his conservator. I didn't know he'd be angry about it or fight it. I'm sorry about that. I didn't want to hurt him. All I wanted was to help him."

Don looked at Jerry Snapkin.

"Thank you, Mr. Chambers," said Jerry. "You may step down."

Don did, gladly, and stumbled slightly as he did.

"Did you want the witness, Mr. Goldberg?" asked the judge.

Goldberg rose. "Reserve recall, Your Honor, but I have nothing at this time." He turned to his client. "May we now hear from you, Mr. Chambers." Solicitously he helped Harry up into the walker and to the stand, then waited on the Clerk of the Court.

The oath taken, Harry turned to the lady on the bench, bared his dentures, and gave her his most conspiratorial I'm-no-spring-chicken - and - you're - no - spring - chicken - so - we - know - what - shitheels - our - kids - can - grow - up - to - be - don't - we - Ma'am? smile. "Good morning, Judge," said he.

Her Honor smiled benignly. "Good morning, Mr. Chambers. Mr. Goldberg?"

Goldberg approached his witness with his own smile. "Please be at ease, Mr. Chambers. You are among friends here. It will first be my duty to establish your name, residence, and relationship to the Petitioner." That done in due course, he leaned on the side of the witness stand. "And how are you this morning, Mr. Chambers?"

"Why, fine," said Harry. "Fit as a fiddle."

'Glad to hear it, sir. I regret to see that your mobility is somewhat limited. How is your hip, by the way?"

"Improving, Mr. Goldberg. I have therapy on it twice a week at the hospital. There's a lady therapist there who really knows her stuff. She says I'll be back playing golf any day now."

"*Golf?*" Don hissed in Snapkin's ear. "He never played golf in his life!"

"Fine." Goldberg beamed. "And how do you do your banking these days, Mr. Chambers?"

"Well, I've kept books all my life. And there's a lady next door—Mrs. Bustard—a good friend and good at figures. She helps me, and I pay her well. So I have no trouble at all."

"He hates her!" Don hissed in Snapkin's ear. "He pays her a dollar a day!"

"Capital, sir, capital." Goldberg moved away from the stand and folded his arms. "Now, Mr. Chambers, will you please tell the Court what occurred in your apartment the night of August twentieth last?"

Harry was well coached. "Well, that's a sore subject, Your Honor"—addressing the judge—"but I'll do the best I can. Donald came over and asked me to lend him ten thousand dollars. I couldn't believe it. But he said he was in bad shape, and he expected the loan. Well, I had to say no. I told him children were supposed to help their parents in their old age—not the other way round. He's had a good income for years, and if he'd squandered it, he wasn't going to squander my savings, too. I said hard times would teach him a lesson. And he wasn't too old to learn. When he went home he was pretty hot under the collar, I could tell. I guess I didn't know how hot. I guess I didn't know my son at all. Because a few days later, here came a man notifying me Donald was taking me to court. I couldn't believe it either. I asked him on what grounds, and he said something about 'mental deficiency.' Well, Your Honor, that just about broke my heart." Harry paused, hauled out a grubby handkerchief, took off his cataracts, and wiped his eyes.

"Take your time, Mr. Chambers," Goldberg purred. "We know how painful for you this must be."

Don stared at his father. It occurred to him suddenly that there was no need to be ashamed, either of himself or of Harry. He had in fact done his father a favor. Harry Chambers was having the time of his life. A nobody man, he had suddenly been snatched out of anonymity and a studio audience to be a contestant in a game show on national television. To every question posed him by Goldberg, the MC, he was giving the correct answer, and he had already won a bonanza of merchandise—suitcases of self-satisfaction, home appliances of sympathy, and a complete wardrobe of approval by his peers. Now the camera zoomed in on him for a closeup. Now, in the last minute of the show before the last commercials, the Owosso Kid had a shot at the Grand Prize—an all-expense-paid trip to triumph over the brat grown too big for his britches, the son who tried, in public, to take unfair advantage of his years. To shove the snotnose into the woodshed one last time and spank the hell out of him.

Harry put away his hanky and adjusted his specs. "So I decided to fight. I decided *nobody*—not even Donald—was going to call me a senile, broken-down old man who couldn't look after himself. I'm only eighty-three. He's going to inherit all I've got anyway—why couldn't he wait till I'm dead and gone?" Harry snuffed and sniffled. "Donald's all I have in the world—my only child. I don't understand it, Your Honor. I don't understand how a son can do something like this to his father. How he can be so greedy and ungrateful. I just hope it never happens to you, Your Honor. I just hope your children . . ."

His attorney cut him off. "Thank you, Mr. Chambers. That's all I have, Your Honor."

Judge Lawhon looked at Jerry Snapkin. "Your witness, Mr. Snapkin."

"Ask him how much he's worth!" Don hissed.

Jerry jerked from his chair. "Just one question, Mr. Chambers. Will you please tell us your net worth—in round figures?"

"Objection!" This from Goldberg.

Her Honor rubbed her chin. "I think I'll overrule. The witness will respond."

"What was the question?" Harry asked.

"I'll repeat it, Mr. Chambers," said Jerry. "What is your net worth?"

"Oh," said Harry, and then, proudly, "well, around two hundred thousand dollars."

"Thank you, sir," said Jerry Snapkin. "That's all I have, Your Honor."

Goldberg had remained on his feet. "I reserved recall, Your Honor. May I have Donald Chambers now?"

"Cross-examine," the judge assented.

Goldberg assisted Harry from the stand back to the table.

"What's this for?" Don hissed at his attorney.

"How should I know?"

Don took the stand again, and was reminded by the Court that he was still under oath. Gustave Goldberg moved toward him, a Chicago of a man on little cat feet. "I have several questions, Mr. Chambers. Your father has told us how deeply he is grieved by this action against him. He . . ."

"No," said Don. "It's not an action *against* him. It's an action *for* him. To protect him."

"I haven't asked . . ."

"I love him," Don said. "It isn't easy sometimes, but I do. I've tried . . ."

"Can the witness be instructed, Your Honor?" Goldberg appealed to the bench.

"Wait for the question, Mr. Chambers," instructed Judge Lawhon.

"Yes, ma'am."

"Very well, Mr. Chambers," said Goldberg. "Will you please give us an idea of your net worth?"

"Objection!" This from Jerry Snapkin.

"I'll overrule," said Her Honor. "If it's germane for Protected, it's germane for Petitioner."

Goldberg turned back to his witness. "I repeat, Mr. Chambers. What is your net worth?"

"All right," Don said. "I have an equity of just over sixty thousand in a condominium. And about twelve thousand in an automobile. Oh, and a membership in a private club worth two thousand."

"What private club?"

"Objection!" shrilled Jerry Snapkin.

"Your Honor, I'm only trying to establish motivation for the Petition," said Goldberg.

"Overrule," said the judge. "Witness will answer the question."

"The Squaw Peak Racquet Club," said Don.

"Very exclusive," said Goldberg. "And what kind of automobile do you drive, Mr. Chambers?"

"Objection!" shrilled Jerry Snapkin. "Irrelevant and immaterial!"

"Motivation, Your Honor," Goldberg reminded.

"Overrule," said the judge.

"A Cadillac Sedan de Ville," said Don.

"Very elegant," said Goldberg. He turned again to the witness. "Now, Mr. Chambers. I have been attempting to establish your motives. First, for begging a loan of ten thousand dollars from your father. Second, for the filing of a Petition with this Court which would enable you to take total charge of his assets. I have a series of questions. Please answer yes or no." He paused. "If you fail to make payments on your home, your condominium, it will be foreclosed, will it not?"

"Yes."

"If you fail to make payments on your automobile, it will be repossessed, will it not?"

"Yes."

"And if you fail to pay dues to your club, your membership will be forfeited, will it not?"

"Yes."

"My final question, sir." Gustave Goldberg nailed the witness to the chair with his eyes. "How prepared are you to meet these obligations? In short, how much cash have you on hand at present—in your bank and in your pocket?"

Don looked at Jerry Snapkin.

Jerry Snapkin looked in awe at Gustave Goldberg.

Don looked at the judge.

Hangin' Hannah frowned at him over her granny glasses. "Witness will respond," said she, sharply.

"Eight hundred dollars," Don heard himself say.

Goldberg raised his eyebrows. "Eight *hundred* dollars." He let the figure hang in the air like a noose. "Thank you, Mr. Chambers. I have nothing more, Your Honor."

"Witness may step down," said the judge. She rose as Don returned to the table. "Court will recess for five minutes."

She left the bench. The Bailiff and Clerk of the Court disappeared. Goldberg and his client conferred. Jerry Snapkin was writing something out on a sheet of blank paper.

"Eight hundred bucks?" he hissed at Don. "That's really all you've got?"

"You heard me."

"Well, dibs on six hundred of it. I'm writing out a bill right now."

"Forget it. Sue me."

Jerry went on writing. "You're getting off cheap. Goldberg'll hit your old man for a couple thou, minimum."

"My old man'll sue him."

Jerry Snapkin shook his head. "I give up. I just can't figure old people. Like my mother—she doesn't know what day it is, but put her on the stand and she's an intellectual giant."

Bailiff and Clerk of the Court returned. The Bailiff banged his gavel twice. "All rise!"

All rose.

Enter Judge Lawhon. She leaned back in her chair and gathered her black robe about her. "Chambers versus Chambers," she said.

All waited.

"Petition denied."

She rose. "Hearing is concluded. Court will recess for lunch."

Jerry Snapkin reached into his briefcase for the sandwich.

"Thank you, Judge!" cried Harry Chambers, on his feet and in his walker. "Judge, I'd like to tell you a little story. I've lived all my life in the town of Owosso, Michigan. Thomas E. Dewey—ran against Truman in 1948. Well, while he was campaigning, he came home and we gave him a big day, parade and all. I was introduced to him. We shook hands." Harry Chambers's face lit up like that of a boy who has just landed a big fish. "And d'you know what, Judge? Tom Dewey remembered me!"

||| 5 |||

"Do it now. Go in Ron's room and see if his clothes are there." Jenny was on the phone to Don, but the voice wasn't Jenny's. It was that of a woman trying desperately to get a girdle on her emotions.

"Dear, listen," he said. "I've had one hell of a day. I lost this morning. The court denied my petition. My old man won."

"Don, right now that's not important. Go in Ron's room and see if his clothes are there."

"Okay, okay." Don left the phone and went to Ron's room and opened the closet door. He returned to the phone. "They're gone."

"I knew it!" Jenny wailed.

"Bobby's here, though."

"I knew it!" Jenny wailed.

"Then this afternoon, second-mortgaged," he continued. "I had to. Good old Friendly Finance—all they'd give me on my equity was eight thousand, the bastards. Anyway, the check's in the bank—how about dinner?"

"So are Sue's!"

"Sue's what?"

"Clothes! Gone!"

"So?"

"Don't you see what this means?"

"Moths?"

"They've moved out on us!"

"Who?"

"Our children!"

"Oh. Well. Great. Free at last. We can make it Mr. and Mrs. and settle down and make legal love. Your place or mine?"

"They're living together!"

Don held out the phone, staring at it as though he were counting the twelve touch-buttons, then put it to his ear again. "Living together?"

"What else?"

"They can't be—they're too conservative."

"My virgin girl! That stud son of yours!"

"Now wait a minute, Jen. Ron's no stud. He wouldn't know a fe from a male."

"Ha!"

"They can't be," Don insisted. "They promised us to wait—not to marry till we do."

"So they're not married—they're living in sin! My darling daughter! Twenty years old and ruined! I called a friend of Sue's and she had an address—they've taken an apartment. I'll pick you up. We're going over there this minute!"

"I haven't even had a mart!"

"You're going with me!"

"Jen, I don't know if I can handle this now. Not after the day I've had."

"Donald Chambers, if you love me . . ."

"Okay, okay. Shall I bring a shotgun?"

"Not funny!"

*

It was and it wasn't. Funny. Because when located, near the intersection of Hayden and Indian School Roads, the studio apartment now occupied by Ronald Chambers and Sue Staley was unfurnished except for carpet and drapes and, in the center of the living room floor, a brand-new waterbed and two Snoopy sheets and pillows. That was funny. What wasn't, what was the shocker, was Sue's appearance and attire. She was eye-shadowed and lipsticked and wore a see-through blouse cut indecently low and buckskin hip-hugger shorts cut indecently high and her shapely legs were encased in tights. On her head was a cowboy hat, on her feet were cowboy boots.

"Hi, Mom," she said.

"Hi, Dad," said Ron.

"Is that you, Sue?" asked her mother.

"Like my uniform? I got a job at the Crystal Pistol—cocktail waitress, starting tonight. Real big tips. I have to leave in a little— pulling the six-to-two-in-the-morning shift."

"The Crystal Pistol?"

"You know, north, out on Shea Boulevard," said Ron. "It's a honky-tonk—country-and-western music, you know."

"How nice," said Jenny.

"Sorry we don't have more furniture yet," said Sue. "Sit on the bed, why don't you? You, too, Don."

Don helping Jenny, they sat down on the end of the waterbed, only to rock from side to side in the cradle of the deep. Ron and Sue remained standing, moving warily round and round their parents like muggers.

"How's Bobby?" Ron asked his father.

"Oh, fine."

"How's Windy?" Sue asked her mother.

"Oh, fine."

"How's Gramps?" Ron asked his father.

"Fine."

Ron checked his wristwatch. "We have to take off. I'm going with her this first night—you know, protect her from concrete cowboys."

Don was dying of thirst, but knew there would be no Stolich-naya here. "Take off? In what?"

"Oh, we've both got cars," said Ron. "Let's say transportation, not cars."

"You have? How?"

"Windy," said Sue, circling.

"Windy!" gasped Jenny.

"I know, it's incredible. But we were out at Happy Hours one night last week and we told her we were in love and the only thing keeping us from living together was that neither of us had wheels. You won't believe this—remember those old saddlebags she took along? Well, she got them out and inside she had two thousand dollars. She said she'd hidden it in those bags for thirty years—she didn't trust banks."

"Are you saying," Jenny interjected, "are you saying my grand-mother—your great-grandmother—gave you money so you could live together?"

"You got it, Mom. Isn't it super? She gave us each a thousand and said to buy cars and be happy."

"Damn her," said Jenny. "I will never forgive her."

"Anyway, we did," said Ron. "They're junk—what can you buy for a thousand these days? But they run."

"And now you're happy," said Jenny.

"All the way," said her daughter.

"Well, I'm not," said Jenny, rocking.

"Second the motion," said Don, rocking.

"Dad, let me explain," said Ron, circling. "Sure, we agreed to wait to get married till you two could be and we will. That's a promise. But we didn't say anything about not living together, and neither did you. So we haven't broken our word."

"Maybe not, but you've broken my heart." Jenny searched her purse for a Kleenex and found one. "No, I will not cry, I'll be modern mother." She stuffed away the Kleenex, snapped the purse shut, and looked at her daughter. "Sue, how could you?"

"Mom, it was easy."

"I've worked so hard, so many years, and this is the thanks I get. I wanted you to have college."

"I'll have college."

"I'll tell you what else you'll have. A reputation. As a pushover."

"I resent that."

"In a relationship like this, the girl always loses. After the boy uses her, he moves out and in with someone else. Then she lives with another boy, and another. After a while, you're ruined. You're not a car anymore, you're just transportation."

"I won't move out on her," said Ron stoutly. "I love her."

"And I love him," said Sue stoutly.

"Call it anything you like," said Jenny also stoutly, rocking, "you're living in sin."

"Oh, come on, Mom," said Sue. "Get with it. Everybody's living together these days."

"That's right," said Ron, circling. "What about you and my father?"

"Now just a damn minute!" Don barked.

"I will not cry," said Jenny, rocking.

"We're not living together!" Don barked. "Even if we'd wanted to, we couldn't! Her damned place was full of people and mine was full of rabbits!"

"But you're *not* sleeping together," smiled Sue.

"Goddammit, we are not!" cried Don.

"I will not cry," said Jenny.

"Oh come on, Dad." Ron grinned.

"Goddammit, we are not!" cried Don, rocking. "We can't get married and we can't shack up and we can't even sleep together! We've tried!"

Ron and Sue stopped circling. "Try again," said Ron, checking his watch. "Listen, we've gotta go."

"Can't be late my first night," said Sue.

"Here, try a waterbed." Ron grinned.

"They're terrific!" Sue smiled.

They started for the door hand in hand.

"Alone at last." Ron grinned.

"Be our guests." Sue smiled.

"Have fun." Ron grinned.

"Just close the door when you go." Sue smiled.

"You're only as old as you feel." Ron grinned.

"See you later." Sue smiled.

They closed the door behind them.

Father and mother sat like bread upon the waters in the empty apartment. After a time Don turned and crawled onto the bed and stretched out on his back, causing the bed to roll so violently that Jenny was almost thrown over the side. To save herself, she clutched her purse and crawled up the bed and tumbled supine beside him. At first they tossed and pitched, but finally the storm beneath them calmed, and they lay together on a tranquil sea, heads at rest on Snoopy pillows.

"Bushed. I am bushed," Don said. "This might be the worst day of my life. Had the hell beat out of me in court by my old man—he'll never speak to me again. Then had to second-mortgage and my kid starts playing house with a girl." He folded arms under his head. "I have to admit, though, that girl is something. Good-looking. Sharp. Cool under fire. Like a take-charge guard on a champ basketball team."

"I will not cry," said Jenny. "But I am exhausted. You've had a hard day? I showed a couple from Memphis five houses. They told me their price range, and I showed them five—I must have driven fifty miles. Then, when they settled on one and we got down to talking numbers, they couldn't possibly qualify. Five houses."

She asked him why his petition was denied, and Don said because he had a wimp for a lawyer and Harry had a shark. They made it appear that the son wanted a conservatorship for the sole purpose of getting his greedy hands on the father's assets. "I must say my old man was a star on the stand. I was the heavy, and because he turned me down for a loan, he was the hero." Jenny asked him if he'd really had to second-mortgage, and he said yes, that came out at the hearing, too. "I was down to about eight hundred in the bank. And just between us, I was a day late shipping Carol another five hundred alimony. One more day and she'd have had me in the slammer." He asked Jenny what about Windy and the two thousand she'd given the kids. Jenny said she was flabbergasted and furious. "Many's the time I could have used that money. I was so short I was actually frightened. She'd led me to believe she hadn't a penny." Don said no, you couldn't have guessed, they were unpredictable. For that matter, Don said, what about the young? How could they have foreseen his son and daughter would fall in love and buy a waterbed and start house-keeping? Jenny said Sue's uniform was obscene. Don yawned. He said this whole experience—everything that had happened since the night he proposed to her in the balloon—which seemed like ten years ago and was really only four months—had changed him. Life, which had once been a piece of cake, he now had to swallow on schedule like a pill. And he had begun to suspect himself. His mind might be going. Much more and he might be a candidate for a happy academy. Or he might buy a three-cornered hat and go live on an island like Elba. Jenny yawned. She was changing, too. She was stressed, she woke up every morning sweating about what the day might bring. She was aging rapidly. New lines had appeared around her eyes and on her upper lip. She'll be a hag soon. At least she'll have to have a lift. Don yawned. "This is weird. Here we are, like an old married couple. Lying in bed sorting out the day's events. And we're not married. We could be now, you realize. I hope. We are free at goddamned last. Harry's taking bows. Windy's hibernating. Our kids have flown the coop. You've got a bedroom, I've got two bedrooms. We've both got borrowed money in the bank. This is what we've been waiting for, babe.

How about it?" Jenny yawned and pushed off her pumps. No, she was in no mood for matrimony. She still blamed his sex-maniac son for the ruin of her daughter. Don yawned and stretched and said it took two to tango. She said let's wait and see.

They fell asleep.

*

The phone woke Don.

It was two or three nights later, and he'd fallen asleep in a chair with Bobby on his lap. Don was beginning to feel that Bobby was the only one in the world on whom he could depend.

"You asked me to keep an eye on your father," said Mrs. Bustard. "Well, here's one for you. He had company tonight. A lady caller."

"A lady."

"She dropped in on him about nine and just left. She was there an hour. And here's the snapper—they pulled the living-room shade."

"They what?"

"Pulled the shade. I couldn't see in."

"No."

"Yep. It's dark out, I can't describe her, but I thought you'd want to know."

"You thought right."

"By the way, Mr. Chambers, you haven't been over here lately—you sent my last stipend in the mail. Anything wrong?"

"Well, the fact is, Dad and I aren't on very good terms these days. We're not communicating."

"Sorry to hear it."

"So am I. Are you helping him with his banking?"

"I have to. He still can't add or subtract for sour apples—not that he pays me for it."

"I see. Well, thanks for the info, Mrs. Bustard. Will you give me a buzz the next time he has company?"

"Yep."

The next time was the next night.

"I don't know how long she's been in there," reported Mrs. Bustard. "I was watching PBS and didn't see her arrive. But her car's still parked in front."

"Shade pulled?"

"Yep."

"Damn," said Don. "What in hell's the old boy up to now, I wonder."

"You better wonder what she's up to."

"I know. Keep calling me, will you?"

"I will, but I have to be careful. Otherwise I'll blow my cover."

On impulse Don drove over to the Eventide, but the car in front of his father's apartment was gone, and with it the dark lady, and the shade was up.

*

Mrs. Bustard was a perfect private eye. After her next alert Don reached the Eventide in eight minutes and parked the Sedan de Ville a hundred feet from the car parked in front of Harry's apartment and cut his lights and engine. Her car was a Plymouth sedan, a junker eight or ten years old. He waited. Half a hot hour later the shade in his father's living room went up, the door opened, and a woman hurried to the car. Don practically detached a retina, but it was simply too dark to get a good look at her. When she drove away, he tailed her. She turned south on Sixty-eighth Street, crossed McDowell Road, turned east on Continental, and pulled into the carport attached to a small tract house half-hidden in overgrown bottle brushes. Don idled past it, then kept on going and thinking.

He thought most of the night, scratched his forearms. In the morning they had an unsightly red rash. He scratched them that day and that night and the next day called his doctor, who referred him to a dermatologist who diagnosed the rash as *lichen planus,* a common stress syndrome, prescribed an ointment, and told him to read the New Testament.

*

Several nights passed uneventfully. Don applied the ointment to his forearms and wore long-sleeved Oleg Cassini shirts. Then Mrs. Bustard set off the alarm again and he slid down the pole and clanged over to the Eventide and this time parked his car right behind the Plymouth and walked to the door of his father's apartment. The shade was pulled. He hit the door chime and waited. He heard voices inside, music from a radio, but the chime went unanswered. He knocked. He heard the clump-clump of the walker. The door was cracked.

"Who is it?"

"Don, Dad."

"Oh. What d'you want?"

"Well, I was passing by and thought I'd drop in and say hello."

Harry opened the door and delayed Don's entrance by having difficulty with his walker. Just as Don was finally admitted, he heard the back door of the apartment slam. He strode through the combo living dining room into the kitchen. A light was on, and on the table were two tall glasses empty except for melting ice and curls of lime. Don turned, strode into the living room, and raised the windowshade. He could make out only the outline of a woman getting into the Plymouth. There wasn't time to get outside before she'd started the car and gunned away. Harry stood near the door watching all this, swaying and blinking. It suddenly struck Don that his father might be in the bag. He walked over to him. He could smell booze on his father's breath, and behind the cataract lenses Harry's eyes were slightly bugged. Don suggested they sit down, and taking Harry's arm, helped him to the davenport and turned him, whereupon his father let go of the walker and fell back onto the cushions like a sack of wet noodles.

"You had company," Don said. "I hope I didn't interrupt anything."

"How are you, Son?"

"Why did the lady leave in such a hurry? I'd have liked to meet her."

"Son, d'you know how much that damned Goldberg wanted? Two thousand dollars! Well, I wouldn't pay it. So we compromised—he took a thousand and I made him executor of my will."

"You did what?"

"Made him executor. Saved a thousand."

Don looked at him. "Dad, that wasn't a smart thing to do. He'll take a lot more than a thousand out of your estate for his fees."

"I know that—but it won't pinch me, will it? I'll be gone."

"Besides, I thought you'd named me as your executor."

Harry took out his upper plate, rubbed his gums with a forefinger, then reset the plate. "Donald, I've been meaning to ask you. Haven't you found me any red raspberries yet?"

Don shook his head, sat back in a chair, and made himself comfortable. "Who's the lady, Pop?"

"Why, she was my therapist at the hospital. Really knows her stuff." Harry went on to explain that she'd been let go at Scottsdale Memorial Hospital, he'd got her phone number from them, and called her and asked her to come to his place and work on his hip. "She really knows her stuff. Done me a world of good."

"I'll bet she has," said Don. "About ready to play golf again, aren't you?"

Harry's response was to remove his lower plate and massage his gums.

"Tell me about her," Don invited.

To his surprise, Harry quit beating around the bottlebrush bush. She was a wonderful, wonderful person. Her name was Mrs. Maria Kirchner, she was fifty-one and Italian by birth, to get to America she'd married a soldier, they were divorced and she'd married again and been divorced again, she had a daughter nineteen, and both her brute husbands had really rooked her on settlements. Upshot: Her life in what she had expected to be the land of opportunity had been the pits—and now that she'd lost her hospital job, she scarcely knew where her next month's rent and car payment were coming from.

"Sounds like me a while back," Don said. "When I asked you for a loan."

Harry ignored. "Well, she's a wonderful, wonderful person. She's done my hip a world of good."

"Tells you her troubles, does she?"

"I'm glad to hear them."

"You didn't care to hear mine."

"Makes a mighty fine gin and tonic, too. Puts plenty of stick in 'em."

"I thought you didn't drink."

"Well, I didn't—not till you started me the night we went out to that damned cowboy place with that crazy family." Harry peered at his wristwatch. "I'm missing the ten o'clock news. Turn on the TV for me, will you?"

"In a minute," Don said. "I assume you pay her for the therapy."

"Of course I do."

"And after you've pulled the shade and had a couple of belts and heard her troubles, do you give her a little extra?"

Harry fidgeted. "Well, I help her a little."

"But you wouldn't me. How much? Rent? A car payment?"

Harry bristled. "That's none of your damned business! I won't have you coming over here questioning me! I'm not on a witness stand—I won't make a horse's ass of myself the way you did! Now turn on my news!"

Don budged not. He sat back in his chair and crossed his legs. "No. Not yet. We need to talk. You need to hear what I have to say. Pop, remember your diamond deal? If you'd only called me, and let me check it out, I could have saved you a lot of bucks. I could have warned you. Well, I'm warning you now. Keep your sharps—be careful of this woman."

Harry sniffed. "Hmpf. I don't know what you're talking about—and neither do you."

"Dad, Phoenix and Scottsdale are full of retired people, and they get taken every day of the week. People prey on them. Lonely old ladies fall for young men and buy land or thousands of dollars' worth of dancing lessons. And lonely old men listen to sob stories and get sold a bill of goods by younger women. It's one of the saddest situations in the world. And I don't want you to be ripped off by this Kirchner broad. She sounds like a foxy operator to me. She's been divorced twice, and she . . ."

"A lot you know about women!" cried Harry. "You left a good one, and you're about to make another damned big mistake!"

Don ignored. "Okay, okay. But do something for me, Dad. Test her. Let her come for therapy a couple more weeks, and pay her for it. But don't give her an extra dime. Then see if she still shows, see if she's still nice to you. Test her."

His father looked at him, and then, inexplicably, bent forward, covered his face with his hands, and began to sob. When he could speak, it was blubber. "That's what I'm afraid of—if I don't help her, she won't come see me! And I need her! I need her!"

Harry found a grubby handkerchief and pushed off his specs and swabbed at his eyes while Don looked away, embarrassed and guilt-eaten, cursing the gods and the mortality tables. His forearms itched. He scratched them through his shirtsleeves.

"I'm sorry if I hurt you, Dad," he said. "But you hurt me not long ago, just as much. Anyway, I love you, I want you to know that. And no matter . . ."

"The hell you do!" Harry bawled. "Or you'd never have dragged me into court!"

He dropped his specs. Don jumped, handed them to him, and reseated himself.

"Dad, I was only trying to protect you. I'm trying to protect you now."

"The hell you are! You've insulted me! I'm mentally deficient!"

"That's just a legal term. But wouldn't you agree your judgment of people and situations maybe isn't what it was a few years back?"

"You shut up!" Harry suddenly took hold of his walker and hauled himself to his feet, unsteadily, dropping both glasses and handkerchief in the process. "I try to straighten out my hip so I can walk and you come over and lecture me! I won't have it!" he shouted, his face raspberry red with rage and gin. "Now you turn on my TV and get out of here!"

Don rose. "I don't believe it. I can't believe this is happening to us. I . . ."

"Get out!"

Don stood uncertainly. His forearms itched. His stomach did acrobatics. This was yet another father, Harry Chambers IV, and Don was torn between falling on his knees and begging forgiveness for whatever or decking the old devil on the davenport and letting him sleep it off. He went to the door and turned there. "All right, Father, I'll go. Just tell me one thing." He pointed at the front of Harry's $29.95 Sears polyester slacks. "If the Kirchner woman's working on your hip, how come your fly is open?"

*

"I forgot to tell you. Remember the night we were in the shower and he called and he'd broken his hip and I caught a redeye to go to Michigan and say good-bye?"

"Do I."

"Well, on the plane beside me was a woman on the way to Elkhart, Indiana, to celebrate her mother's one-hundredth birthday. Boy, was she bitter. Anyway, she said someday I'd wish my old man were dead. It made me mad then, but not now. I see her point. I wish he would sleep away some night."

"Don, you don't mean that."

"I do. Yes, I do. I hate myself for saying it, but I do. He's of no use to anyone. There are activities at the Eventide—bingo and movies and parties—but he won't participate. He just sits in that apartment and sucks his thumb. He's of no use to anyone—to me, even to himself."

"He's evidently of use to her—what's her name again?"

"Maria Kirchner."

"Do you know anything about her?"

"Only what he told me."

"Suppose you find out more."

"I don't care to. The whole thing stinks. I don't even want to talk about it. How're our kiddies and their waterbed getting along?"

"Swimmingly, I guess."

"That's funny."

"Sue called me the other day—they have a phone in now. She took in three hundred dollars in tips her first week at the Crystal Pistol."

"My God, that's better than real estate. Say, you'd look terrific in one of those cowgirl outfits. How about a mother-and-daughter act out there?"

"Oh, sure." Jenny frowned. "One thing I don't like—suddenly she's become very profane. I suppose it's the language level in a place like that."

It was a Sunday night. Don had brought a big pizza and a six-pack over to Oasis North and they'd drunk beer and devoured the pizza—Jenny gave him all the anchovies, which he adored—and now he lay on the davenport in the living room with his head in her lap.

"I haven't told you the worst part," Don said. "When I left—when he threw me out—I pointed to the front of his pants and said, 'If she's working on your hip, how come your fly is open?' "

"Oh, no."

"Oh, yes. Obscene. In addition to everything else, he's a dirty old man. You know, I don't mind his being leeched by some bitch out of a few bucks from his current income. What I don't want happening is that he becomes more and more infatuated, more and more dependent on her, and starts giving her stocks and bonds and everything but the kitchen sink—including my inheritance. Which of course is what she's after. Tell me, why are women so predatory?"

Jenny refused to take the bait. "If it's true confession time, now I can tell you what a problem Windy was these last years. I don't know how I stood it. She'd have spells, and say terrible things to Sue and me. She was cruel to me about the jobs I took and the men I dated. When she simply had to have a bath, we gave her a Valium first, and then it took the two of us to get her into the tub. When she couldn't sleep, she'd come out here and watch a late, late movie on TV and keep us awake. Why do they become so self-centered? Why is the whole world bounded by their skin? I really didn't know Windy any more, she'd changed so much."

"I don't know this father. This one's about number four."

Jenny sighed. "God knows, I still love her, but Lordy I'm glad she's gone." She sighed again. "They're just living longer now."

"Longer and not better."

"And we have to grin and bear them and wait them out."

Don had a horrible thought. "He'll outlive me!"

Jenny laughed.

"He will! He's just contrary enough to bury me! Or one of these days the men in white jackets'll come and take me away—and he'll visit his wacko son, with Kirchner, and they'll make faces at me behind the wire and laugh like hell!"

Jenny tousled his hair.

"I mean it! Look—look at my arms." Don unbuttoned his cuffs and pushed up his shirtsleeves. "I've broken out in a rash—the doc says it's a common stress syndrome. Ointment takes care of it most of the time, but when I'm around the old man, or think about him, it burns, it drives me berserk. Jen, we've gone through the fires the last four months. My nervous system's shot. I can't take any more."

"Poor dear."

"If I didn't have you and Bobby, I'd put on my tennis clothes and go out to the club and hang myself from the backscreen. With a sign: 'He Lost Life by a Love Score.' The first doubles match in the morning could cut me down."

"Poor darling."

"Even if you said full speed ahead, we'll marry tomorrow, I couldn't do it. Mentally. When the Reverend said 'Repeat after me,' I couldn't. I couldn't remember the words."

Jenny was silent.

"An anchovy for your thoughts."

"I was thinking about how you saved me that night behind the Whataburger, when I fell apart. And wondering what I could do for you now, when you need help. I wonder about sex."

"Sex? What's that?"

"It's what a man and a woman do. Or a boy and a girl, unfortunately."

"Oh."

"The time is right. We're alone, and we have a bed. Are you interested?"

"I might be."

"If you are, how come your fly is closed?"

Don sat up frowning, shaking his head. "Sex? It's been so long I've forgotten how."

Jenny smiled and said "I'll show you." She put an arm around him and kissed him passionately and with the other hand unzipped his fly and ascertained his interest. "Why, you are, aren't you? Then let's."

He kissed her experimentally. "Will you show me? Everything?"

She stood and took his hand and he stood and she led him. To his bedroom. When they were there, she said, "Now we undress."

When they were undressed, he asked, "Don't we take a shower first?"

"No. Takes too long."

"Why?"

"You have to squeegee the water spots." She looked him over. "You're lovely."

"Thank you." He looked her over. "You have a beautiful bod. It's possible you have the most beautiful bod in the world. Certainly in the developed world."

"Thank you."

"Now what do we do?"

"We lie down on the bed together."

They lay down on the bed together.

"Here's where I forget," he said. "From this point on, I draw a complete blank."

"Well," said Jenny, "as you can plainly see, men and women are constructed differently, and they use different parts of their bodies while engaged in the act of love. You use this." She touched him. "And I use this." She touched herself.

"Gee whiz," said Don. "I really don't know what you're talking about."

She frowned. "All right. I'll try again. I lie on my back and you mount me."

"Mount you?"

"So that you can enter me."

"Enter you?"

Jenny groaned. "Lordy. Don, do you remember trying to put toys together for little Ron on Christmas Eve according to the directions? I used to have awful times trying to do it for Sue. 'Insert Part A in Part B (see diagram)'—and so on?"

"Do I. I used to swear and carry the directions around and drink and get half-smashed trying to assemble the damn things before Santa was due."

"All right. Just the same, you're a man, you're supposed to have a mechanical mind, so let's pretend it's Christmas Eve and we're assembling a toy."

"Naked?"

"Never mind that. Now this is Part A." She touched him. "And this is Part B." She touched herself.

"I still don't get it. Where's the diagram?"

"There isn't one."

"You mean they didn't send . . ."

"Hush. This is Part A." She touched him. "And this is Part B." She touched herself. "Now the whole idea is to insert your Part A in my Part B."

"And then what?"

"Then what?"

And then Don Chambers's and Jenny Staley's straight faces shattered and they collapsed in laughter, throwing arms and legs around each other and rolling back and forth on the bed like cubs. And then they stopped laughing and started kissing madly and she lay on her back and lifted her legs and he mounted her and was about to insert Part A in Part B when, outside her condo, there was a loud report. It was unmistakably a gunshot. There was a second gunshot. And then voices, and a loud, prolonged battering on the front door.

"What in hell!" Don fell sideways.

Jenny sat up. "It's a shooting!"

"Pay no attention!"

"You'd better go!"

"And get shot?"

"They may need help!"

"What about me?"

There was a third gunshot, followed by more battering on the door.

"Get dressed!" Jenny jumped off the bed and seized her smalls.

"Oh my God," groaned Don, sliding off the bed and grabbing a sock.

They dressed in nothing flat as the voices and the door banging continued and rushed into the living room and just as Jenny unlocked the door Don found his bikini briefs in his hand and stuffed them into a pocket and in came Windy Coon with the old Colt in one hand and the rattlesnake cane in the other and in came Ron carrying her suitcase and in came Sue carrying her saddlebags.

"I'm home!" cried Windy Coon, waving the revolver. "I busted out!"

"Oh, Gram, I'm so glad to see you!" cried Jenny, going to her grandmother and embracing her and at the same time relieving her of the weapon, which she laid aside on a table.

"We sprung her!" cried a proud Ron, smashing the suitcase.

"We've planned it for a week!" cried Sue, slinging the saddlebags.

"Let her tell it," said Jenny. "Come, dear, here's your chair. Sit down, you must be exhausted."

Windy was ensconced in her chair. "You've moved my TV," she accused.

"We'll move it back," Jenny assured her. "Now tell us all about it."

The old lady was on an achievement high. Her eyes swam wildly about the room. Her wig leaned to one side of her head. Her hands shook as she placed the cane across her lap. "Oh, goddamn, if we didn' pull it off, though! Time was ten o'clock—all them old folks'd be watchin' the news—an' I knew my darlin' Ron'n Sue'd be outside with one of them cars I bought 'em. I was dressed an' had my bags packed an' Wade Will's gun loaded— kep' cartridges in them saddlebags for years. Well, I rung the bell an' when a nurse come I says, 'Missy, I'm riding' outta here.' She says I can't an' tried t'jolly me out of it. So I pulls my six-gun an' tells her t'tote my bags, we're movin' on out. She still don't b'lieve me. Well, I point that cannon straight up an' boom! I let one off right through the ceilin'! Then I says, 'Missy, pick up them bags an' lead the way or I'll give you a gutful!'—an' say, didn' she shake a leg! Well, we're outta the room an' all them old folks hollerin' an' stampedin' around an' we get t'the main hall by the door an' here comes a bunch of nurses an' a sonovabitch male nurse t'stop me an' I raise my persuader an' let off another one through the ceilin'. Boom! Then I says, 'Everybody back off an' open that door—me'n my bags we're a-goin' t'town! You try t'stop me an' I'll blow holes in you big enough t'throw a bucket of shit through!' Oh by God, that settled their hash! Them yahoos backed off an' opened the door an' me'n Miss Fat-Ass sashayed out an' there was Ron'n Sue'n the car waitin' an' this ol' girl was a free girl again for good! I'm home! Home t'stay!"

Jenny sat down on the floor before her and took her trembling hands. "That's an amazing story, dear. But what I don't quite understand is—I thought you liked Happy Hours. Every time I came to see you, you said you did."

"Hated the damn place!" cried the old lady. "Bunch of old folks settin' around waitin' t'die! Well, not me!"

"Attagirl, Gram!" cried Sue.

"Hang in there, Mrs. Coon!" cried Ron.

"I'm so proud of you!" cried Jenny.

"No," said Don.

They stared at him. Until he spoke, it was as though he'd been a piece of furniture.

"No," he said. "She can't stay here. She's got to go back."

Now it was as though he'd peed in public.

"Don, you should be ashamed," said Jenny.

"What a nerd," said Sue.

"This is my father?" asked Ron. "This is actually my father?"

Don's back was to the wall. "That's right, everybody gang up on me—but I'm only saying what's obvious. Jenny, you can't handle her alone, she's too much for you—and you've served your time." The more he said, the angrier he became. "You gonna take her, Sue? You, Ron? With a telephone and a waterbed? And what about me? I paid twenty-two hundred dollars for her first month in that home—down the drain!"

"Booo!" cried Sue.

"She's my grandmother, she's welcome here!" cried Jenny.

"Turn on my TV!" cried Windy. "Push that set over to me!"

"And what about Jenny and me?" demanded Don, undeterred. "We waited, we finally got everybody out of our hair—we were going to be married! What in hell do we do now? Take her on our honeymoon?"

"Gimme my gun!" cried Windy. "I'll shoot that dude sonova-bitch!"

"Goddammit, this is impossible!" cried Don. "Everybody's so proud of themselves—all you've done is open up a crate of snakes!"

"Here, I'll move the TV for you," said Jenny to her grandmother, and with the strength of ten, pulled and pushed the console to its accustomed place. "There, dear," she said. "You're home again indeed—and you shall stay here as long as you're able." There were tears in her eyes, but she gave Don a defiant glare. "I'm sorry, Don. Just because you're estranged from your father doesn't mean that's the way I must live. Maybe you can harden your heart, but I can't. I love this dear lady, and I intend to do my duty to her, and willingly, till the day she dies."

"Yaaaay, Mom!" cried Sue.

"Applause, applause!" cried Ron.

Don looked from face to face.

"I am the turkey of all time," he said, and stalked out on them. As he opened the front door he heard the TV audio rev up, theme music from "Lifestyles of the Rich and Famous." He also heard Windy Coon's famous last words.

"Die hell!" she cried over an ingratiating invitation from Robin Leach. "I'll live t'be a hundred!"

||| 6 |||

It was an old saw in real estate. When deciding which house to buy, you should first consider three things: location, location, location. It was equally prudent, when deciding where to move to or vacation during the summer, that you should at any cost avoid three locations: Phoenix, Phoenix, and Phoenix. And its suburbs. It was late September now, in the Valley of the Sun, but the sun gave no sign of abdication. Daytime temperatures exceeded 110°, the nights 90°. People who had stayed indoors all summer came down with claustrophobia or, thanks to conditioned air, serious sinus problems. Husbands beat on wives with beer cans. Women stabbed lovers with nail files. Fender-benders ended invariably in fights, from which fatalities ensued. Riots started at bus stops. Gophers got delusions of grandeur and chased dogs. Senior citizens keeled into swimming pools and sank like stones to the bottom, gladly. Groups of children tore Good Humor men from their trucks and beat them to drippy death with Nutty Buddies.

Don Chambers, a man with a rash, put out his "For Sale" signs and sat afternoons in houses with eight to ten thousand square feet under roof and selling for half a mil to a mil and waited for buyers, pigeons from back East, their pockets crammed with cash. What he got—and even these infrequently—was "lookers," curious couples who couldn't put their ass up for a down payment but were determined to see where the rich would live. He could spot them in a minute. They used the johns. They stole his time, his patience, and the ashtrays if any were available. Don Chambers hated growing old in empty rooms. That was what his life was now: an arrangement of empty rooms. He'd rather have been in cool California, strolling the beach and eating a peach.

One afternoon, just at five, just as he was folding the wooden signs and stowing them in his car trunk, a dust storm struck. These broke the monotony of the weather in summertime Phoenix. Thunderheads would rear up in the skies every few days, tornadic winds would be created, and a huge engine of dust and sand would roll in from the desert and crush the city, skeltering traffic and blowing mobile homes and infiltrating lungs and charging the air with such ionic tension that the residents that night fell upon each other with renewed ferocity. He drove home through the storm, and sprinted into his condo. He showered and washed his dusty hair and sat down to a sumptuous TV dinner.

Later that evening, Bobby hopping at his heels, he roamed his empty, second-mortgaged rooms. He turned on a light in his son's room and opened a door to look into his empty closet. What was that? He went to his knees. In a back corner of the closet an urn had been tipped over. His father, when he moved out, had forgotten the urn. Typical. Bobby, exploring the closet or seeking refuge from Ron and the Rabbit Rabbit, had tipped it over. His mother's ashes were strewn on the carpeting. His mother, dearest Lila, the girl with class who had settled for less and gone too soon. Who should have been asleep in Michigan, in the earth from whence he had come. Whom a greedy husband had cremated and carted what was left of her around the country. Don looked over his shoulder at Bobby, who gave him a twinkle of the nose and a big brown blameless eye. Don broke into tears. "Oh, Mom," he choked, "I am so sorry, so damn sorry." He sat on the floor in the closet and cried for five minutes.

When he had cried himself dry, he found his Dustbuster Plus, a hand-held, battery-operated vacuum cleaner, removed the sack from inside, and washed it thoroughly at a bathroom bowl. He then used his hair-dryer to blow the sack dry, and replaced it. Then, on hands and knees, flashlight in one hand and Dustbuster in the other, he vacuumed up every trace of ash. Finally he removed the sack from the vacuum and returned the ashes to the urn, which he put reverently away on the shelf in his own closet.

The phone. Mrs. Bustard.

"Mr. Chambers, d'you want me to keep calling you when she comes over to your father's?"

"No need to."

"Well, I won't then—she's over there three or four times a week. She's there tonight, and she came in style. I thought you might be interested. She had an old jalopy—now she's driving a big new car. I don't know what kind."

"She is, is she?"

"Yep."

"Thanks, Mrs. Bustard."

Don put down the phone and stood there, his forearms heating up. This was just what he needed tonight. This really pulled his trigger.

*

He parked a hundred feet from the car parked in front of Harry's apartment and waited. Her big new car looked to be a Ford Crown Victoria four-door, a year or two old at most. He waited only ten minutes this time. The shade in the apartment window was raised, Maria Kirchner came out, got in her Ford Crown Victoria and drove away. Don followed. But tonight, rather than heading south on Sixty-eighth, she turned north, crossed Thomas and Camel-back, turned east into a better residential area, and pulled into an enclosed garage on a house set on a well-landscaped half-acre.

Thinking back, Don appraised her old tract house at seventy-nine-five. This one would go, if you could find a buyer, for over a hundred thou. Therapy, like crime, paid well.

He parked and walked to the front door and rang the bell. Lights went on.

"Who is it?"

"Donald Chambers. Harry's son."

"Whatta you want?" A slight accent.

"I'd like to talk to you."

"Go away."

"We'd better talk."

"Go away or I call the police!"

*

Don backtracked to the Eventide. He drove with caution, for a great engine of anger had rolled over him, sweating his palms and blurring his vision and laboring his breath. He must not have a fender-bender now. He'd fall upon the other driver ferociously.

He hit his father's door chimes and waited. He heard the ten o'clock news on TV, then the clump-clump of the walker. The door cracked.

"Who is it?"

"Don."

"I don't care to see you."

"No? Well, goddammit, you will!"

Don bulled through the door, banging it into the walker and almost bowling his father over, strode across the living room, and turned off the TV.

"I told you, I don't care to . . ."

"Sit down, Pop. I'm sitting, right here. Sit down and relax. I must tell you I am very, very burned. But I'm going to sit here and control myself and we're going to have a calm, intelligent discussion."

||| 163 |||

Harry glared at him, then shut the door and clumped to a chair. He didn't appear to Don to be ginned. Perhaps the local news, the beatings and stabbings and drownings, had sobered him up.

"Glad to see your fly's closed," Don observed.

"Now if you're going to start . . ."

"Sorry, Pop. Slip of the tongue. All right, let's begin the discussion. I warned you about this woman. I told you I was afraid she'd get into you deeper and deeper—well, she has, hasn't she? I notice she's driving a practically new Ford. Did you give it to her?"

"None of your business."

"And she's upgraded her housing. I figure her new place was almost twice the price of her old. Did you buy it for her?"

"I'm missing sports," said Harry. "I want to know how the Tigers did today—they played Boston."

"You're not answering my questions, Dad."

"I don't have to—I'm not in court."

Don scowled. "You would bring that up again. Let's stick to the subject. I want to know how much that broad's put the bite on you for."

Harry clamped his choppers shut like a vise and began to twiddle his thumbs, an old and irritating habit. Not only that, he pretended to be alone, looking about his living room as though he'd just occupied it. Not only that, he began to hum. The tune, as far as Don could make it out off-key, was "Old MacDonald Had a Farm," which was probable since Harry's repertoire was as limited as his ability to carry a tune.

"Dad, for God's sake, can't you see she's making a fool of you? And there's no fool like an old fool, you know."

Harry twiddled and hummed. " 'And on his farm he had a duck.' "

"She's the lowest. One of the lowest things anybody can do is prey on old people—work on their loneliness and kindness. For money."

Harry twiddled and hummed. " 'With a quack-quack here, and a quack-quack there.' "

"And she'll never be satisfied. The more you give her, the more she'll ask. And the more dependent on her you get, the more you'll give."

" 'Here a quack, there a quack, everywhere a quack-quack.' "

"You may need your money. What if you have to go into a nursing home someday? You know what they cost."

Harry saw an opening. "I'd expect you to pay for it."

"Maybe I couldn't."

"Couldn't? If you can pay for that crazy old Coon, wouldn't you pay for me?"

Don sat back, stabbed. "All right. I just don't want you to get in over your head."

"Suppose I love her?"

Don saw an opening. "Love shit! That's exactly what you said to me!"

" 'Old MacDonald had a farm, ee-i, ee-i, o.' "

"You can't love her," Don pressed. "It'd be unnatural. You're old enough to be her father. If you want to know, the whole thing's disgusting—she's got a sugar daddy and you've got a sugar tit."

Harry stopped twiddling and humming and looked as though he'd been beaten with a beer can. "If I didn't have this hip, I'd wash your mouth out with soap. You want to discuss, all right, we'll discuss. You don't give a shit about me. All you care about is getting my money as soon as you can and any damn way you can."

Don shook his head. "That's not true and you know it."

"But you better get one thing straight, Sonny. It's my money, and as long as I'm alive, I'll do what I please with it!"

"Keep it! Shove it! But I want my mother's because she'd want me to have it. I honestly don't give a goddamn what you do with yours—if you have to throw it down that bitch's bottomless pit, why, throw it—but don't you dare give her my mother's! I warn you! If she hadn't worked and saved you'd have damn little in the first place!

"At least I didn't divorce her!"

"No, she didn't divorce you! And looking back, I don't know why! She was twice the woman you are a man! At least now! You sicken me—the only way you can get affection is to buy it!"

"You had mine, but you don't anymore! You've lost it!"

"If I had it, you sure as hell didn't show it!"

Suddenly they ceased to shout at each other. They had worn themselves out. The air in the room was charged with positive ions, residue of the duststorm earlier that evening. Don's forearms were on fire. He scratched them. Harry stared at the dark TV screen.

"You abandoned me," Harry said.

"Abandoned you?"

"Yes, when you moved out here, away from home."

"You mean, children can't grow up and live their own lives?"

"I don't mean any such thing."

"Stick to the subject, Pop. I invited you out here and you accepted. I brought you out to a healthy climate and thought you'd be happy."

"Healthy climate? This place is hotter than the ass end of a bakery."

One of them would speak, the other would respond, and then there'd be an interval. There was nothing between them now but the bare bones of relationship. And the bitter dregs of resentment. And the ions, hanging in the air, of remembrance.

"You've changed, Dad. I don't think you realize how much."

"I wonder how the Tigers did."

"I don't know you anymore. It's like I've had at least four different fathers, and I don't know which one you are."

Interval.

"I'll never forget the things you've said to me tonight, Donald. *Never.*"

"You've become a mean, cheap, stubborn, selfish, stupid, hypocritical old SOB."

"I am so tired. I don't know if I'll have the strength to go to bed."

Interval.

"Well, you've lost a son and gained a whore. Jesus H. Christ."

"You're not sorry enough for me."

"Sorry enough?"

"I'm eighty-three years old."

"You're lucky, Pop. The average man in America lives to be seventy-two."

Interval.

"I could have used a father lately. To talk to me and help me. You've failed me."

"You're the failure. You're broke."

Interval.

"There's a bear in the woods, Dad."

"What?"

"And he's killed us both."

Interval.

"The Bible says to 'Honor thy father and mother.' I do honor my mother, and love her, and I always will. But I can't honor you, or love you—not anymore."

"You wish I was dead, don't you, Donald?"

"Yes. No—I don't wish anybody dead. But the father I'd like to respect and remember is already dead. He died about five years ago. In the afternoon, in the sunshine. At a ballgame out here with me. Remember how I used to take you to the exhibition games here in the spring? And buy us hot dogs and peanuts?"

"I remember."

"And the good times we had?"

"I bought the peanuts."

*

Late the next afternoon, after Don had come within twenty-five thou of getting buyer and seller together on a $600,000 house, and both parties had finally gone away mad, not at each other but at him, and he had as a result lost twenty thou in commission, his door chimes chimed and there was Ron, carrying two suitcases and a conservative expression and wearing a T-shirt that said on its front "God Bless Ralph Waldo Emerson."

Don did one double-take at his offspring, at his suitcases and expression and T-shirt and, leaving the door open, turned and walked through his condo to the kitchen. When he came out, after several minutes, he wore over his head a brown paper sack in which he had cut two eyeholes.

"Squattez-vous, Son," he said, seating himself, his voice muffled by a sack.

Staring at him, Ron sat down.

"Let me guess," said Don. "You and Sue are Split City."

"Yes."

"Over money."

"How did you know?"

"Well, you're a two-income family. And she makes more than you do. So she started calling the shots. Is that about right?"

"That's about right."

"Which involved your macho. So you had a big fight and you walked out on her."

"Yes. Dad, the older I get, the less I know about women."

"I say the same. When you and Sue sprung Windy from Happy Hours the other night, and Jenny took her side, against me, I almost had a hernia. I couldn't understand it. Not half an hour before that, she'd told me she was glad her grandmother was gone." Don adjusted the sack over his head so that his eyes matched the eyeholes. "But that's neither here nor there. But Sue's there. And you're here. And I assume you want to stay here. To move in with me again."

"Yes. Can I?"

"Par for the course. Windy's back with Jenny and you're back with me and we'll all back to square one. Well, you're welcome as usual. But this time there'll be some conditions."

"Conditions? Like what?"

"One. Bobby's my bunny from now on. I need a friend."

"Sure. Okay."

"Two. You work for your room and board. Cooking, cleaning, laundry—for both of us."

"Geez."

"I'll expect to come home and find the place immaculate, the candles lit, the wine chilled, and a gourmet dinner in the oven. Swanson's."

"Geez, I don't . . ."

"Or hit the road, Sonny."

"Well, okay."

"Three. Stay away from your grandfather. I don't want you on his team at this point. I don't need that."

"What's with Gramps? I haven't seen him lately—been too busy."

"On the waterbed, no doubt." Don told him about Mrs. Maria Kirchner, and in the telling started to scratch his forearms through his shirtsleeves.

"Oh, wow," was Ron's assessment.

"Well said," said Don. "Well, you've bought my three conditions. You may now unpack and suck some oxygen. I may have some myself."

"Okay, tell me, Pop. Why the paper sack?"

Father looked at son gravely through the eyeholes. "This is not a sack. It is a tomb," he said, his voice muffled. "I am the Unknown Son. Also the Unknown Father. Known but to God. The bottom line is—I have come to the end of the line. Life has hit on me so long and so hard that I am beaten to a bloody pulp. My ex-wife hates me. The woman I love hates me. Her grandmother hates me. My father hates me. His ladyfriend hates me. I suppose my son's ex-live-in hates me. I haven't sold a property in four months. I second-mortgaged my house, that money's running out, and I have nowhere to turn. Looking down the road, I'll inherit nothing because my father will have blown it all on a woman he's known for a month who gives him genital therapy. Now my kid comes home and gives me a rabbit. To top it off, my good vodka is gone." Don turned the paper sack so that the eyeholes were at the back of his head and his face was totally masked. "So I am dropping out. I am withdrawing from the world. I am a tragedy with an itch. And the tragedy is, I have done nothing to deserve my fate, I really am a fine man. So tell me, my boy, why should God bless Ralph Waldo Emerson?"

"Who? Oh." Ron looked down at the front of his T-shirt. "Well, he wrote a really terrific essay, 'Self-Reliance.' Everybody in the U.S. ought to read it and live by it."

"I will," said Don.

*

He had but walked in the door late the next afternoon when his secret agent was on the phone.

"Been trying to get you all afternoon, Mr. Chambers. Bad news."

"Bad news, Mrs. Bustard, is my meat and drink."

"It's your father. I found him on the floor again around two o'clock. I thought he was dead. I called the paramedics and they said heart attack. I rode in the ambulance with him to the hospital and then started calling you. I can still hear those sirens. I'm so sorry."

"Scottsdale Memorial?"

"Yep. Coronary Care Unit. Myocardial infarction—that's the medical term. Will you be going right over? Do you want me to meet you there?"

Don hesitated. "No to both."

"Both?"

"No, don't meet me, because no, I'm not going."

"You're not?"

"Thank you, Mrs. Bustard."

Don put down the phone as Ron walked in hot and dusty after a hard day installing sprinklers and reflecting on Emerson.

"Harry's in the hospital—heart attack. I just got the call."

"Oh, geez, that's too bad. Damn. We going right away?"

"Not me."

Ron stared at his father as though he still had a paper sack over his head. "You're not going?"

"I am not."

"He might die!"

"So?"

"What about me? I know that's one of your conditions—stay away from Gramps—but Jesus, this is different. What about it?"

"Go if you want."

Ron went. Don had a happy hour with Bobby and a vulgar vodka and the bad news on TV and got his own frozen gourmet dinner.

*

Harry hovered for three days. Ron brought back bulletins from the hospital. One day the prognosis was reasonably good, the next it was not.

"He's in and out. One time he'll open his eyes and I think he recognizes me, the next time I don't think he does at all. His heartbeat's not regular yet, they tell me. That's the problem—it hasn't settled down into a normal, steady beat. And hey, guess who I met? I introduced myself. Mrs. Kirchner. A nurse told me she's there every day."

"You damn betcha she is," said Don.

"Really?"

"If he goes, there go her goodies."

Sunday. Ron was about to leave for Coronary Care and Don was slouched in his living room chair reading the latest best-seller,

Jojoba Farming for Fun and Profit, when Jenny called. Don got the phone, and on recognition of her voice, his own heartbeat instantly became irregular.

"I know you're not speaking to me, and I'm not speaking to you," she said. "Is Ron there?"

"Yes."

"Hold him. Sue and I will be right over. I can leave Windy for a little. The four of us have something to discuss."

"A calm, intelligent discussion."

"Yes."

"But I don't think Ron's speaking to Sue."

"Well, she isn't speaking to him, either."

Don's brow furrowed. "But if you and I aren't speaking, and Ron and Sue aren't speaking, how can we discuss anything?"

She hung up on him. Ron was in his room, headphones on over his backwards baseball cap, boning up on Kafka. In five minutes they were there, mother and daughter, looking calm and intelligent and smashing, but Don sensed that this was the calm before the storm. He went to get Ron, informed him they had company, and accompanied him to the living room.

"Jesus," said Ron.

"No," said Don. "Ron, this is Mrs. Staley and her daughter, Sue. Mrs. Staley, Sue, this is my son, Ronald."

Jenny bit her lip.

"Nice to see you again, Sue," said Don. As host, he believed he should break the ice. "How's it going out at the Crystal Pistol? Really raking in the tips?"

Sue stared out a window.

"Nice to see you, too, Mrs. Staley," said Don. "How're things in real estate?"

"Sue is pregnant."

There was a pregnant pause. Even though everyone knew everyone, the four of them stood around like total strangers.

"Oh my God," said Don.

"Jesus," said Ron, and left the room abruptly. When he returned he was carrying his oxygen tank and tube. Jenny and Sue were seated in uneasy chairs. Don had sunk almost out of sight in the davenport. Ron placed the tank in front of the davenport and sat down beside his father. The tank was a bright green Puritan, a size D cylinder packed with pure oxygen under two thousand pounds of pressure per square inch.

"Would you repeat that?" Ron asked of Jenny.

She addressed Don, not Ron. "To put it coarsely, your son has knocked up my daughter. She didn't wish to come here at all, but I insisted. I want to know what he intends to do about it."

Ron clapped the plastic cup at the end of the tube from the tank over his nose and mouth, opened the flow meter, and inhaled deeply and loudly.

"You were addressing me?" Don asked of Jenny.

"I was. You're his father."

"That's true," said Don. "But in this situation, I don' see why I should be involved. I've got a lot cooking myself right now."

Jenny blew. "You will not talk yourself out of this, Don Chambers—I won't let you!" she cried. "You are his father—*you* should have taught him about contraceptives—*you're* responsible!"

"Oh my God," said Don, and rising, left the room abruptly. When he returned he had a brown paper sack over his head, with two holes for eyeholes. He seated himself beside his son.

"Mom, will you tell me why he has a sack over his head?" Sue inquired of Jenny.

"I have dropped out," Don said to her, his voice muffled. "I have withdrawn from a cruel world. I am a tragedy. And the tragedy is, I do not deserve my fate, I am really a fine man."

"I have never heard such . . ." Jenny began.

"Bullshit," said Sue. "There's no reason for us to be here at all. I'm going to have an abortion."

"Abortion!" cried Ron, horrified.

"Abortion!" cried Jenny, horrified.

"Tomorrow!" cried Sue, resolved.

"Murder!" cried Ron. "Remember—in the beginning, everybody was a fetus!"

"I'm a woman, a human being!" cried Sue. "What I do with my body is my own affair!"

"Taking an innocent life is society's affair!" cried Ron.

"I have freedom of choice!" cried Sue.

"The unborn don't!" cried Ron.

"Tomorrow!" cried Sue.

"Tennis, anyone?" asked Don.

"Ron Chambers, you marry her!" cried Jenny.

"Marry her? Jesus," said Ron, and helped himself to the tank again.

Sue looked at father in the sack and son on the tank, then at her mother. "These aren't men," she said acidly. "They're clowns."

"Laughing on the outside, crying on the in," said Don.

"I *insist* they marry," Jenny told Don. "He's ultimately responsible, he's the father."

"This is unfair as hell!" cried Ron, stung. "What the hell am I charged with? In Kafka's *The Trial,* the poor guy's never charged with anything, he's just . . ."

Sue interrupted. "All this is academic. I wouldn't marry that oxygen-sucker if he . . ."

Don interrupted. "I don't think we're programming our computer properly," said he, his eyes solemn through the eyeholes. "The main thing we have to consider is, How will Sue look in that Crystal Pistol outfit six months from now?"

"Besides," said Ron, "I'm not ready for marriage, I have to raise my consciousness and find myself. And besides that, I wouldn't marry a cocktail waitress. I'm not . . ."

"Oh, oh, oh!" wailed Jenny. "I just realized! This is Bucky Staley and me all over again! I made the mistake of marrying him and it blighted my whole life! No, they must *not* marry!"

"Who's Bucky Staley?" Ron inquired.

"Her no-good ex-husband," Don explained. "She had to get married, too."

Jenny went white. "May you suffocate in that sack, Don Chambers."

"Oh. Well, Sue's too far into feminism for me," Ron continued. "I go along with that stuff to a point—equal pay for equal work. Though I must say she makes a hell of a lot more serving underage drinkers than I do digging my ass off."

"She *will* have the child!" declared Jenny dramatically. "She *will* be a modern, single mother! I will stand by her and . . ."

"Digging underground sprinklers," said Sue to Ron, scornfully. "Coolie labor. If you have no more ambition than . . ."

"Keep 'em in the kitchen!" cried Ron. "Barefoot and pregnant!"

"You sexist bastard," said Sue.

"We have a swell tennis court here," said Don. "My game's a bit rusty, but . . ."

"But you *will* pay child support," Jenny warned Ron, waggling a long fingernail. "You'll pay through the nose."

"Child support!" cried Ron.

"Miss one month and you'll be behind bars!"

"Jesus!" cried Ron, and helped himself to oxygen, breathing deeply and loudly.

"What I don't understand," said Don, "is how she can be pregnant. After all, they've only lived together two weeks."

"You idiot!" snapped Jenny.

Sue jumped up. "I thought I was in love—and he loved me! Love, shit!" She burst into tears. "I won't be manipulated! I'm the one having this baby—I mean, aborting this baby! I'm a human being, not a dumb animal!"

A concerned Bobby hopped into the room.

"Are we sure about this?" asked Don. "Has she had a rabbit test?"

Jenny jumped up. She put a motherly arm about her daughter. "Darling, I've changed my mind. Have the baby or not, it's entirely up to you—but you must *never* marry into this family."

Ron jumped up, overturning the tank. "Now just a damn minute! What's wrong with this family?"

"Bad genes!" cried Sue.

Don jumped up, but rather than retorting, he took Jenny's arm with a hand and pulled her forcibly toward the front door. "Come, Mrs. Staley," he said, "come with me. Let us let these sterling young people have a calm, intelligent discussion." To his surprise, she did not resist him. He opened the door and pulled her through it. "As the Good Book says, 'There is a time to sow, and a time to reap.'" He closed the door behind them. "These sterling young people have sown their seed. Now let them go thither, into the fields, and . . ."

"Shut up," said Jenny. "And take off that insane sack before someone sees you."

"Oh," Don said. "Yes." He pulled the sack from his head. "Bad genes?"

*

From his door they faced the rocky rump of Camelback Mountain, behind which the sun had now retired. To their left was a walkway, covered with a ramada, which led to the Oasis South swimming pool and sauna. Since the evening was still hot, they sought relief under the ramada, seating themselves on a wooden bench. Don folded the sack and offered it.

"Can you use this sack?"

"For what?"

"Storing things?"

"For example."

"Dead mice?"

"It has holes in it."

"That's right, it does."

A lizard stuck its snout out of a bush before them and observed them beadily.

"Harry's in the hospital again," Don said. "Heart attack."

"Oh, Don."

"Ron says it's nip and tuck with him."

"You haven't been there?"

"No."

"Why not?"

"We had a real shoot-out the other night, over Kirchner. A lot of things."

"Could that have contributed?"

"I doubt it."

"And you won't see him?"

"No."

"That's not like you."

"He'll never die. He'll just mean away." Don unfolded the sack and thought of something. "Wouldn't that be the capper, though?"

"What?"

"If they patch it up and get married before we do. Here we've been trying all summer, and our two kids could beat us to it."

"I'd rather not talk about marriage."

"Now or never?"

"Don, I don't know. We're not speaking, remember? In any case, I'd want to wait till the baby, if she has it. And then there's Windy."

"How *is* Windy?"

"In and out, up and down. One day she's high, proud as the dickens of having escaped from the home, waving her six-shooter around—I've taken care to hide the bullets. The next day she's depressed. She'll cry and say she's wrecked my chance of happiness—you know, our getting married."

"Well, she has. But who hasn't? And hey, how come you took her side that night? Against me?"

"What was I to do? Say you were right, she had to go back, and carry her kicking and screaming out to the car? An old lady, ninety-one?"

"Call the Humane Society. They'd throw a net over her and . . ."

"Be silent." Jenny was annoyed. She looked at the lizard. Don folded the sack.

"C'mon," he said. "Let's go peek in my window and see what's going on."

She was willing. They sneaked around the corner of his condo, and then, in order to see into the living room without being seen, they had to insinuate themselves into a big cassia bush, snagging her hose and his Sergio Valente shirt, then thrash through the bush to the other side, where they tripped and almost toppled and wound up close together, Jenny before Don, his arms about her tightly, torso to torso, pelvis to pelvis, embowered by the cassia bush. They peeked into the living room. Ron and Sue stood by the oxygen tank in a matrimonial embrace, their eyes closed, their lips locked in a long kiss, both of them breathing, it could be supposed, deeply and loudly.

"Thank God," Jenny whispered, and began, softly, to weep.

"Thank the fetus," whispered Don into the nape of her neck. "Well, looks like there's going to be a wedding. Will you go?"

She couldn't answer.

"Can I come?"

She couldn't answer.

He pressed his pelvis to hers. "My old man's getting it but I need it, too. Coronary care. I still love you. I still lust for you. Tell me, what were those directions again?"

"What directions?"

"Was it Part A into Part B?"

He tightened arms about her and part of the bush. She was crying on the outside, but he could feel her laughing on the in.

"Hey, Jen, I got it!" he whispered. "A great idea—a sure way we can marry! We'll make it a double wedding!

"How?"

"Let me knock you up!"

*

Ron, Sue, and their waterbed resumed residence together. Ron called his father Monday night to report that he'd just come home from Scottsdale Memorial and there'd been no change in Harry's condition. And also that Mrs. Kirchner had been there. Don said of course she had. Harry couldn't write checks now, so she was probably going through his pockets for loose change. He suggested they talk about something else. Had they set a wedding date yet, Ron and Sue? Ron replied not yet, they were thinking about it. It would be in the afternoon, probably, so he could work in the morning, and Sue would take off work just that one night. They couldn't afford a honeymoon. Then he threw his father a curve.

"You really won't go see Gramps?"

"No."

"What if he dies?"

"He dies."

Ron wound up again and fired. "You'll be old someday, Pop. What if you're dying and I won't see you?"

"I asked you to talk about something else!"

Ron had two strikes on him, however. "Well, if you want to know, Dad, I think this is really turdy of you."

"It takes one to know one," said Don.

*

Mrs. Bustard checked in with Don at the Rancho Grande Realty office on Tuesday. She said she'd made sure his father's apartment was locked, and she'd watered some plants of his. She'd also been at the hospital. Twice. Today she asked the nurses if Mr. Chambers's son, Donald, had been in to see his father, and they said no, not as far as they knew, just his grandson, and a woman. Was that right? That was right, Don said. Mrs. Bustard said well, she had no right to stick her nose into family matters, but she was going to anyway. She said he should go. She knew as well as anybody how difficult his father had been. But if he died, and Don hadn't seen him, he'd regret it the rest of his life. Don said thanks and hung up and sat there scratching his forearms through his shirtsleeves.

*

The call Wednesday morning came from Dr. Bud Biller. "About your father."

"What's the story?"

"Okay, to be medical, he's been in here five days. His hospital course has been characterized by numerous episodes of erratic heart rhythms—fast and slow, fast and slow—which are basically minor extensions of his original infarct, and which do further injury to the heart. And during these episodes his blood pressure fluctuates radically."

"Translate."

"I don't think he'll make it."

"Why not?"

"One, that heart should have settled down by this time. Two, since it hasn't, it probably won't. We've got him on everything—Foley catheter, intravenous drip, running EKG, the works. But asystole at any time wouldn't surprise me."

"What's that?"

"The heart stops. Stops."

"Oh. What're you saying?"

"He's had two episodes since midnight. Close calls. His lucidity is variable—in and out of semi-comas. I've just seen him. He asked for you. If I were you, and cared to say good-bye, *Vaya con Dios,* I'd get over here. Now."

"You would."

"Look, Chambers, this isn't the lottery. This is life and death."

*

It was a clear, hot morning. Don Chambers stood outside the entrance to Scottsdale Memorial for a minute, counting. Until his father's stroke he'd been in a hospital only three times in his life: when Ron was born and when his father broke a hip and when he'd visited a buddy after an appendectomy. He brought the buddy a copy of *Hustler* and a martini in a paper cup. He looked up at the sky. Cloudless, it seemed to glitter and bong like a great blue gong. He entered the hospital.

Coronary care. Nurses everywhere. EKG City. A nurse showed him into a small room in which, in bed, was a very small man. Beside the bed was a big machine with a computer screen. Leads were attached to the patient's chest, and the wires stretched out to the machine which printed out on the screen a running electrocardiogram. A catheter tube ran from the bladder out of the bed into a container on the floor. Above the patient hung a bottle on a stand, and a tube to the patient's arm. The intravenous drip for medication. The nurse removed an oxygen mask from the patient's face and said Don could pull up a chair by the bed. Don pulled up a chair. The nurse vamoosed. Harry's eyes were closed. Don waited.

After a while Harry's eyes opened. "Donald? Donald?" It was less a whisper than a faint, blowing sound. "Where's my son?"

Don pulled the chair closer and bent over his father. "I'm here, Dad. I'm Donald."

His father's eyes did not move. They were fixed on the ceiling. "Ohwo. I'm so glad."

Don covered his father's cold hands with his warm.

"Donald. You see Goldberg. My executor."

"I won't need to, old scout. You'll pull out of this."

"Nowo. Donald, so sorry. Should've given you that loan."

||| 181 |||

"It's all right, Dad."

"Been hard on you."

"No, you haven't."

"When I go, you'll have it all."

"I'm fine now."

"Ohwo."

Harry opened and shut his jaws, massaging his gums with his tongue. His dentures were out, and the lower half of his face was babylike.

"Donald?"

"Yes, Dad?"

"Will I see your mother?"

Don began to cry.

"Will I?"

"Sure you will, Dad," Don sobbed, not at all sure his mother would forgive Maria Kirchner.

"I still love her."

"Mom loves you."

"Love you, too, Donald."

"I love you, Dad!"

"Ohwo."

Harry closed his eyes. Don's tears blurred his father. But suddenly Harry went rigid, and his right leg extended as though the accelerator of the Pope-Tribune had stuck and he was trying to slam on the brakes.

"Whoa!" he blew.

Then, suddenly, under Don's hands, he was lifted upward as though his soul were being vacuumed out of his body by a divine Dustbuster.

Then he fell back, and lay limp, and the Owosso Kid was gone.

Then suddenly there was an ear-splitting BEEEEEEEP from the EKG machine, and Don, terrified, leaped from his chair.

Then suddenly a team of nurses, male and female, rushed into the room rolling a cart of apparatus including a defibrillator and bustled in around the bed and Don was bustled against a wall as they began cardiac-arrest procedures. He pushed and shoved and defended himself and fought his way out of the room past the nurses' station and down the hall to the elevator.

When he got downstairs and outside the hospital he stood for a moment, hyperventilating and rubbing his eyes, and when he could see clearly, he looked up at the sky. He couldn't see a soul. Cloudless, it seemed to glitter and bong like a great blue gong.

All he could think of was—he's gone, tell Jenny; he's gone, tell Jenny. He lunged into the Cadillac and squealed out of the parking lot onto Osborn Road until he was red-lighted. Then he drove north on Scottsdale Road and through town across Camelback and past his place, Oasis South. When he was within a block of Jenny's place, Oasis North, he heard sirens behind him. He obeyed the law. He pulled over to the right-hand curb and stopped and waited impatiently until two fire engines rumbled by, and then a third fire engine.

As soon as he turned into Oasis North he saw smoke, a straight black column built into the blue sky. And Don knew. In his bones he knew. He slowed his car to a crawl and crept to the fire engines and the people and got out of the car in the middle of the street as though handicapped, like an old man with a walker. Heat enveloped him. The condo was a living, breathing thing of flame. Two pumper trucks were already hooked to hydrants, and firemen in boots and helmets directed arcs of water at the condos on either side of Jenny's. It was too late to save hers. Don stood in the street, confused by people running and shouting and hoses snaking and sirens screaming down and the awful roaring of the fire. Then a woman ran toward him, at him, and he scarcely recognized her face. It was only an open mouth, screaming like a baby's.

"You! You! You!" she screamed, and hurled herself at him and struck him with her fists, striking his face and shoulders and arms. "You killed her! You killed her!"

Don grappled with her in the street. He had to use utmost force or she'd have injured him. He got both arms around her and trapped her between his body and the side of his sedan.

"Jen, I didn't kill her, I didn't!" he yelled. "She must've left the stove on!"

"She turned it on high! She killed herself! It was what you said! She burned herself up for me!"

Jenny twisted her head back and forth and struggled and it was all Don could do to hold her.

"Did you have bacon for breakfast?" he yelled. "Did you leave grease in the pan?"

"No—yes, we did—no, she killed herself for me, goddamn you!" Jenny screamed.

Suddenly there were loud bangs from the burning condo, and whizzings in the air, and firemen and people crouched and ducked. The sounds were like those of big bullets being fired from the flames and whizzing everywhere.

"I hate you!" Jenny screamed in Don's face.

"My father died!" he yelled in hers.

"What your son did to my daughter! What you did to my grandmother! What you've done to me!"

"My father died!" Don yelled.

"I'll never see you again! Murderer! Clown! Turkey! Loser!"

"My father's dead!"

"I wish you were!"

Don let her go. She sank to her knees, released and exhausted. He swung open the car door, threw himself inside, and slammed the door. The motor was running. He inched away, slowly, over the hoses, through people, around the fire engines, but she was beside him again, striking his window with her fists. He drove half a block before the woman outside the car stopped striking his window with her fists.

*

When he reached Oasis South and eased into his parking slot he couldn't remember driving. Instead of going into his condo he walked under the ramada past the bench on which he and Jenny had sat and he'd offered her his paper sack and on into the green landscaped center of the development. He walked under palm trees to the shallow end of the 20×40-foot swimming pool. No one else was about. The other owners swam early in the morning during the summer or in the late afternoon. He stepped into the water and down the steps and waded into the pool toward the deep end, slowly, so as not to make waves. When he reached the depth at which his chin rested precisely on the surface, he stopped and stood motionless.

After a while something occurred to him. Raising his left arm out of the water, slowly, so as not to make waves, he unbuttoned his shirt cuff and looked at his wristwatch. His father had given up the ghost about half an hour ago, he knew that for sure. Jenny's grandmother had probably hung up her spurs about half an hour ago. This coincidence meant that, mortal enemies though they were, Harry Chambers and Windy Coon had gallivanted into eternity together. He wondered how they got along. Had she a cane with which to punch him? Had he a harp to throw at her? And when they reached the Pearly Gates together, had the gentleman allowed the lady through them first?

Something else occurred to him. Raising his right arm out of the water, unbuttoning the cuff, pushing up both wet shirtsleeves, he examined his forearms. They itched no more. The red rash was gone.

Don made funeral arrangements for his father. A shattered Jenny made some for her grandmother, with the same Scottsdale mortuary, Ron the rest. Her condo had burned to the ground. She had lost everything, but she was adequately insured. Windy's remains had been found opposite the remains of the TV set in what remained of the living room. Since she had already been practically cremated, the undertaker had undertaken to finish the job. Don might theorize that she had accidentally punched the stove on high under bacon grease, and that the grease had flared to ignite the kitchen curtains and so on, but Jenny, Sue, and Ron would go to their graves convinced it had been deliberate, that

Don's heartlessness was entirely responsible for her suicide. While she was slugging it out with the insurance company, Jenny had sublet the apartment of a friend who was taking an extended vacation on the Coast. Ron and Sue had at last set their wedding date.

This info came from Ron to Don via several phone calls. It could have only come from Ron, since neither Jenny nor Sue would communicate with Don by any means—telephone, telegraph, carrier pigeon, or drums.

"Okay," said Don to his son, "if that's the way they want it, the hell with 'em. The hell with everybody. Just the same, all four of us will have to be at the wedding whether we like it or not. Some wedding this'll be—mother of the bride hating the father of the groom's guts. But the funerals, my God. Attendance is going to be pitiful. Windy's friends are all dead, and dear old Harry didn't have any. You three'll be the only mourners at hers because Jenny and Sue won't want me there, and you and I'll be the only mourners at his because Jenny and Sue won't show if I'm there—three mourners at one and two at the other won't say very damn much about the loss of loved ones. Of course, they're just graveside services, but it'll be a sad show. So let's cut a deal. You tell Jenny and Sue that I'll come to Windy's last rites if they'll come to Harry's."

Ron relayed this offer and got back to his father. "It's a deal, Pop. That means four of us at each funeral, plus the reader, plus the mortuary man. Which is a real improvement."

"Okay," said Don. "Now to the brighter side. Where and when is the wedding?"

"Old Maricopa County Courthouse, downtown Phoenix. Justice of the Peace. This Saturday afternoon, two o'clock."

"Wait a minute. Son, say that again."

"Saturday afternoon, two o'clock."

"Goddammit, it can't be!"

"Why not?"

"Harry's funeral's Saturday afternoon at three o'clock!"

"Oh," said Ron. "Well, change it."

"I can't! This mortician's booked the rest of the day! We can't go right from a wedding to a funeral! You change the time!"

"Sorry, we can't. This J.P.'s very popular—they call him 'Speedy Steve'—we only got the two o'clock slot because they had a cancellation."

Father and son considered. Each could hear the other's mental machinery.

"All right," sighed Don. "I guess we can handle it. If the girls cry at the wedding, they can just go on crying at Harry's funeral. Anyway, you talk it over with Jenny and Sue. See what they say."

Ron called back in ten minutes.

"Dad, you won't believe this."

"Now what?"

"Well, Sue and I forgot to ask Jenny when she's having Windy's funeral. Guess when."

"Saturday."

"That's right. One o'clock."

Don clutched the phone like a drowning man a straw. "Do you mean . . ."

"That's right. She can't change it either—it's the same mortician as yours, and you just said it—he's booked solid that day."

"Do you mean . . ."

"That's right. We bury Windy at one, Sue and I marry at two, and we bury Gramps at three."

Don went up the wall. "Jesus *H.* Christ! I am going back in my sack!"

"What's the problem, Pop? We're just jammed up a little."

"A little! Have you ever been to a wedding?"

"No, I haven't."

"Have you ever been to a funeral?"

"No, I haven't."

"Have you ever drunk beer on whiskey?"

"Yes."

"What happened?"

"I got sick."

"You'll be sicker on Saturday, goddammit! Weddings and funerals do *not* mix! We can't—we *cannot*—sandwich in a wedding between two funerals! Why in hell didn't you and Sue consult with us before you . . ."

Ron resented. "How did we know Gramps and Windy'd kick the bucket the same day? Why in hell didn't you and Jenny ask us when we were getting married before you set the funerals?"

"I am losing my mind," said Don hollowly. "They are gone but they are getting their revenge. Do you actually mean that . . ."

"That's right, Pop."

"Stop saying 'That's right!' "

"Windy at one, us at two, Gramps at three."

"Jesus Christmas!"

Don dressed in his best for the funeral-wedding-funeral. He wore his Christian Dior suit, a Giorgio Armani shirt, an Oscar de la Renta tie, Nino Cerruti socks, Pierre Cochon shoes, and underneath, a Givenchy ball bag.

He picked up Ron and Sue first. He had never seen his son in a sportcoat. This was one of tan poplin, and he wore a white shirt and a knit tie and white jeans and sandals with white socks—the perfect ensemble in which to mourn and marry. She looked more bridal than funereal in an aqua crinkle-gauze dress, but it was evidently her best shot. Then they picked Jenny up at her friend's apartment, and in a blue linen short-sleeve suit and blue pumps she was so fetching that Don almost commented. There had been some controversy over transportation, Jenny and Sue refusing at first to ride with him, but Ron's tires were bald as hen's eggs, Sue's heap had thrown a rod, the AC in Jenny's Cutlass was temperamental, and in the end, the Sedan de Ville was the only sensible solution.

They rode in detonative silence through the October heat to Green Memories, the nearest Scottsdale cemetery. It was a charming boneyard, with orange and grapefruit trees and a view of the majestic Superstition Mountains to the east, an Arizona Public Service coal-fired power plant to the south, a Tastee-Freeze stand to the north, and to the west a drive-in movie double-featuring *Sex Cruisers* and *Senior High Sluts*. Don could see the white hearse parked down a lane—hearses were always white in Arizona to refract the sun's glare—and two men in dark suits waiting. He parked behind the hearse, and all dismounted and moved sedately to the burial site. The mortician introduced himself and introduced the mourners to Mr. Cornwell, the reader. So far as the family knew, Windy Coon had no religious affiliation, and the mortician had suggested a lay reader for both services. Cornwell was a dainty, red-faced man who wore dark glasses and seemed to be suffering acutely from the heat. In one hand he had several sheets of paper, and in the other a wicker fan with "Dr. Pepper" in large lettering. Mortician, reader, and the four bereaved positioned themselves. In the pit, three feet square and three feet deep, stood a metal stand covered by a green felt cloth, and on the stand a white ceramic urn. Two floral offerings leaned against the stand. Jenny, Ron, and Sue had supplied a handsome spray of two dozen red roses. To express his grief, and make amends to Jenny, Don had popped for a big horseshoe of red and white carnations, with a ribbon across it on which was printed "Happy Trails, Windy!"

"Shall we begin?" the mortician invited.

All nodded. From a short sleeve Jenny pulled two Kleenexes, one of which she handed to Sue, and held the other at the ready.

Mr. Cornwell shuffled his sheets, cleared his throat, and began to read. For so small a man, he had a sonorous voice.

" 'Trust thyself: every heart vibrates to that iron string. Accept the place the divine providence has found for you, the society of your contemporaries, the connection of events. Great men have always done so, and confided themselves childlike to the genius of their age, betraying . . .' "

"Mr. Cornwell," Jenny interrupted.

"Ma'am?"

"What in the world are you reading?"

"I believe it's from Emerson, ma'am."

"Emerson who?"

"Ralph Waldo Emerson," said Don.

"His essay called 'Self-Reliance,' " added Mr. Cornwell.

Jenny was close to tears. "Why in heaven's name would you read that?"

"Jenny, listen, it was my idea," admitted Ron. "They asked me what to read—how did I know what Windy'd like to hear?"

"But why couldn't we have something from the Bible?" Jenny cried.

Ron hung his head.

"May I go on?" asked Mr. Cornwell, fanning himself with his Dr. Pepper fan.

"Or a psalm?" Jenny demanded.

" '. . . Betraying their perception that the absolutely trustworthy was seated at their heart, working through their hands, predominating in all their being. And we are now men, and must accept in the highest mind . . .' "

"This is simply dreadful!" Jenny wailed, dabbing at her eyes. "My poor grandmother . . ."

"Ralph Waldo Emerson was a great American writer," said Don the scholar.

" 'Self-Reliance' is a terrific essay," argued Ron. "Windy would really go for it."

"How would you know? You and your underground sprinklers!" cried Jenny somewhat irrelevantly.

"May I go on?" asked Mr. Cornwell.

"Mom, please don't be nasty to Ron," Sue requested. "Not today."

"Everyone should read and live by it," said Don.

Mr. Cornwell, the good Christian soldier, marched on. " '. . . Accept in the highest mind the same transcendant destiny; and not cowards fleeing before a revolution . . .' "

"Stop! Stop!" cried Jenny, waving her Kleenex.

"How much more of this shit do we have to listen to?" inquired Sue.

"Shit?" cried Ron. "You may not be exposed to *culture* in computer programming, but . . ."

"Please, please, I'm almost finished," agonized Mr. Cornwell.

"Well, okay," said Sue, "but if we fart around here much longer, I'll miss my wedding."

"Wedding?" asked the mortician, startled.

"We're a little jammed up this afternoon," said Don.

"Jammed up?"

"We have a wedding at two o'clock," Don explained. "In downtown Phoenix."

"But you have another service here at three, Mr. Chambers! For your father!" cried the mortician, aghast. "Why would you schedule . . ."

" '. . . Not cowards fleeing before a revolution,' " read Mr. Cornwell, " 'but guides, redeemers, and benefactors, obeying the Almighty effort and advancing on Chaos and the Dark.' " He fanned himself violently with his Dr. Pepper fan. "There," he said, "that's it, thank God."

"We better get on the stick," said Sue to the other mourners.

"Shouldn't we have a moment of *prayer*?" appealed the mortician, by now extremely distressed.

"Indeed we should," Jenny agreed, bowing her head.

All bowed heads, and stood in silence. But when a moment had passed, and another, and no one had uttered an appropriate word, Don came to the rescue with the only prayer he knew.

" 'Dear Lord,' " he intoned, " 'bless this food to our use and us to Thy service.' Amen."

All raised heads and stared at him.

Jenny was furious. "*This* man," she said to the mortician and Mr. Cornwell, pointing at Don, "drove the woman in *that* urn to suicide."

It was an unkind cut, and Don retaliated. "And *that* lady's daughter," said he, pointing at Sue, then Ron, "for reasons which'll be apparent in about four months, is marrying *my* son."

The mortician and Mr. Cornwell stared in turn at Don, Jenny, Sue, and Ron.

"Not if we don't get downtown I'm not," said Sue. "How about we haul?"

The four moved toward the Sedan de Ville. Sue skipped back to the urn and took a rose from the memorial spray. Don turned and waved at the two men in dark suits, who were still staring. "So long! Be right back!"

He directed Ron to take the wheel, and stepping to the rear of the Cadillac, opened the trunk, and carried around to the front seat a large styrofoam cooler which he placed between himself and Ron.

"Fire 'er up," he ordered. "We're running late."

Ron eased out of Green Memories and cut north to McDowell, then west between the Papago Buttes and down into the metropolitan valley.

"Well, one down and two to go," said Don cheerfully. "We gotta change the mood." He took the top off the cooler. Inside it were four plastic cups and, under ice, three bottles of Hanns Kornell. "What say, guys, some giggle-water?" He extracted a bottle, and after some delay, popped the cork and put it in his pocket and poured, offering the first cup to Jenny, who looked out her window, then to Sue, who sniffed her rose, then to Ron, who kept his eye on the road. "Okay," said Don, rebuffed. "Ralph Waldo says be self-reliant, so I'll drink alone." He raised the cup. "Here's to the bride and groom!"

Ron changed his mind. "I'll drink to that, Dad!"

Don beamed, passed the cup, and poured himself another. They touched cups and drank. Don poured them another. He was merely trying to turn things around. He'd been looking for two signs. One, that the young man beside him had at least an inkling of what he was getting into, of what vows and a wife and father-hood would mean, of how his life would in a few minutes be ir-remediably altered. Don couldn't catch a trace. Ron was still the tall gangly son with the lopsided grin who needed to get his head on straight. Two, for a hint that Jenny was mellowing, that she no longer laid all the guilt on him, and that at last, on reflection, with her grandmother under the ground, she might, if he were a good boy and behaved, love him again. No hope there either. He had lost her. Windy and Harry were really having their revenge. The dear old dead might *be* dead, but they were still, by God, kicking.

Don poured himself and Ron another. By the time they crossed Twenty-fourth Street, father and son were well into the bottle.

"Hey, just thought of something," said Don. "There's five of us going to the wedding, not four!" He raised his cup. "Here's to our new relative!"

"I'll drink to that!" Ron enthused.

Don offered a cup in the rear. "Care to join us, girls? Toast the little bugger?" Noses high, mother and daughter gave him the get-lost.

"You better have a boy, not a girl," Don confided to the driver. "Girls are damn difficult to raise."

*

By the time they reached downtown Phoenix, and Ron maneu-vered a route among the vagrants, transients, and indigents indig-enous to downtown Phoenix, father and son had almost polished off the bottle. Thinking it wouldn't do to let the well run dry, that he might need a reserve at the wedding, Don emptied the bottle into his cup. They parked in a municipal garage and crossed First Avenue to the old Maricopa County Courthouse, Don hiding the reserve in his hand.

On the second floor they were jammed up again. Ron gave the Clerk of the Justice Court the license and the thirty-four-dollar fee, but when she showed them down a narrow corridor to the door of the judge's chambers, two other couples were ahead of them. The clerk said sorry, there'd been an emergency wedding, but the judge was a "fast marryer," his average tie-the-knot time was under five minutes, so it wouldn't be long. They waited. The first couple went in. Now first in line was a scuzzy young couple with long hair and a baby. The mother-and-bride-to-be obviously had another one in the oven. She held her baby so that its head stuck up over her shoulder and its face was close to Don's. It stared at him. He stared at the floor. Still the baby stared. Finally the door opened and the couple and baby entered the judge's chambers. Don relaxed, uncovered his drink for a sip.

"Cheer up, everybody. These are momentous moments, the first day of the rest of our lives."

Ron nodded enthusiastically, Sue grinned and even Jenny managed a tight smile. But then there were screams through the door and the pregnant bride burst out and shoved the screaming baby at Don and asked him to please hold it till her ceremony was over. Don was the worst person she could have asked. To spare Ron and Sue and Jenny its screams, he took it to the far end of the corridor, and holding it with one arm, tilted the baby's head and his cup and trickled some champagne into its open mouth. The kid loved champagne. It stopped screaming and widened its mouth for more and in a minute had chug-a-lugged the last of his reserve. He pitched the cup into a trash basket and returned to his party. The baby's eyes began to roll. It made gurgling sounds, and to stop them, Don stuck the cork between its lips. Just then the scuzzy young couple, now husband and wife, emerged and took possession of the baby without so much as a thank you and Don and the others moved quickly into the chambers.

Judge "Speedy Steve" Craig had a machine-gun delivery, and might have set a record that afternoon, but just as he reached the line "I do therefore, by virtue of the authority vested in me by the laws of the State of Arizona," the pregnant bride charged into his chambers behind him clutching her gurgling baby.

"You pig-fucker!" she screamed at Don. "You've got my baby drunk!"

"Why, ma'am, I assure you . . ." Don began.

"Young lady, leave my chambers!" cried Judge Craig. "That's an order of this court!"

The baby's eyes rolled at everybody. Its head rolled on its shoulders.

"You screw my wedding up, you bitch," Sue warned the pregnant bride, "I'll beat your buns off."

"He had this cork in his mouth!" yelled the pregnant bride, brandishing a cork.

"Was this your first marriage, ma'am?" Don inquired of her.

"Or I'll have my bailiff hold you for contempt!" threatened the judge.

"Don Chambers, how could you!" cried Jenny.

"My husband's waiting!" the pregnant bride warned Don. "He'll punch the piss out of you!"

The instant the door closed behind her, Judge Craig finished the line, and before Ron could kiss Sue, he had them out a side door, where they skulked down a flight of stairs and outside and double-timed across First Avenue to the car.

Don insisted the bride and groom sit together in the front seat, and moving the cooler into the back, slid in beside Jenny.

"Two down, one to go," he said cheerfully, as Ron headed them up Central Avenue. "Time to celebrate!" He uncovered the cooler, extracted another bottle, popped the cork, and poured a cup for Ron and one for Sue. "Oh-oh, only three cups," he noted. "Here, Jen—I'll drink outta the bottle if nobody minds." He offered the cup. Jenny looked out her window, frowning, then at the cup. Don held his breath. If she were ever to allow him a little hope, to call even a temporary truce, it had to be now. And then, to his joy, but still frowning, she accepted the cup.

"Very well, a little," she said.

"Hey, great!" Don cried, raising the Hanns Kornell high. "Here's to the bride and groom! Many happy returns!"

They drank. Ron and Sue drank and kissed. Ron turned east on McDowell and started the long trek back to Scottsdale. Don started proposing toasts.

"Here's to the mother of the bride!"

They drank to that, Jenny excepted.

"Here's to the father of the groom!"

They drank to that, Don included.

"Here's to Judge Craig!"

They drank to that.

"Here's t'Windy!"

They drank to that.

"Here's t'Harry!"

They drank to that. By the time they zoomed between Papago Buttes they had killed the second bottle and Don had opened the third. He poured and leaned forward to the front seat.

"Now lissen, you two," he said. "I don' have a wedding presen'. But maybe I do. As you know my ol' man has gone t'his reward— whatever that is—which is why we're goin' t'this fun'ral. Obvious. But as you don' know, he was very well-fixed, an' yours truly's the only heir. Which means as of Monday morning, when I go see the exec-ya-tor, I come into big bucks. My fi-nan-shal problems are over. Bye-bye. Well, I want you two t'finish college. Don' care where you go, but after you have the babee, want you t'go. Gradu-ate. Ron's gonna be a great writer, Sue's gonna program them 'put-ers. I'll pick up the tab. Everything. Tu-ition, books, 'partment, car, babee food, the works. Okay?"

"Oh, Don, that's super!" cried Sue, leaning to kiss her father-in-law on the chin.

"Thanks, Pop!" cried Ron, and stuck a hand back for Don to shake.

"That's very generous of you, Don," said Jenny, bestowing a smile.

Dizzied by this applause, and by his offer, which he had just now thought of, Don sank into the rear seat and lifting the bottle celebrated his philanthropy with the last of the bubbly until they reached Green Memories. Ron idled them down the same lane as before, past the markers and orange and grapefruit trees, toward the same white hearse and the same two men in dark suits, waiting. This time, however, after Ron had parked behind the hearse, rather than stepping sedately from the Sedan de Ville, they bumped and bumbled out of it as though they were being hit over the heads by the three o'clock heat. In fact, they were. In fact, in that fiery afternoon furnace, the four of them were instantly smashed.

"Jussa minute," said Don, gathering them. "I 'pologize for Windy's fun'ral. Weird. But this my father's. All that money, don' forget. So we gotta do better. Be respec'ful. Put on a class act. Shape up. Get with it. Okay, everbody?"

The other three nodded repeatedly, and then in a group they swayed like penguins to the burial site and positioned themselves about Harry Chambers's urn while the mortician and reader stared at them in apprehension. Harry's urn was made of dark wood, and carved, and stood on what was undoubtedly the same green cloth draped over the same metal stand. Leaning against the stand were a spray of a dozen red roses, courtesy of Jenny, Ron, and Sue, and a construction of red and white carnations which formed letters and words into a headline, the blossoms reading "In Loving Memory, Don."

"Well, hey," said Don cheerfully to the mortician and the reader, "here we are again. Right on the ol' button. Let 'er rip, Cornwell!"

The dainty reader was by now on the verge of heat prostration. He shuffled some sheets and tried, simultaneously, to fan himself with his Dr. Pepper fan. "Ahem." He began to read. " 'Logic is doubtless unshakable, but it cannot withstand a man who wants to go on living. Where was the Judge whom he had never seen?' "

"Jussa minute," Don interjected, jerking at his tie to loosen the knot. "What'n hell's that?"

"Why, it's from Franz Kafka's *The Trial,* Mr. Chambers."

"Kafka? Who's Kafka?" asked Sue of everyone.

"One of the greates' writers of all time," said Ron.

"You asked me to read from *The Trial,* Mr. Chambers," reminded Mr. Cornwell.

"But why in hell that part?" Don demanded. "Why not somethin', uh, upliftin', for Chrissake?"

A bead of sweat hung from the reader's nose. "Mr. Chambers, I read the entire novel, and I simply couldn't find anything fitting. The truth is, I couldn't make any sense of it whatever. So I chose these few lines—the last lines in the book. Don't blame me if . . ."

"Lordy, Don," said Jenny, "why in the worl' would you say Kafa?"

"Kaf-*ka,*" Sue corrected.

"Ron," said Don. "He's high on ol' Kafka. He's been tellin' me . . ."

"I'm going on," Mr. Cornwell interrupted. " '. . . Where was the high Court, to which he had never penetrated?' "

"My God," said Don, unbuttoning his shirt collar. "I don' unnerstan' any of this stuff. Will somebody please 'splain t'me what . . ."

"It's about this poor guy charged with a crime," Ron explained. "But he never knows *what* crime! An' he never goes t'court—he can' even *find* the court! An' then they ex'cute 'im!"

"Poor bastard," said Sue, touched.

"Soun's like me," Don mused.

"But why Kafa?" Jenny repeated. "Why not po-etry?"

"Kaf-*ka,*" Sue corrected.

" 'Cause Ron knows lit, thas' why!" Don was becoming embarrassed and steamed. "Whaddo I know 'bout lit? Ron's gonna be a great writer! So I took his word, an' . . ."

"Don' you see the symbolism?" Ron appealed to the mortician.

"I shall proceed, no matter what," declared Mr. Cornwell, fanning the bead of sweat from his nose. " '. . . He raised his hands and spread out all his fingers. But the hands of one of the partners were already at K's throat, while the other thrust the knife deep into his heart and turned it there twice.' "

"Oh, your poor father!" cried Jenny at Don.

"Father hell," he groaned. "M'poor mother."

Instant silence.

"M'poor, dear mother," he groaned again.

"Your mother!" gasped Jenny.

"Your mother!" cried Sue.

"Your mother!" mumbled Ron.

All continued to stare at Don as a champagne tear trickled down his cheek. He sopped it up with one end of his Oscar de la Renta tie.

"Yeah, m'poor mother," said he mournfully. "I wasn' gonna tell."

Only now did the mortician get the dreadful drift. "Mr. Chambers, you engaged me to cremate the remains of, and to provide the last rites for, one Harold Chambers, whom I understood to be your father." He pointed a manicured finger. "I must know—I demand to know—*who* is in that urn!"

"Lila Chambers," Don confessed. "My mom."

"Lila Chambers? Your mom? That's impossible!" cried the mortician. "It may even be unlawful!"

"*What* a switcheroo!" cried Sue.

Mr. Cornwell was confused. "Then who did I read Emerson for?"

"Then where's ol' Gramps?" cried Ron.

"In my condo, in a closet," Don revealed. "His ashes."

"Oh, Don, how *could* you!" cried Jenny.

" 'Cause my ol' man was s'pose t'bury her back home, in Michigan, twenny years ago," said Don defiantly. "But he was too cheap—he sold her plot for a lotta money an' brought her out here, damn him. So I thought I'd plant her in a nice place—whas' wrong with that?"

"Whatcha gonna do with Gramps?" asked Ron.

"Beats me," Don admitted. "I'll think of somethin'."

"This is disgraceful!" cried the mortician. "This is an insult to my profession!"

"And mine!" cried Mr. Cornwell. "I'll charge you *triple* for this blasphemous . . ."

"Mr. Chambers, you've made a travesty of one of mankind's most solemn ceremonies," said the mortician sternly. "I may have grounds for a lawsuit, sir, and I shall . . ."

"And such profane language I have never heard!" added Mr. Cornwell. "To think that people mourning the loss of . . ."

"Aw, shut up, you fartknockers!" swore Sue, the Crystal Pistol waitress, and taking a step toward mortician and reader, put one foot upon the green cloth, which gave way, plunging her leg into the pit.

"Whoooaaa! Ooooh, my leg!" She kept her balance, but stood with one leg in the pit and the other doubled at the knee on the grass.

Ron and Don rushed to her aid, placing hands under her armpits. But Sue was a big girl, and though she jumped up and down in the pit, they were unable at first to extricate her.

"I knew it!" Jenny wailed. "I knew we couldn't make it! Mos' unspeakable day of my life!"

"Ow, my leg!" wailed Sue.

" '. . . With failing eyes K could still see the two of them immediately before him . . .' " Mr. Cornwell had decided to read again, as the *Titanic*'s orchestra had decided to play again. " '. . . Cheek leaning against cheek, watching the final act.' "

Sue was hauled from the pit. She came up with a fistful of red and white carnations, which she hurled over the urn at the reader. "C'mon, Cornwell!" she cried. "Get this goddamned show on the road!"

" 'Like a dog!' he said,' " the reader shouted. " 'It was as if the shame of it would outlive him.' " He tossed his sheets and his Dr. Pepper fan triumphantly in the air. "There, I'm done! Damn Kaf-*ka!* Damn you common drunks! Mr. Chambers, I hope with all my soul your father returns from the Hereafter to haunt . . ."

"I didn' even know Lila Chambers!" cried Jenny.

"Returns?" cried Don. "He better not! My ol' man gave me fits! I'm glad he's . . ."

"Ladies! Gentlemen!" cried the mortician. "Let us conclude with a *silent* prayer!"

"Gone!" Don continued. "No, les' pray for m'poor, dear mom!"

"Please!" implored the mortician.

All bowed heads, even a reluctant Don. All stood in apprehension, fearful of what Don might say. Instead, what they heard was the crunch of car tires on gravel. Heads were bowed, but eyes were irreverently raised.

A big Ford Crown Victoria crunched to a stop behind Don's car, which was parked behind the hearse. The engine died. The driver, a stranger, a middle-aged woman in black with a lavish bouquet of flowers in her arms, opened the door, got out, and seeing the mourners, all of them staring at her now, hesitated.

Don knew.

Jenny knew because Don had told her.

Sue knew because Jenny had told her.

Ron knew because Don, Jenny, and Sue had told him.

But none of them, Don included, knew what Don would say or do.

"No!" he bellowed.

He tore off his suitcoat and threw it down and pawed the

ground. He bellowed at the woman like a bull. "He's gone! Party's over! Now you get the hell outta here, you bitch!"

The dark lady dropped her bouquet, scrambled back into the sedan, started the engine, and began to reverse down the lane. Don wasn't satisfied. Horns lowered, he trotted after the slow-moving car.

"No more money! Go, goddam you!" He grabbed a green orange from a tree and wound up and pitched it wildly at her car and missed. "No more bucks!"

He grabbed a green grapefruit from a tree and threw it at the car and missed and fell down. He got up and galloped reeling after her as she backed the Ford faster and faster. "Outta here! Go on! Party's over! Get outta here, you gol'digger bitch!"

*

Don Chambers sat opposite Gustave Goldberg at ten o'clcok on Monday morning. Jerry Snapkin had called him a "shark." With his massive head and mane of white hair, the attorney reminded Don more of a lion.

"Well, Mr. Chambers. You're here of course about the estate."

"Of course."

"I have the will here." Goldberg indicated a document on his desk. "It's also on file with the county."

"I know about the will—only child, only heir, he told me," Don said. "What I'm really curious about is the Kirchner woman. I warned Dad about her time and again, but I was just spinning my wheels."

"I see."

"How much did she take him for? The car, for instance. Do you know?"

"I do. Your father conferred with me regularly, by phone." The attorney leaned back in his chair and clasped hands behind his head. "He traded her vehicle in on a newer one, the Ford. I think the difference was something over ten thousand dollars."

"Swell. Great." Don shook his head. "What about the house?"

"A similar arrangement. She put hers on the market, priced it reasonably, sold it, and bought the better house. With her equity in the first house, and twenty thousand dollars he provided additionally, she was able to make a substantial down payment on the new one."

"Twenty thousand?"

"Twenty thousand."

"Twenty and ten. In about five weeks, then, she tapped him for thirty thou," Don said. "Not bad for a little hip therapy. You approved all this?" Goldberg gave Don a look like a hook. His eyes were a brilliant violet. "It was not for me to approve or disapprove. A man may do with his money whatever he wishes—don't you agree?"

Don smiled. "Sure, why not?" He crossed his legs. "Okay, she lucked out. She hit the old man in the right place at the right time. I won't fight—I've been known to be generous myself. But where do we go from here? What does the estate add up to? I can use some good news."

"Around $180,000. Including the house in Michigan, which is under land contract."

"About what I thought. How long before I actually see some of it? I may want to keep some of the stocks, by the way."

Gustave Goldberg lowered his arms and sat forward, looking directly at Don. "Before we get into that, Mr. Chambers, there's something of which I should apprise you."

"Oh?"

"Three weeks ago your father called me and asked me to come see him and bring his will. This I did, the following day. He then dictated to me a codicil to that will—an appended clause which changes and supersedes a clause in the original will. I took it to a public steno, had it typed into the will, and returned it to him. He then signed the codicil in the presence of two witnesses"—the attorney picked up and glanced at the will—"a Mrs. Bustard and a Mr. Burton. The codicil is legal and binding."

Don waited.

"In it, your father has left one-half of his estate to a Mrs. Maria Rizzo Kirchner." Goldberg waited for a response.

"Half?"

"Half. As I said, the codicil is legal and binding. You may therefore expect to realize about ninety thousand, less my fees as executor, burial expense, so on."

"Ninety?"

"Ninety. Not twice that."

"Ninety."

Don Chambers made a face. But when he tried to compose himself, he couldn't. He jumped from his chair and went to a window, turning his back to Goldberg, and still couldn't erase his stricken face. Keeping his back to the other man, he walked from the office.

||| 8 |||

Don believed the act of shaving with a safety razor could be elevated into a performing art. And that he had hit this elevation. He used Barbasol, in the tube. His father had put him onto tube Barbasol when he started shaving, at fifteen, and though it was as difficult to obtain as noble martini olives, he had set up a deal with a drugstore which ordered Barbasol for him a dozen tubes at a time. First you washed your face with soap and very hot water, opening up the pores. You then massaged Barbasol into the skin with the tips of the fingers. You let it lay for no more than thirty seconds, during which the cream took the stubble in amorous hands and caressed it into a condition of complaisance. Meanwhile you readied your razor by rinsing it in cold water—cold, never hot, for hot dulled the blade edge—and tightening it. After exhaustive research, Don had come to prefer a Gillette razor with a Platinum-Plus blade. You commenced below the right sideburn, shaved that cheek, turned on the cold water, rinsed the razor, turned off the water, shaved the chin, rinsed, shaved the left cheek, rinsed, shaved the left and right sides of the neck, and rinsed. Then, holding the razor delicately, as though you were shaving your ass by means of a mirror, you shaved your Adam's apple, then rinsed the razor for the fifth and final time and loosened the blade. Finally you massaged the remainder of the Barbasol into the skin and congratulated your second self with a smile. Ecologically, you had saved water and steel. Cosmetologically, you had an impeccable face. Psychologically, you had begun the new day with an upper. Spiritually, you had turned the mundane into the divine.

This morning, however, he cut the hell out of himself. With one stroke of the razor he was furious at his father. With the next, bitter at the Kirchner bitch. With the next, his hand shook with self-pity. In the end, the butchery done, blood on the cheek, chin, and Adam's apple, he slapped wet scraps of toilet paper on his wounds and went to the phone and called a smart guy he knew in the El Rancho Realty office who was an authority on everything from pro football to oil leases and asked him to recommend an attorney.

"What for?"

"Contest a will."

"Oh. Sure. My guy is Charles Sturm—Sturm and Drang. One sharp cookie. Give him a bang on the pipes. Use my name."

"I'll do that. Thanks."

Don did that.

*

"Half?"

"Half. Around ninety thousand. And he'd already given her ten thousand for a nearly new car and twenty thou toward a house."

"How long had he known her?"

"I think four to five weeks. She was a damned fast worker."

"I see." Charles Sturm reflected. "Did she care for him during that period? I mean, live with him, nurse him, cook and clean for him, that sort of thing?"

"No," Don said. "She came to his apartment two or three nights a week, maybe more, a couple hours, to give him hip therapy. Whatever that means. Why?"

"If she had, tended him that is, she could file what's called a 'quantum merit' claim against the estate. Payment for domestic and other services rendered. I think, on the basis of what you told me, we can eliminate that possibility."

"We sure can. Peanuts compared to what she thinks she's got coming."

It seemed to Don he'd spent too much time lately around lawyers. These offices were handsome. The chair he sat in was real leather.

"Let's talk about the grounds for contest in a will case," said Charles Sturm. "There are four. First, testamentary capacity. Was your father competent, mentally, to add a codicil to his will?"

"I suppose he was. He'd had a stroke. He was having trouble signing his name and doing arithmetic."

"That wouldn't affect competency, not if he was lucid. Second, was there due execution of the codicil? Was his attorney present? Did witnesses sign?"

"Yes. He dictated it to Goldberg in the presence of two neighbors, who signed."

Sturm nodded. "That's out, then. So's the third—validity. Forgery, et cetera. That brings us to the fourth. Whether or not the addition of the codicil was an act of free will. In other words, was the testator, your father, acting with freedom from duress, menace, fraud, mistake, restraint, lack of intent, or undue influence?"

"That's it," Don said. "Undue influence. That's where we nail her. She influenced the hell out of him. She had to."

"Why d'you say?'

"Because my father was tighter than an ant's asshole. Undue influence, you know it. She even made him drinks. Gin and tonics. He never drank, but she got him sloshed and gave him a sob story and zingo—out came the checkbook."

"A good point." Charles Sturm made a note of it. "I must tell you, though, that undue influence is hard to prove. There are at least eight factors the court will be interested in."

"For example."

"All right, a quick rundown. Did she make false representations to him? Was the codicil a hasty act? Was it concealed from others? Was she active in seeing that he added it? Is it consistent with his prior declarations? Is . . ."

"Hold it." Don gestured. "Dad told me three times—on the way out here from Michigan, once during an argument, and once on his deathbed—that I'd have it all. And that's how the original will reads."

Sturm nodded. "Another good point." He made a note of it. "To continue. Is the codicil reasonable or unnatural in view of his circumstances, attitudes, family? Was your father the kind of man who'd be susceptible to undue influence? How would you answer those Mr. Chambers?"

"Well, he was probably lonely."

"Undoubtedly."

"And a loner. He didn't make friends easily. I tried to get him to participate in things at the Eventide, but he wouldn't," Don said.

"The last one. Were the testator and the beneficiary—the woman—in a confidental relationship? I gather they were."

"Were they? Over a hundred thousand bucks? I'd call *that* confidential."

Charles Sturm was a sober man in his early fifties. He wore a sober suit and tie. He was long and lank and gray at the temples. Don had not seen him smile, even in greeting, but his handshake was solid. He belonged in a courtroom, before or behind the bench. He was also the kind of man Don would have liked to have with him on a dark night down a dark alley.

"Very well," said the attorney. "We'll try for undue influence." He referred to his notepad. "We have the drinking and your father's prior declarations. Not much to go on, I'm afraid. I must ask—you're determined to contest?"

"I am."

"Why?"

"Because I've been raped. Really ripped the hell off. Because I'm damned mad—at him *and* her—wouldn't you be?"

"I expect I would. Hard to tell, though, what the elderly will do."

"You can say that again. What happens now?"

"Several things already have, I'm sure. The executor has already filed a petition with the court for formal probate of the estate. This was to establish testacy—that a will exists and that it's valid. And just as Goldberg's apprised you of the contents of that will, so he's let the woman know. Given her the good news. And informed her of her rights."

"Her rights?"

"She is now a beneficiary—she therefore has certain inherent rights. She can defend them. She can defend the codicil. My guess is she's already looking for counsel, just as you are. And that they'll immediately file a petition in support of the will. For the same reason we'll immediately file one objecting to it."

"I see. Then what?"

"In about two weeks there'll be a preliminary hearing to determine the facts. Before either Judge Howard or Judge Witliff—they're both on probate this term. A hearing is like a minitrial. Testimony, so on—but brief, an hour or two. The court then decides—the matter before it is trialworthy or a waste of time. If the former, there'll be one."

"When?"

"Six weeks, two months."

"Damn," said Don. "I'm scraping the bottom of the barrel. Money-wise. I've had to second-mortgage my condo. I sell real estate, but nobody's buying. Now I've inherited but I haven't. What am I supposed to do?"

"Wait."

"Damn."

"Sorry."

"Why does everything legal have to be so damn complicated?"

Sturm almost smiled. "If we kept it simple, how would we make a living?"

Don almost smiled. There was a long recess. The attorney found a piece of paper in a desk drawer, laid it on his desk, and closed the drawer.

"Let me make you a little speech," he said. "I've been involved in perhaps a dozen will contests. They are the nastiest, most vicious, most degrading pieces of litigation to come before a court. Families are literally torn apart. Parents and children and brothers and sisters go to the grave with murderous last words. Let me read you something. We had a lady justice on the Arizona Supreme Court some years back, Lorna Lockwood, a very smart gal. A will contest was appealed all the way up to her bench. I'll read a quote from her decision. 'No matter how much we may reprobate the conduct of a testator from the standpoint of natural justice, or even of humanity, we may not on that account permit his will to be set aside unless it clearly appears that he did not fully realize what he was doing with his property, for it is his to dispose of as he pleases.' "

"So?"

Charles Sturm put the paper away in his desk. "What she's saying, what I'm saying, is—of course you've been raped, of course you've been ripped off, but in the eyes of the law, that's irrelevant. Justice is irrelevant. Humanity is irrelevant. We have a whole body of judicial precedent by now. Male or female, if decedent knows what he's doing—and does it of his own free will—he can do any damned thing he wants with his property. *Anything*. Unless it's a community-property state, he can impoverish his wife of fifty years. He can make his cat a millionaire. He can buy a whore a bunch of gold bars. He can light cigars with his stocks and bonds. Anything. And the hell with his rightful heirs. And the court will let him do it."

The attorney stood a silver pencil on end on his desk and looked at it, then looked at Don. "Still intend to proceed?"

"Yes. Oh, yes."

"Even though, win or lose, I warn you you're walking into an emotional buzz saw?"

"Even though."

"Why?"

"Because I'm my father's son," Don said. "And I'm a good man."

Charles Sturm smiled, and stood, and extended a hand. Don got a solid shake.

"I can't promise a thing," Sturm said, "but I'm with you all the way. Let's go, good man."

*

Don picked up the Rabbit Rabbit and placed it by his front door. "Take this sucker home," he said to Ron. "Bobby goes into shock every time he sees it. He'll never ride in it again, I gave him my word. He and I are going to lead a quiet life together, reading, playing old Elvis Presley records, and thinking deep thoughts." He went to his bedroom, pulled Bobby from under the bed where he had fled when Ron arrived, brought him back, and stretching out on the davenport, draped his pal across his chest and gave him a Milk Dud. "How's Jenny?"

"Fine."

"How's Sue?"

"Fine."

"How's the fetus?"

"Fine."

Ron was Don's only source of info about them. Neither mother nor daughter would touch Don Chambers with a ten-foot pole. He was bad luck. He was a pestilence. He was the human pits. According to Ron, Jenny still blamed him for what she was convinced was Windy's suicide. Sue was mad at him for screwing up her nuptials and getting them all bombed and making a farce of the funerals, and besides that, her leg still hurt from stepping into Harry's final resting place.

"Guess what?" Don said.

"What?"

"Last week, after the funerals, I went to see Gramps' executor, a lawyer named Goldberg. To find out how much I was coming into."

"And?"

"He's given half his estate to the Kirchner woman."

Ron had been sprawled in a chair, long legs and long arms. Now he assembled himself upright and stared at his father.

"Half," Don said.

"He hasn't," Ron said.

"Oh, yes, he has."

"He wouldn't."

"But he did."

"Oh my God."

"My sentiments exactly."

"That's the shits!"

"My sentiments exactly."

"But *why* would he?"

"You tell me. Dear old Gramps—you were always in his corner. You stuck up for him, you stabbed me. Well, defend him now, Sonny Boy."

Ron swallowed so hard Don could hear him. "I can't. What a cruddy trick. Unless he didn't know what he was doing."

"He knew damned well. He did it a month ago. But here's the payoff—on his deathbed he told me I'd have it all. He lied to me. Through his teeth. No, his choppers were out. But he lied."

"He must have changed some way."

"Did he ever. Three or four times in three or four months. I could tell you other things he did that would curl your hair, but I won't. Anyway, the father we didn't bury isn't the father I care to remember."

Ron was thinking. "Does this—I mean, you won't be getting as much as you thought—I mean, what about your sending Sue and me back to school for our last two years? You won't be able to now, will you?"

"I said I will and I will. I'll find the money. Maybe I'll go into real estate and get rich."

Ron shook his head. "I can't believe it. After all you did for him."

"And that's not the worst." Don stroked Bobby's battered ear. "My dear mother, your grandmother, Lila, worked just as hard as he did while she lived. Half of what he had was hers—she'd earned it and saved it. So what I'm getting is her half—she'd have wanted me to have it. Which means my dear father gave me absolutely nothing of his. Disinherited me."

"Geez. That must really hurt, Pop."

"It does. Believe me."

"The old bastard," Ron said. "Isn't there anything you can do about it?"

"I can fight. I've got a lawyer and we're going to court. I'll fight that woman on the beaches, in the hills, in the streets, I'll never surrender."

"Terrific." Ron smote a palm with a fist. "It's really a jungle out there, isn't it, Dad?"

"Two things," Don said, warmed by rabbit fur and by the shift in his son's allegiance. "Don't tell Jenny and Sue about this."

"Why not?"

"Just don't. I don't want sympathy. I can take care of myself."

"Well, okay, if you say."

"And let this be a lesson to you. I'll be old myself someday. I'll turn cheap and crabby. All I'll give a damn about is my old bones. I'll have a will. You'll be my heir. Between now and then, you get your act together and be a loving, dutiful son or I'll cut you out of my will. I'll leave every cent to Bobby."

*

The night before the hearing a storm front that had formed in the Pacific off Alaska roared down over Washington and Oregon and Nevada and blew summer and insanity out of Phoenix. The temperature dropped twenty degrees in two hours. Instant autumn. In the morning hospitalized males tore out their tubes and goosed their nurses. Pimps on East Van Buren enlisted in the Marines. Good Humor men gave away Nutty Buddies. Senior citizens turned off TV and read good books and sent back Social Security checks uncashed. Husbands and wives made up and started beating manners into their children. Dogs at the dog tracks refused to run after rabbits. A religious cult announced it had deferred the end of the world for a week. Sons and daughters went to court damned if they'd let some bitch or sonofabitch screw them out of their inheritance.

Probate Division 2 of the Maricopa County Superior Court was on the fourth floor of the building, a courtroom identical to that of Division 8, in which the late Harry Chambers had zilched his son. Don Chambers entered it at ten of two that Tuesday afternoon to meet Charles Sturm, who stood at an attorney's table and greeted his client with another solid shake.

"Hullo, Tiger. You ready?"

"For raw meat," Don said.

"We've drawn Charley Howard, as judge. A sound man, no nonsense, likes to keep things moving. Ever been in court before?"

"Sure, couple of months ago." Don gestured. "A room just like this, two floors up."

"Oh? What was the occasion?"

"I filed for conservatorship of my old man."

Sturm frowned. "You did? You didn't tell me that. Presumably you lost."

"Yup. Dad put on a great show on the stand. Not a dry eye in the house."

Sturm was still frowning. "I wish you'd told me. That won't look very good on the record—it provides him with motivation. I'll steer clear of it, but you can be sure the other side won't."

"No problem—how would they know?" Suddenly Don did a triple-take. "My God!" he whispered. Maria Kirchner had just entered the rear of the room, and her counsel with her. "That's the guy I hired for the conservatorship!"

Sturm had a look. "Don't think I've run into him before."

"Jerry Snapkin!" Don took his attorney's arm and ear. "A wimp! She must've seen his ad in the paper!"

Jerry Snapkin smiled and waved at Don, who nodded back and deliberately did not look at Kirchner. He sat down beside Sturm, who opened a real leather attaché case. "I tell you," he whispered, "it'll be amateur hour. I don't know how that guy got admitted to the bar. We're in! We can't lose!"

"That remains to be seen" Sturm was still frowning. "Didn't you just ask me how the other side could possibly have knowledge of the conservatorship?"

Gustave Goldberg showed, and exchanged nods with Don. The Bailiff and Clerk of the Court took their places near the bench. Don continued to avoid looking at Kirchner. He had seen her several times, at a distance, at night, getting into her car in front of Harry's apartment, and through drunken eyes at Harry's funeral, but he hadn't really seen her. He knew anyway what she'd look like. Purple hair, cheap makeup, over the hill, a ten-dollar broad who'd have to work dark bars and undemanding men. He despised her. He hated her. He was afraid that if he saw her clearly, that if their eyes met, he might freak out. Strangle her with his bare hands. Or better yet, stand her up, turn her around, and kick her sleazy, unscrupulous ass.

The Bailiff banged his gavel twice. "All rise!" he proclaimed.

"This Maricopa County Superior Court, Probate Division, is now in session, the Honorable Judge Charles Howard presiding!"

Charles Howard was a man of medium age and height with a neat brown beard. Even in raven robes, he gave off a kind of kinetic energy. "Good afternoon," he said into his microphone as all were seated. "This is a preliminary hearing *in re* the estate of Harold Chambers. Court has the will. Court has also received from the executor a petition for probate. Testacy has been established." He referred to notes. "Petition in support of the will has been filed by Mrs. Maria Kirchner, represented by Mr. Jeremy Snapkin. Petition objecting to said will has been filed by Mr. Donald Chambers, son of decedent, represented by Mr. Charles Sturm." The judge glanced at one attorney, then the other. "As I said, gentlemen, this is a preliminary hearing. I don't intend to go up hill and down dale. I expect counsel for both sides to get the salient facts in the record, period. Court will then determine whether or not the matter goes to formal proceeding." He leaned back in his chair. "Mr. Goldberg, I'll hear from you first."

The executor was sworn in and testified that decedent was, to all appearances, in full possession of his faculties on September 14, on which date he dictated and signed a codicil to his will in the presence of two witnesses, who also signed.

"Thank you, Mr. Goldberg," said the judge. "You are excused. Mr. Sturm?"

Charles Sturm rose. "Your Honor, I will call upon Donald Chambers, son and only child of testator. It is Mr. Chambers's petition objecting to the codicil to the will which the court has before it. Our objections are based upon two issues that have been traditional grounds for contest, issues of judicial concern— namely, prior declarations and undue influence. And I shall ask witness to speak only to these issues. Mr. Chambers?"

Don was duly sworn and took the stand. He decided to look either at his attorney or at the judge. He was much more at ease this time around. This time he wasn't taking on his father and his walker and his tears. And he wouldn't have to face Gustave Goldberg as inquisitor. He had, he believed, a case as plain as the nose on anyone's face, and besides that, justice and humanity must tip the scales in favor of a surviving son or what was civilization all about?

Charles Sturm stood at his table. "Mr. Chambers, did your father ever declare to you his intentions regarding the disposition of his estate?"

"Yes, three times," Don said. "In June, while we were driving from Michigan to Arizona, he told me what he owned and said it would be all mine someday. Again in September. Then week before last, after a heart attack, just before he died he said the same thing. This had to be after he'd already added the codicil, giving away half. He must have forgotten it. I can't believe my father would lie to me on his deathbed. He just wouldn't . . ."

"Objection!" cried jumping Jerry Snapkin. "Opinion of the witness is not—"

"Sustained," said Judge Howard. "Witness will confine himself to fact. Proceed, Mr. Sturm."

"Now, Mr. Chambers, let us address the issue of undue influence," said the attorney. "Will you tell us what you know of the relationship between your father and Mrs. Kirchner?"

Don made it as simple as he could. Mrs. Bustard's alerts. Kirchner's drop-ins as his father's apartment at the Eventide, at night, supposedly to administer *hip* therapy. The living room windowshade was pulled. "I went in one night after she'd left to ask him what was going on. There was liquor on his breath, and he didn't drink. He said she made them gin and tonics, with plenty of 'stick' in them: I warned him how some people prey on old people, taking advantage of their loneliness and trust, conning them out of whatever they can. But he wouldn't listen." Don hesitated. Now or never. But his mother wouldn't want him to, Jenny wouldn't want him to, and his conscience wouldn't let him, so he went on without mentioning Harry's open fly. How he'd gone in the front door one night just as Kirchner took off out the back. "Then I found out he'd bought her a newer car. None of these things were things my father would normally do. He never even had liquor in the house. He never spent money freely, on himself or anyone else. I talked with him again, trying to make him understand what was happening, how he was being used, but I couldn't make a dent. He was eighty-three. He knew better than I did." Finally, his discovery, from Mr. Goldberg after his father's decease, that in addition to the car, his father had helped Kirchner buy a bigger, better house and added a codicil to his will. "And all this in a few weeks," he concluded. "Around thirty thousand dollars in gifts, plus half of everything else he had. I was shocked. I'd done a great deal for him, I was his son, but he—"

"Thank you, Mr. Chambers," Sturm interrupted, and turned to the other table. "Your witness, Mr. Snapkin."

A new and improved Jerry Snapkin approached the witness, a suburb of Chicago on little legal feet. His eyes bored into Don's. "I have only a few questions, Mr. Chambers. Please answer them yes or no. First, did you this summer ask decedent, your father, for a loan of ten thousand dollars?"

Don had a hot flash. This was one from left field. "Yes," he said.

"Did your father refuse you?"

"Yes."

"And did you, not long after that, petition the court for conservatorship of your father?"

Don could have torn a telephone book in two. "He had a stroke. He couldn't do arithmetic, couldn't sign his name. He couldn't do his banking. I—"

"Yes or no, Mr. Chambers."

"Objection, Your Honor," said Charles Sturm, rising. "I don't see what this line of questioning—"

"Motivation, Your Honor," argued Jerry Snapkin. "And if the relationship between testator and my client is pertinent, then relationship between testator and his son is also pertinent."

Don waited. Charles Howard reflected. "I'll overrule, Mr. Sturm," said the judge. "Sauce for the goose. Proceed, Mr. Snapkin."

Mr. Snapkin advanced on the witness like a wolf on the fold. "I'll repeat, Mr. Chambers. Yes or no. Did you, not long after your father refused you the loan, petition the court for conservatorship?"

"Yes," Don said.

"And what was the outcome?"

"Petition was denied."

"All right. Now. These talks you had with him relative to Mrs. Kirchner. On two occasions. When you warned him about her, and he wouldn't listen—I'm quoting you. These weren't 'talks.' They were bitter quarrels, weren't they, Mr. Chambers?"

Don sat mute. Harry had told her everything, then, as he might have a wife. He'd told her more than he had his own son.

"Mr. Chambers?"

"Yes," Don said.

Jerry Snapkin smiled. "Thank you very much, Mr. Chambers."

Don could have used a walker to get from the stand to a chair at the table. He sat down heavily. He heard Snapkin call Mrs. Maria Kirchner. He heard her sworn in, and her attorney address her.

"Mrs. Kirchner, will you please tell us about your relationship with Harold Chambers, the decedent?"

Don heard her speak, and at last, looked at her. Hard. And could scarcely accept what he saw. If this was a *femme fatale,* he was Albert Einstein. This was a dumpy woman in a nothing black dress. Her face was round and ordinary, and her hair, black though streaked with gray, was drawn into a peasant bun at the back of her head. She might have been a chambermaid at a motel. She might have worked in a laundry. She might have hired out for housework by the day. This was what his father had settled for at eighty-three. This was what the last year of his life had offered him, and like a child he'd thrown his arms around it. She spoke with an accent. Don listened.

"I couldn't do nothing for his hip. I told him so, at the hospital, but after I was fired he called me up and asked me to come over. I told him I couldn't do nothing for his hip, but he said he didn't care, he was just glad to have me around. Somebody to talk to, you know." She spoke in a monotone. "He asked me to come at night when I could, so maybe the neighbors wouldn't notice. We had good times. He asked me to buy some gin and tonic—he'd like to try that. I didn't drink neither, but I did for him a little. He was awful lonely, you know. His wife had gone and left him alone. He told me about when he was a boy, and how he liked to fish and grow berries. He asked me about myself. I was just fired from the hospital. I told him times was hard for me. My car was broke down almost. He wanted to buy me a newer one, but I said I couldn't, it wouldn't look right. He did, though. I was worried about my house payments, and he sold my house and gave me enough for a new one I found. He wouldn't take no. I told him about my girl over to the University of Arizona nursing school, how I couldn't pay for her much longer. He said he'd take care of that. I didn't know what he meant. I didn't know what he was gonna do with his will. He must of thought he was gonna die, and he wanted to fix it so she could finish nursing school and I could have a nice house." She paused and looked down at the hands folded in her lap. "He was the nicest man I've ever known. He told me he loved me. He said if he was twenty years younger, he'd marry me if I'd have him. I'm fifty-one." She took out a handkerchief and swabbed at her eyes. "He was the nicest, kindest, loneliest old man. He didn't ask for nothing himself. Just me being there. I'd kiss him on top of his head. That's all I ever done. He'd hold my hand, and kiss it, and cry."

Maria Kirchner continued, but Don didn't hear her, nor did he see her. He heard the purl of water over a semisubmerged log. He saw the deep dark hole in Honey Brook, his father's glory hole, and heard his father's voice, instructing him. The line went taut in foam, and moved. He heard a voice hollering to high heaven as son hauled from Honey Brook the fish of his father's life. It was not the voice of a boy, but that of a man, his own.

"Judge, Your Honor." Don Chambers was on his feet at the table. "Sir, I'd like to drop this whole thing. I don't care to fight it anymore."

All fixated on him—Judge, Kirchner, Snapkin, Sturm, Bailiff, Clerk.

"Are you certain, Mr. Chambers?" asked the judge.

"Yes, sir."

Howard nodded. "Mr. Sturm, Mr. Snapkin, come to the bench, please."

The attorneys approached the bench. In low tones the three conferred. Then the attorneys returned to their respective tables. Maria Kirchner was still on the stand. Don remained standing.

Judge Howard leaned to his microphone. "Petition of objection to the will of Harold Chambers is withdrawn. This hearing is dismissed."

Charles Sturm moved toward Don, hand extended. "Chambers, this is a generous, intelligent . . ."

Don brushed past him.

Jerry Snapkin raised his arms high. "Thank you, Mr. Chambers, thank you! The first case I've won! I'm calling my mother and . . ."

Don brushed past him and through the gate and up the aisle and was surprised to see a single spectator seated in the back row on the aisle. Jenny stood up to meet him. He brushed past her.

*

He started walking around the four block-long sides of Patriots Square, a small downtown park with green grass and flags and benches for winos. Suddenly he felt he was being followed. He turned his head, and there was Jenny, following him. He walked the westside block, crossed the street with the light, and started walking the northside block. He was a wet noodle. It was as though he'd taken one of his old man's nuclear laxatives and finally been purged of Old MacDonald and his goddamned farm and Franz Kafka and Happy Hours and Ralph Waldo Emerson and Aunt Min and flying steaks and burning condos and bears in the woods and wills and pills and codicils. Jenny was still following him. He crossed the street with the light and walked the eastside block. Jenny was still following him. He walked faster. She walked faster. He walked slower. She walked slower. He ducked into the Jackalope Bar.

*

No one was in the Jackalope Bar but a bartender. Don walked up to the bar and sat down on a stool.

"What'll it be?" asked the bartender.

"I don't know," said Don. "When you get right down to it, none of us knows."

"Knows what?"

"What it'll be. Tomorrow, next year, an hour from now. How can we know?"

The bartender looked at him. "What, would, you, like, to, drink?"

"I don't think I'd like to drink," said Don. "If you don't mind, I'd like to sit here and meditate."

"Meditate," said the bartender.

Don elbowed the bar and looked at the jackalope sitting in a glass case on a shelf over the mirror. It was a white jackrabbit with a set of antelope horns on its head. "Y'know," he said, "I'm glad to see the Jackalope Bar's got a real jackalope. That's one of the things wrong with the world today."

"What is?"

"Well, you go in a bar called the 'Blue Goat.' Or a restaurant named the 'Pink Pony' or the 'Crystal Pistol.' That bar doesn't *have* a blue goat—those restaurants don't *have* a pink pony or a crystal pistol. You've been had. It lets you down."

The bartender leaned on the bar. "Never thought of it. Guess you're right, though."

Don looked over his shoulder. Jenny was standing in the street doorway looking at him.

"But you've got a real jackalope," he said to the bartender. "A white one at that."

"Albino. Pink eyes."

"Albino? They must be pretty rare."

"Sure as hell is," asserted the bartender. "There can't be more'n eight, ten jackalopes left in the whole West. Prob'ly no albinos."

"Where'd you get him?" Don asked.

"Right out back here," said the bartender. "One night about two years ago."

"Out back?"

"Yep. I close up here at 2 A.M. Well, my pickup was parked out back. I went out and there was this jackalope eating on one of my snow tires."

"How'd you get him?"

"He musta been *real* hungry. I walked right up to 'im and picked 'im up and shook 'im. He closed his eyes and died. Just couldn't take it. So I had 'im stuffed and changed the bar's name."

"I'll be damned," said Don. "Done much for business?"

"Not much. People seen everything these days."

Don nodded. "Well, listen, I'll tell you something. I agree a pink-eyed albino jackalope's rare all right, but I've got something at home just as rare."

"What's that?"

"A live rabbit, a regular brown-eyed rabbit with one bum ear who drives a car."

"I'll be damned," said the bartender. "What kind of car?"

"A Rabbit Rabbit."

Jenny sat down on the stool beside Don.

"Hi," she said.

"Hi," Don said.

"What'll it be?" the bartender asked her.

"May I buy you a drink?" she asked Don.

"Why not?" he said. "I drink, in moderation. I'll have a double vodka mart, on the rocks with an olive," he told the bartender.

"I'll have a Coors draft," said Jenny.

They hadn't seen or spoken to each other for three weeks, since the funeral-wedding-funeral. They watched the bartender make the martini and draw the beer.

"I just wanted you to know," Jenny said to Don, "that that was just about the finest thing I've ever seen a human being do."

"Thanks," Don said.

"Why did you do it?"

The bartender served them, and they sipped without toasting anyone or anything, not even "Cheers."

"Well," Don said, "my old man was only generous two times in his life I know of. This was one. To her. So I suddenly decided not to fight him, not to spoil it. If somebody wants to be generous, let 'em."

"When was the other time?"

"I told you. He gave me his favorite fishing hole once, when I was a kid. And the trout of his heart. I remembered."

They sipped. So as not to eavesdrop, the bartender had retired to the far end of the bar.

"How'd you know about the hearing?" Don asked.

"Ron told us."

"He wasn't supposed to."

"He couldn't help it. You're his father."

They sipped.

"We did have bacon that morning," Jenny said. "I must have left the grease in the pan. She must have punched the wrong burner. I remembered."

"That's what I thought," Don said.

They sipped.

"I sold a house," Jenny said.

"Hey, great," Don said.

They sipped.

"I'm starting a new organization," Don said.

"Oh? What?"

"Children Ruined by Aged Parents. CRAP."

They sipped.

"What about their children?" Jenny asked.

"Let's see. Children Ruined by Aged Parents and Pampered Youth. CRAPPY."

They sipped.

"You still living in your friend's place?" Don asked.

"Yes, but I have to be out in two weeks, she's coming back from Carmel. And guess what—tomorrow Sue and Ron are moving in with me. She had to quit at the Crystal Pistol, she's starting to show. So on one income they can't afford their apartment. I don't know what I'll do. Rent, maybe. Or buy. The insurance company's settling with me next week."

"What'll they do with the waterbed?"

"Store it."

They sipped. Don could smell her Patou. The bartender came down the bar to Don.

"What's a Rabbit Rabbit?"

"A little go-cart, battery-powered. On command Bobby gets in it—Bobby's his name—and you buckle him in and on command he puts down the pedal with his paw and off he goes—*bang,* into a wall."

The bartender looked hard at Don, then retired again to the end of the bar.

"I suddenly decided something myself," Jenny said. "This afternoon."

"What?"

"You can wait your life away."

"That's about right," Don said.

There should have been two olives in his double mart, but there was only one. He fished it out of the ice and examined it. It had size and shape, but the pimento protruded, so it lacked nobility. He frowned and buried it under the ice.

"And something else," Jenny said. "Last April you asked me to marry you. Now it's my turn. In a minute I'm going to ask you to marry me. But before you say yes, I want you to . . ."

"I might say no," Don said. "You did."

"I know. It was the dumbest thing I've ever done. But if you might say *yes,* I want you to think what it means. I won't rent or buy. We'll live in your place. But so will Ron and Sue."

"And the fetus," added Don.

"And the fetus."

"And Bobby."

"And Bobby."

"Six of us."

"Six."

"Water spots."

"Squeegeed."

They sipped.

"Also, if you say yes," Jenny said, "I don't want to make a big production out of it. Please. I'd like to come downtown here, the way Ron and Sue did, and be married by the same J.P.—two 'I do's' and that's it. Five minutes. No production, no problems. Please."

They sipped.

"Will you marry me, Don?" Jenny asked.

He looked at her, then slid off his stool and stood. "Ask me again."

Jenny looked at him, then slid off *her* stool and stood. "Will you marry me?"

Their arms encircled one another.

The bartender, a silent witness, had now truly seen and heard it all.

"Pinch me," said Don, dreamily.

Slowly, suspensefully, her hand descended, to the posterior region of his slacks, hesitated—hesitated—thumb and forefinger parted—and pinched—tenderly.

As the finally engaged were ambling out hugging each other tightly, the bartender yelled after him. "Hey! Why *does* that rabbit hit the wall?"

"Don't we all?" Don replied, over his shoulder.

The bartender just stared after him.

*

Cramp City. They were packed into the basket of the balloon like sardines—Don Chambers carrying a burnished can and Jenny Staley and the pilot, Max the Beard, and the Reverend Ray Ufer with his guitar over his shoulder and, cowering on the bottom of the basket between their legs and the propane gas tanks, Bobby. The bride-to-be was ravishing in a red silk shirtwaist dress and a baseball cap with "Oakland A's" over the bill, which her groom had provided to protect her new hairdo. Ray Ufer was a Unitarian and played the guitar and sang folk songs and was the only minister Don could think of who'd make music and go for a high-altitude service both. Don had once attended Ray's church a few times, but dropped out because the minister was a born martyr who crucified himself every Sunday for some social cause and also because all the Unitarian hymns seemed to be about the Industrial Revolution, not God.

The five of them were suspended beneath the same balloon, yellow and white and purple and seven stories high, and as they sailed along the south slope of Camelback Mountain through a carbonated autumn afternoon, Max went into his pilot routine about burning and deflating and rate of climb, etc.

"No, goddammit, we heard all that before!" Don shouted over the roar of the dual burners flaming in the throat of the bag. "We gotta move it—I only rented this sucker for half an hour! Just shut up and gimme a minute and then Ray'll sing and we'll get married!"

He squeezed around and leaned out over the side of the basket. Jenny squeezed around with him. They drifted low over a posh section of Phoenix, over big homes and walled patios and swimming pools. Don unscrewed the cap in the top of his burnished can, and turning the can upside down, spilled a stream of fine gray ash which filtered through trees and onto rooftops and into pools.

"What's that?" cried Jenny.

"My old man's ashes!"

Had she not grabbed the grab bar, Jenny might have fallen out of the basket.

"I said I'd think of somewhere!"

"Oh my God!" cried Jenny.

Don shook the last of the ash at a telephone pole. "Pop won't mind! He loved Arizona!"

He let cap and can fall away. "Urns a hundred bucks up! Got that can for fifty!" He grinned at Jenny. "Half the estate—half the price!"

He squeezed around just in time to catch Max the Beard kicking at Bobby. "Don't kick that rabbit!" he shouted. "He's my best man!"

"He was trying to get up my pantleg!"

"He's scared!" Don shouted. "He's never been up in a balloon before!"

Young Ray Ufer had planned to sing his socko numbers, "Shoo-Fly Pie" and "The Wreck of the Edmund Fitzgerald," before the ceremony, but now he seemed to be turning green around the gills.

"You okay, Ray?" Don shouted.

The minister was hyperventilating and turning green. "I can't sing! Guess I can't take the height!"

"Let's move it, then, before you urp!" Don helped Jenny turn, and shoved an arm around her waist. "And hey, Ray, make it the minimum, will you?"

"I have to."

Jenny adjusted her skirt. Don freed the seat of his Jean-Paul Germain slacks, which had snagged in the wicker.

"Do you, Donald William Chambers, take Jenny Staley as your lawful, wedded husband?" shouted the minister.

"Wife!" Don and Jenny corrected.

"Wife!"

"Do I ever!" Don shouted.

"Do you, Jenny Turner Staley, take Donald Chambers as your lawful, wedded husband?"

"I do!" cried Jenny, taking off her Oakland A's cap, waving it, and putting it on again. "Yeeaaay!"

"Get your ass outta here!"

Everyone but Bobby looked over the side. Below them, a buck-naked bald-headed man with a big belly and a small lobopreem stepped out of his pool and shook a fist.

"Watch your mouth!" Don shouted down. "We're getting married!"

"First time?" Fatso shouted back.

"Second!"

"Nothing! I been around the track four times!"

"I can see why!" Don shouted.

That really steamed the skinny-dipper. He shook his fist again. "Outta here, you trespassing bastards!"

"Up yours, skinhead!" Don shouted down.

Jenny pulled Don in and around. The minister was shouting at Don. "Do you have a ring?"

"Here!" Out of a pocket Don pulled a small leather pouch.

"Unset diamonds!" he shouted at Jenny. "My dad bought 'em—I got half—fifteen hundred bucks worth! You can have 'em set any way you want! Okay?"

"Okay!' she cried.

The couple faced Ray Ufer, who was hanging on to a rope and appeared about to toss his cookies.

"I do therefore!" he shouted desperately over the hoarse blowing of the burners. "By virtue of the authority! Vested in me by the laws! Of the State of Arizona! In the presence of God! And these witnesses! Pronounce you husband and wife!"

"Half-hour's up!" shouted Max the Beard. "I'm rippin' the top! We're goin' down!"

And then, as the great hand of God gentled the balloon down, down, divinely down to earth over the parking lot of a church, where the chase pickup waited with *mucho* champagne and Ron and Sue and the fetus, and as Jenny shed a joyous tear and Don shed a joyous tear and the pilot shut off the gas and the Reverend finally unslung his guitar and gave it a game go with his showstopper, a Gordon Lightfoot classic.

> *The legend lives on, from the Chippewa on down,*
> *of the big lake they call Gitchy-Goomy.*
> *The lake it is said, never gives up her dead,*
> *when the skies of November turn gloomy . . .*

"Ray, why in hell'dcha pick that one?" Don yelled at him.

"It's my best song!"

Below, their kids waved up at them from the truck as the newlyweds returned their enthusiasm.

The good green Reverend, really into it now, wound up for a boffo finish.

> *The Captain wired in, he had water comin' in,*
> *and the big ship and crew was imperiled,*

And later that night, when their lights went outta sight,
came the wreck of the Edmund Fitzgerald!

And while the newlyweds planted their feet among the propane tanks for the landing and a terrified Bobby tried to get up Don's pantleg, lifting the bill of her baseball cap so they could finally, at long last, get their torrid lips together, Mr. Chambers kissed Mrs. Chambers and Mrs. Chambers kissed Mr. Chambers as a great, golden Southwestern sun set behind them.